Bloody Scalps and Cuckoo Clocks

Copyright © 2018 Michael L. Phegley

Michael L. Phegley

BLOODY SCALPS
AND
CUCKOO CLOCKS

Joe-Pye Press
200 Hanover Road Evansville IN

For my Grand Parents and my Grand Children

Thanks:

To my first best friend:
We finished another one.
Thanks for all your help.

To my children, who make me strive to do better.

To my wife, a true helpmate in everything I do.

To Mr. Mutchmore, who made the study of history seem cool
when I needed a goal.

Disclosure

This story is fiction based upon historic facts. The major events really happened. The settings were authentic and as accurate as I could verify from historic documentation. Most of the newspaper articles and official reports mentioned in the book were drawn from New Jersey and Pennsylvania Archives. I drew some of my storyline from a diary kept by James Young while he inspected the Pennsylvania Forts near the Forks of the Delaware. Many (but not all) of the characters in this story were people who lived in these times and places.

The dialogue, individual character attributes, specific actions and opinions are fictional.

Words

Our past has not always been pretty. I think it important that we not sanitize history. We need to recognize the inhumanity people often show one another. One way is to expose the meanness in words or more precisely the way people *use* certain words.

When writing history or historic fiction I believe we should not remove offensive language. Rather we should expose its various destructive *uses*. We must be true to the reality that existed—good or bad—as we have the ability to know it.

This is not to promote *that* reality. To the contrary it is to demonstrate the ongoing struggle to become civilized. We need to show how difficult a fight it has been, and still is. We must expose the meanness not only in the words but in the casual, unconscious way we use those words to demean others.

I share my opinions on this subject to explain my occasional use of certain words in this text. Some readers may be offended. That is not my purpose. I attempt to be respectful, while being true to the nature of my characters. If I fail in my effort to portray each culture in a respectful manner please accept my apology.

As a writer and a human being I am a work in progress. You may share your opinions with me at **stormsatkendiamong @gmail.com**. Please, be gentle.

Waters

To fully experience this story you must imagine the landscape of eighteenth century North America before highways, railroads and air travel. People and commerce traveled upon or along rivers and streams. Overland trails connected these waterways. Small communities formed in such places and over time some thrived.

The Hudson, Delaware, Susquehanna, and Mississippi Rivers are the major waterways flowing north to south dissecting the area where this story unfolds. They and their tributaries were the transportation routes of their time. Controlling and defending these byways was critical for the people living here.

Even the smallest waterways called runs were important locally. They powered the mills and watered the livestock. Primitive homes required a water source. Springs were particularly valued and most pioneer homesteads were not considered complete until a springhouse was built to cool the milk, cheese, and other food.

It is hard to overstate the importance of such waters. In his famous poem "Snowbound", when a farm family's children search for their brook following a snow storm, John Greenleaf Whittier described it this way:

"We minded that the sharpest ear

The buried brooklet could not hear,

The music of whose liquid lip

Had been to us companionship,

And, in our lonely life, had grown

To have an almost human tone."

Our ancestors fought and died to secure and protect treasured waterways, which today we neglect or hardly notice.

Iroquois

Territories

Delaware R.

Machackemack R.

Coles

Upper Smithfield
Northamton County
Pennsylvania

Brinks

Ft.
Gardner

Nominack

Munsee

Indian

Ft
Johns

Deckertown

Ft
Hyndshaw

Walpack

Dupui

Van Campen

Newton

Ft
Reading

Ft. Hamilton

Ft. Norris

Wind Gap

Ft
Allen

Nazarath

Bethlehem

Delaware R.

Lehigh R.

Easton

Philadelphia

vi

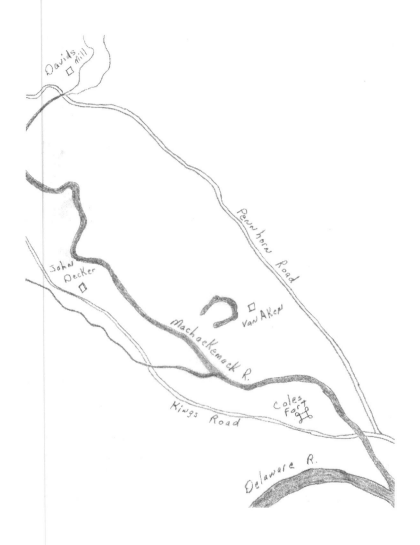

Davids mill

Penhorn Road

John Decker

Machackemack R.

van AKen

Kings Road

Coles Fort

Delaware R.

Chapter 1

(June, Year 168?)

$\mathcal{T}$he small bark canoe surged forward into the current with each stroke of the paddle. Sweat dripped from his brow and shimmered through the gray hair across his sun-browned chest, back, and shoulders. He had been making slow progress paddling upriver for hours. Now he needed to get off the water—quick.

Noticing a small spit of sand on the left bank, he made for that landing. Getting closer with each stroke the old man handled the paddle proficiently never wasting energy to change sides. He also never bumped the gunnels, as less experienced boatmen do, sending that unwelcome loud thump reverberating over the water for half a mile. Christoffel Davids knew his business. He had been at it for over fifty years.

Swiftly the bow of the canoe slid to rest along the sand without touching. Nimbly Christoffel rose crouching as he moved forward, hands on both gunnels, weight balanced low. He placed his left foot to the center of his craft and with a graceful movement stepped his right foot onto the sand. He beached his canoe so it would not drift.

During the approach his eye had caught notice of a small bare tree trunk on shore. It had been conveniently left by the last flood lying on its' side a few feet up in the sand. He now made hastily for that half buried driftwood. Fumbling frantically with his belt he dropped his pants as he wheeled, seating himself over the log, just as his bowels loosened their grip. He heaved a huge sigh of relief.

Damn!, he thought, *that was close, but now what?* Normally when nature called there was time to prepare. Usually there was ample opportunity to pick the right spot and gather necessary supplies. He was presently in no condition to move far in such a search.

Christoffel chuckled. As predicaments go this one wasn't so bad. Pausing a moment, he stepped out of his deerskin trousers. He walked, with a bowlegged gate, to the water's

1

edge. He slipped off his moccasins. Standing naked, he walked straightway a few paces out into the slow moving water. He squatted with a short sudden gasp.

The water's cold.

Waist deep in the river he heard the rapid rhythmic swish of winged flight. Glancing skyward he watched five Whistler Swans fly low over his head winging their way downriver.

Looking to settle in fer the night, he thought, *just like me.*

The only soap Christoffel owned was at his cabin. The old man, promptly, began cleaning himself scrubbing thoroughly with sand and river water. Thankfully it was a warm fall day. The water temperature was bearable and soon he had himself cleaned in as good a bath as was normally required.

Shadows lengthening the old fellow emerged from the water refreshed. Slipping on his moccasins he tied them securely. Then he gazed about as if for the first time. His bare, weathered old hide dried in the afternoon breezes.

A few paces across the sand he glimpsed a narrow game trail heading up the brushy riverbank. Following the faint path, a short way into the fast darkening forest, he found the site he was seeking a few yards inland. It was big enough. He decided it would have to do. There was little time left in the day.

Back at the water's edge Christoffel pulled on his trousers. Shivering slightly, as the day waned, he reached into the canoe for the buckskin shirt. He glanced up and then down river. He pulled the shirt over his head and let it settle around his torso enjoying the sudden renewed warmth. Next he slung about his neck a small knife, kept in a sheath tethered by a leather thong. Here it would be easily accessible for a thousand uses. He reached down again into the canoe retrieving a flintlock pistol and a small tomahawk. Slipping each weapon under his belt on opposite sides he finally felt dressed for being ashore.

Wasting no time the old man hoisted the first bale of supplies out of the canoe onto his shoulder and headed up the narrow trail. He was back and forth repeatedly during the next few minutes. The load was quickly transported to his new camp.

2

Then, glancing up and down river a final time, he headed in. Hoisting the canoe he balancing it on his shoulders. The bow of the little bark parted the pliable willow branches, braking through the forest's edge into the open understory of a big beech woods.

At his impromptu abode the seasoned trader quickly covered his supplies with oiled canvas. Securing the covering with a good hemp rope he knotted it so as not to blow off in the toughest gale. His elk-hide bedroll soon was unfurled beneath the upturned canoe.

A tiny Downy woodpecker watched these odd proceedings from a short distance careful to keep some brush between himself and the stranger. In the distance Christoffel heard the "crrronk" of a bittern. *Probably somewhere in the willows across the river*, thought the old man. Nearby on the ground and in the trees squirrels barked and chattered for a short time and then went about their business. Geese honked and ducks quacked high above. Everything in this world along the river seemed normal. A dampness returned to the woodland air as the light faded.

With darkness settling about him, Christoffel procured his flint and steel from a leather possible bag. From the same bag he produced a delicate, well-constructed wrens nest. He had discovered the bird's tiny shelter of dry grasses that morning abandoned among the red berries and green leaves of a spicebush growing near the river's edge. Now, he placed the nest on the ground and squatted over it with flint and steel poised.

A quick strike sent flashing sparks shooting into the combustible handiwork of the unknown bird. Immediately the old man drew a deep breath and blew a long steady supply of air onto the tiny glowing embers. The delicately formed grasses ignited into a flame. He placed the burning nest on the ground where he had brushed away the forest duff. He fed his fire with tiny sticks, at first, progressing till they were the size of antler tines. Then, he left it burning on its' own and went to gathered firewood, enough at least, to burn through the night. A small fire would not require a big supply. Christoffel believed in thrift and smaller fires attracted less attention.

During his life the old trapper had spent as many nights sleeping under his canoe as under a cabin roof. He had lived a long time and was comfortable in his own skin.

Ringed by giant trees his brightly burning little fire, created a small ring of light illuminating a circle of only a few yards. Tonight, that little bit of light was immersed in millions of square miles of dark forest.

Christoffel relaxed. He laid his back against the canoe and put his feet toward the fire. He watched a thin column of smoke, shoot upward through the leaf canopy overhead. The flickering flames spoke softly to him in that melodious language only very old trappers hear.

He ate a few bites of venison jerky as he listened. Supper was washed down by rum he kept poured into a metal cup beside the fire. He sipped slowly and thought about days past and days ahead.

An Englishman, Christoffel Davids had come to America in 1640 on a Dutch ship. The Hudson River Valley was then the center of a profitable Dutch fur trade in the new world. He was a young man at that time. There was nothing, which drew him back toward the old country and much about the new world, which fit him.

While some left to go home, he stayed. He prospered through the years but not without conflict and not without making enemies. Christoffel had plenty of both.

He was concerned for a while after the British seized control of the Hudson River Valley from the Dutch in 1664. However, no questions were ever asked him by the new authorities. Little changed for common folk except the names of towns and forts. In a short time new opportunities presented themselves. His language abilities were helpful. He was licensed to trade with the savages. The decades rolled by.

The week past Christoffel Davids had traveled downstream to the Manhattan Islands. He sold a farm he owned near Hells Gate on the East River. With the proceeds he purchased supplies and trade goods from the merchants of New Amsterdam. Now he was returning upstream to his cabin on

Rondout Creek near Esopus, which everyone now called Kingston.

In the coming months of snow and ice he would prepare for a trading expedition next spring. He and his grandson Solomon had decided to follow Rondout Creek toward its headwaters in the Catskill Mountains. Here they would cross over to the Machackemack River, which flowed down a different slope to meet another south-flowing river known as the Fishkill. A few miles south of this confluence was Minisink Island home to the Munsee Indians. Christoffel planned to trade for furs with these people..

While other traders took the usual path down the Mohawk River to trade with the Iroquois, he and his grandson hoped to establish a good relationship with the Munsee. The Fishkill was over a hundred miles from his home. The old trapper knew it would be hard and dangerous but his grandson would make things easier. Solomon was a likeable and capable boy of full growth and wise beyond his years. The necessary friendships among the savages had been established during previous hunting trips. At least Christoffel hoped those bonds were strong enough. Often it was hard to tell.

As the old warrior pondered his scheme laying in his woodland lair he slowly drifted into a fitful slumber. The night darkened without a moonrise. An owl called from the inky blackness above. There was the sound of whispering wings, and the owl glided away through the darkness. A log shifted on the slow burning fire sending sparks flying upward. Christoffel Davids died in his sleep, lying under his canoe, alone in the forest.

Chapter 2

(Year 1733)

*T*hird-street was cobblestone now. It shed rain. The rainwater, as all water does, flowed downhill. A few blocks south Dock-street crossed Third-street diagonally redirecting this flow off toward the wharfs and finally into the Delaware River.

Zack Miller was impressed. No cobblestoned streets had existed here, when he came ashore seven years ago. He hadn't seen anything like them since leaving Amsterdam.

Front-street, Dock-street, Second and Third-streets were all being cobbled now at least partially. Work was starting on High-street, but it was slow going there with the markets operating and all the wagons coming and going. It might take years to finish the work on High-street. Someday Fourth-street would be cobblestoned too and that would complete almost the whole town as it now stood.

Progress, thought Miller, *I can walk down the street right after a big rain without getting my boots muddy, that's progress.* He walked at a quick pace enjoying the clicking sound his boots made on the glistening stones. Ahead, on the right, he saw the tavern's sign. It would be warm and dry inside Town Tavern. He was hungry and getting wet. Rain was falling again. He hadn't eaten anything since last evening. It was just now after noon.

Philadelphia was becoming a city. Good streets were just one sign of its success. There were over ten thousand people living here now. Folks said it was the biggest city in America. And it was growing again following the troubles and lean times of the seventeen-twenty's. The Quakers were once more attracting lots of new folks to their colony.

Ships docked regularly at the wharfs bringing almost a thousand settlers every year from the old countries. Five ships had come so far this year. Two docked in the last ten days. Most vessels now-a-days were loaded with Palatine Germans, but a few more Irish were still arriving depending, year to year, on how the crops grew back in their homeland. Most of these immigrants did not want to stay in the city long unless they had a skilled-trade. Some would stay seven years indentured in service as payment for the cost of passage to America.

But land could be purchased near here. Property was almost impossible for a man to buy back in the old country. Most of these folks were farmers or wished to be. Their dream was to own land of their own in the countryside.

Miller noticed a man walking up the street toward him. The man was tall, brown skinned, well-dressed, silver bobbles hung through his ears. The stranger was carrying but not using a cane with a round-shiny-silver-nob on its top. The fellow passed Zack without so much as a nod.

Philadelphia in 1733 was a boomtown. There were Swedes, Dutch and English residing here. They were mostly the ones living in the big brick houses with the gardens and small orchards. Many of those families had been living in the colonies for three generations. Their great-grandfathers had fought each other and burned each other's towns as often as they had battled with the natives. But that was all settled, at least for the time being. The English king ruled now, but he was far away. These days the old families were busy getting rich exporting lumber, grain, flax seed, fur; importing furniture, cloth, and manufactured goods.

African slaves worked in many of the fine homes of the city, even the Quaker homes. There was much debate about that in the Society of Friends but it was legal and it seemed to be the way of things for people who had money.

Miller had never had much money. But he had never questioned those who did. He hoped maybe someday he too would find a way to become rich and live in a fine house with a garden, orchard and servants.

A few *free* black people lived in town. Usually these were cobblers, blacksmiths, hostlers, cabinet-makers and the like. Hell, Miller had just yesterday met a priest named Greaton in Willings Alley who said he was trying to start a Romish Chapel of all things. It was illegal. Everyone knew that. You had to take two oaths when you got off the ships, one swearing

7

allegiance to the English King, the other denouncing the Pope. However, after those oaths were sworn, the Quakers here in Pennsylvania didn't worry as much about that as the officials in other colonies did. Some folks said the Pennsylvania Charter contradicted that particular law anyway.

That printer fellow, Franklin, don't seem to like Germans much or Irish either, thought Miller, *I wonder what he will say in his newspaper about a Catholic Church on his doorstep.*

Even the Indians came to town occasionally. There were a few Delaware Indians from over in the Jersies accepting the ways of the white man. At least they dressed like white folks, raised corn, and wheat, kept cows and horses, and such. Miller had seen them. Likely that was one he had just passed on the street. They kept good farmsteads and grew corn well. But they didn't know much about doing business, and they couldn't hold their rum. Sooner or later they had to sell out, what they had left, to some white man and move up north of the Kittatinny Mountains. Their cousins up that way would always take them in no matter how long they had been living among the whites. Zack's brow began to furrow as he sauntered along. *I guess it's the natural way of things.*

Town Tavern was a popular place. The essence of today's fare greeted Zack as he came up the stone steps in the rain. Baking bread, frying fish, cool ale, called to him through the storm freshened air. The door was open despite the wet weather. He entered shaking the rain from his hat as thunder rumbled off in the distance.

There was a buzz of conversation inside. He hung his coat and hat on a peg in the entry hall. He glanced into the front two rooms—both full—not an empty chair. He moved down the hall. In a third room toward the rear he noticed a man sitting alone near a cold fireplace at a table *with* an empty chair. He guessed the fourth room was likely full too. Other men behind him were hanging up their coats. He feared a wait coming and he was hungry.

Miller stepped over to the empty chair.

"May I join you sir?"

8

The man sitting, looked up. There was an awkward pause and then he nodded once. Zack pulled out the Windsor chair and sat down catching a glimpse of his new tablemate. *Fathers' generation,* he thought, *looks to be about fifty, not as well dressed as some in this room but he's not from here, or the frontier either— immigrant I'd bet.*

The man was eating chowder with a wooden spoon. The bowl steamed. A small loaf of rye bread, half eaten, sat on the table beside some butter, on a real china plate, with a bone-handled knife to spread it. Zack's stomach growled and his mouth watered. Here came the gal to take his order. *What a marvelous place.*

"Zack Miller," he said, looking across the table after he had ordered his food.

"Heinrich," the man responded, pausing for another awkward moment, "Heinrich Feagley."

Zack stuck out his hand and the man shook it from across the table looking him square in the eye.

Farmer, from across the waters, thought Miller.

"How was the crossing?"

"Slow—cold."

"On the Ship Samual or the Ship Elizabeth?"

"I auf 'Lizabeth. Mine son und his fambly auf de Samual." " We vait now de Hope."

"Another ship coming this season?"

"Ya."

"With more of your family?"

"Ya, ya," Heinrich said nodding.

"Been to the courthouse to take your oaths?"

"Ya."

" Got your land legs back yet"

"leetal"

"Know where you're headin?"

"Ya. We go noort ober Goshenhoppen." He paused "place called Schwampp auf Perkiomen creek."

The gal brought Miller's mutton stew. It smelled wonderful. He ate a few spoonfuls pausing to blow on each and enjoying his experience. He tore off a big piece of brown bread, spread on some butter with the knife, started dunking and eating. He did this for a while. He really was hungry. The edge off his appetite, he paused, looking up from his bowl with a wry smile. He took a gulp of ale to clear his throat.

"I know Perkiomen creek and the Schwampp. It's good land, not a real swamp just flat land. Good ground. You should do well there. It's out a ways from here but still well south of them Blue Mountains. The savages are all pretty much up north of those mountains. You know about the Indians?"

"Leetal."

"Well the wild ones are all north or west of those mountains. There may be a few Christian Indians between the Schwampp and those ridges but they're mostly all friendly. You should have thought about crossing the river to the east. Most of the savages are getting pushed clear out of New Jersey at least in the southern part where its flatland—sold their birthright over there. They're moving now up above the forks of the Delaware toward the Minisinks. I hear they ain't all happy about it but they're goin anyway. There is still land can be bought over in New Jersey south of the mountains from them that bought it from the savages. But you'll do well up on Perkiomen Creek. And the land won't cost you as much."

"Das goot."

Got friends goin with you?"

"Ya," Heinrich said nodding his head. "friundin."

"Stay south of the Blue Mountains and the Kittatinnys. You should be safe. There's a road of sorts most of the way from the Schwampp into Germantown, Good road from

Germantown into here. You could sell your extra crop up on High-street maybe get cash money.

"Ya."

Miller paused to concentrate on a few more spoonfuls of his stew. It was good stew. There was some left in his bowl but it was getting thin. When he sopped up the last of the gravy with the last piece of dark brown bread, he savored it a while on his tongue swallowing it with a sigh. He wiped his mouth on his shirtsleeve noticing a cloth napkin the gal had left on the table. He smiled to himself, picked it up, and wiped his mouth again.

He sipped his ale. It was cool. Tasted good. He really liked this place. Too bad he couldn't afford to eat here every day. *Maybe if I had a skilled-trade*, he thought, *but I don't*.

He nursed his ale.

"Myself I'm heading out tomorrow. I'm goin' out to the Juniata River. West of here about five days walk. It's a bit wilder out that way, but I got friends myself on the Juniata. Land is cheapest out there, for now."

He hesitated.

"That's where I'm goin.'"

Forgetting Heinrich Feagley, Zack Miller stared into the dark liquid at the bottom of the cool crock stein. Listening to the thunder mutter nearby, he wondered *what's life gonna be like out on the Juniata River*.

Chapter 3

Shadows stirred inside the longhouse. Two wood fires burned within the fifty-foot long structure. Each fire was located on the ground ten-feet inside either end. Four-foot square smoke holes in the arched roof above, exhausted fumes and admitted additional light. Today, with the sun low in the southern sky, that obscure sunlight cast upon the floor to the north of each blaze a cold gray rectangle, adding little assist to the warmth of the fire.

Outside, it was a relatively warm winter day with low hanging clouds. The wind was still. A misty rain whispered onto the snow-covered landscape. Wood-smoke had trouble rising. A great amount of it hung, like a cloud of its' own, over the Munsee village of four hundred souls spread out along the life sustaining Fishkill—a river which flowed slowly passed with snow covered ice chunks floating along upon its surface.

Inside the longhouse a two-foot layer of smoke hung diffused and striated below the roof, filtering the outside light even more than usual. Occasionally, the east or west door-flap briefly emitted a flash of illumination when people came or went. It was a dank day, but most of this extended Lenni Lenape family of thirty-five people was snug in their dry lodge just as the beaver would be in his', if there were any beaver left along the streams.

Presently a little brown skinned boy stood naked on a large woven-reed mat just where the gray sunlight shown on the floor near the eastern fire. He was no more than eight-months-old and he stood with his legs a bit too far apart.

In his hands the boy held a gourd about the size of one of his mother's small breasts. The gourd's elongated neck was the length and diameter of a cylindrical cattail head in late July, but slightly more curved by the sun than the cattail would be. The gourd had been well seasoned, rubbed with sand, and stained a dull red color. There were several rows of tiny yellow dots painted on its head and black stripes painted around it's long neck. At the top of the gourd, in the center, sketched in black, was the simple outline of a walking turtle.

The boy's eyes narrowed as he focused on the gourd. He stood perfectly still, with his head cocked first to one side and then the other like a woodpecker looking for just the right spot. Slowly he turned the gourd around in his clumsy little hands as brother raccoon handles a crawfish. Then the boy pulled it too him giving it a big open-mouthed kiss, slobbering over it, seeking anything which might resemble a nipple. Finding none he took the gourd away from his mouth and looked it over again. He smiled more to himself than to his mother who watched from across the fire where she ground hominy in a wooden bowl with a stone pestle, transforming it into thin white mush.

Abruptly, the boy gripped the gourd by its neck, held it over his head and shook it several times listening to the dry seeds rattle inside the toy. He crowed with delight in his accomplishment, making his mother smile too. He shook the gourd again, wildly this time, squealing once more but with just a bit of growl mixed in for good measure. With the shaking of the gourd the boy wobbled a bit on his legs but he didn't topple over. He held the rattle out in front of himself and shook it harder this time growling like a dog shaking an unfortunate opossum caught too far from its tree. The toddler leaned forward straining his torso with the extra effort but still he did not fall down. Instead he continued shaking his toy for a few moments more and then stopped. Looking all around him he stood with his head held high as if to say, are you all seeing this?

His mother chuckled and others in the shadows chuckled with her. Stepping closer to the firelight one of the mother's sisters held her sewing out, toward the light, to get a better look at the stitching.

"He has been standing for many days when will he walk?"

"When he is ready," the mother replied. "It is yet early for him to walk. But he stands much."

"Yes, He stands very well," said the sister. "But I think he should walk soon."

"When he is ready," repeated the mother.

Then she smiled once again and thought to herself: *Stands much... He-stands-much?*

As the mother thought her new thoughts a second naked child came running on tip toes across the mat to where the boy stood. She reached out to take the rattle. The boy held fast.

"Le-go!"

The boy gripped the toy tighter and pulled back, still standing, looking the other child, who was obviously a year or so older and bigger, square in the eye. The little girl smiled and released her grip on the gourd. Then, still smiling, she reached over placing the palm of her hand squarely on the boy's forehead and pushed.

Backward he plopped onto his plump little butt, So quickly he didn't seem to know what had happened. He dropped the toy. Swiftly the little girl grabbed it up, dancing away, rattling as she faded out into the dusky interior. There were more chuckles and giggles. The little boy sat on the mat, in the gray light, rubbing his eyes, wondering *where did the rattle go? What just happened? Am I hurt? What's that over there?*

The fire hissed and sputtered from rain falling through the smoke hole. The young mother watched the boy and thought to herself: *He-stands-much? He stands-often?*

Chapter 4

*T*homas Shirby walked up Dock-street in Philadelphia 9 July 1742. He had been on board a ship for eight weeks. His steps were wobbly and awkward. Each time he place his foot down he could not feel certain the ground would be there to meet it. But he was upright. That fact was more than could be said for many of his fellow passengers. It had been a rough crossing. Bad luck all around.

Shirby had been in the best of health when he boarded ship in England. He was one of two-dozen Englishmen replacing a few Palatine Germans who lost their lives or their nerve during a storm at sea, which nearly sunk their ship. The storm forced the Captain to return his vessel to England for refitting. Some of the passengers took the opportunity to disembark and Shirby had his chance to board in their stead. Thomas was only fifteen-years-old when he strode confidently up the gangplank, big for his age, five foot ten, hundred eighty pounds, stout, full of piss and vinegar as they say.

He was still just fifteen-years-old today but he felt older, much older. He had lost sixteen pounds on the crossing of the Atlantic, but had no way to know that. He just knew he didn't feel stout any longer and he was having trouble walking a straight line. The ground seemed to sway under his feet. He was really hungry but he wasn't sure he could keep food down yet.

Presently he walked along in a straggling cluster of thirty-two other men, who were stumbling, with unsteady gate, up the cobbled street. These were all of the immigrants able to come ashore today. Two sailors herded them up Dock-street to take their oaths at the courthouse. Thomas noticed the city streets were wider than he was used to in England. He had been told, and saw now with his own eyes, that except for Dock-street, the other streets of Philadelphia were all laid out on a simple grid pattern. William Penn had planned his capital city well from its very beginning. It was already growing into a reality to match that dream. The buildings were newer than those with which Thomas was accustomed, the houses more substantial than he had expected. No log cabins here.

He took his oaths to the King of England. When Thomas emerged from the courthouse he was a free man and could go where he pleased. Right now he thought he needed something to eat. High-street was north of here. The man inside the courthouse had said the markets were mostly all on High-street. It was Saturday and the population of Philadelphia had suddenly swelled to almost double for the day. Farmers from miles around had come to town to do their trading.

He walked north. Soon he saw High-street ahead. He was astonished at its spaciousness. It was probably a hundred feet wide. Farm wagons were set in the center two wagons deep for several blocks in both directions. They were parked in such a way that two backed up to two others, leaving about twenty feet between them, room for the horses which were resting, out of harness, tied to the rear of the wagons. Wares and produce were displayed along the outside of the wagons some on the ground, others on makeshift tables, or in barrels, or baskets.

This arrangement left room for a wide lane of traffic moving on either side of the temporary open-air markets. Bordering the perimeter of High-street were the regular businesses interspersed with small homes. These were the permanent brick or frame structures for merchants, blacksmiths, tinsmiths, cobblers, print shops, bakers, grog shops, barristers and others. Today they were all bustling with commerce.

There were lots of people. All kinds and classes of people: sailors from the ships docked at the wharfs, new immigrants, farmers from the countryside, tradesmen, slaves, city employees, carpenters, stone masons, traders of all kinds. Gentleman, businessmen, soldiers, government officials, housewives, servant women, and children; all scrutinizing the surprising array of available products.

Thomas turned right and started walking down High-street back toward the river.

He soon noted that the manufactured goods were pretty much the same here as at home except for the prices. My-god how could people afford to pay so much for cloth, hats, dresses and such?

He needed something to eat. In almost every stand he saw peaches. The place reeked of ripe and over ripe peaches. He

16

had never seen so many at one time and they were cheap. How could they afford to sell them so cheap?

A ripe peach sounds good he thought. I think I could keep that down now. I must try to eat something. He bought one and then *what the heck* he bought two. He had never purchased two peaches for one lunch before. Maybe America was going to be an easy place to make a living. At least here it looked like a man might not starve. Plenty of people starved back home every year.

He ate slowly. He had a small knife in a sheath on his belt. He cut slivers off the peach, at first, eating peel and all. When those stayed down, he cut larger pieces. Finally he popped the pit into his mouth sucking on it for a while before spitting it out onto the ground. He noticed other pits all around him. *I guess everybody is eating peaches this week.*

Thomas leaned against the farm wagon owned by the farmer who had sold him the peaches. The second peach was still in the cloth sack he carried. In fact, everything in the world owned by Thomas Shirby was in that sack, and it wasn't all that big a bag. He kept it tied shut and slung over his shoulder with a small rope. He stood a while longer to see if the world would slow down its rocking. It did so long as he stood still beside the wagon.

He decided he was okay to eat the other peach. He unslung the bag to untie it. He noticed a commotion back up the street from the way he had come. A body of men were crossing High-street a block west moving south back toward the courthouse. From hear he could see men with painted faces, and feathers tied in their hair, some looked practically naked, others wore coats or vest flashing with silver accoutrements. The crowd nearby seemed to pause their bargaining and stare.

As these newcomers moved through the crowd the people parted like water does for the bow of a ship.

"Savages!" said the farmer who had sold Thomas his peaches.

The man spat out the word and then spat on the ground to emphasize it. He turned to grab his pitchfork leaning against the wagon, then back to look up the street again. The Indians were disappearing into the crowd and then, gone, out of sight behind a small brick home.

"Damned Indians," he said looking at Thomas.

"Have you had trouble with those Indians?" asked Thomas.

"No I havn't," said the man. "But they're no good. None of them are any good fer nothin."

"Why they here in town?"

"Governor is meeting with 'em. They're Iroquois. Supposed to be friendly."

"Why does the government meet with 'em?" asked Thomas.

"I been told they uses 'em to keep the other Indians in line. Iroquois come to visit from time to time to get presents and argue about things. Takes a week or more to have a big council like their having now. It's been goin on fer several days already. They start at the courthouse every afternoon. Takes time to get some of 'em started in the morning, they're like sailors ashore when they get to town. And don't none of 'em move without 'em all being ready fer the talks. Myself, I think they just like to drag it out to get more stuff."

The peach seller paused a moment. He spat again on the ground.

"Hell, in a month or so some of the other red devils will show up begging fer a council of their own. They will whine in meetings fer a week about how unfair *Brother Onas* has been to 'em. That's what all the savages call the Pennsylvania Government, *Brother Onas*. Aint that somethin. The Indian agent will give them presents too. They just all need to stay up in the mountains where they belong. All this giving of presents just encourages 'em to come begging again. I don't like 'em. Unless they're ready to sell more land they just need to stay to home."

Thomas Shirby ate his second peach sauntering back up the street toward the courthouse. He thought the ground under foot might be swaying a little less.

Chapter 5

$\mathcal{T}$homas Shirby walked back to the courthouse in Philadelphia. A crowd of on-lookers stood outside. The doors were closed but the windows were open. A small knot of men hung close under each of those windows trying to hear what was being said inside. Thomas stopped in the shade of a big sycamore near enough to watch but not close enough to hear inside unless someone shouted.

A young man, a bit older than Thomas, sat nearby with his back against the tree.

Thomas stepped closer to him.

"What's going on inside?"

"Indian council with the authorities."

"Yeah, I been told that but what do they want?"

"Well *Brother Onas*—you know who that is?"

"Yeah, the Pennsylvania government."

"Well Brother Onas wants to learn what the Iroquois know about the French in the Ohio country and how cozy the Frogs may be getting with the Indians out that way. All the traders have been talking about it lately. Everyone is worried. *Old Brother Onas* wants assurances from the Iroquois that they can control their cousins, the Delaware, the Shawnee and a bunch of other tribes you never heard of."

"How do you know I never heard of 'em," asked Thomas?

"Cause you ain't from around here. Just come off a ship I'd say. About right?"

"Maybe," said Thomas.

The older boy smiled.

"My name's Elias Knepp. I live up on High-street when I'm in town. I know all about Indians."

"Is that so?"

"Yep."

"I'm Thomas Shirby. I may need to learn about Indians and other things I might encounter here in Pennsylvania."

"You alone," asked Knepp.

"Yeah. My Pa died when I was three. Ma gave me my passage money before she died last year. Got two older brothers somewhere at sea. I hadn't heard from either, for over two years, so I left word, and come here. Likely, I'll never see 'em again, but that's okay."

"Any money left?"

Thomas looked Knepp over again.

"Just askin. I don't need any right now."

" I got a few shillings left, that's all. No more to follow."

"Any kin here in the Colonies? Any job? Are you indentured?"

"No job or indenture. I got cousins out on the frontier. A place called the Juniata River Valley. Do you know it."

"Yeah it's west of here about a week's walk. People lookin fer cheap land have been movin out there fer a few years now, but not many folks. These days most of the Germans are settling up the Schuylkill River. Most of 'em comin off ship, if they ain't indentured, head right out toward Perkiomen, Skippack and Swamp creeks."

"Why they go to a swamp?"

"Tain't really a swamp just called that. I've been there."

"Is that where you learned about Indians."

"No. I went there to hear Count Zinzendorf preach to the settlers. But only a few of 'em was really interested in his ideas so he don't go there much now. You ever hear about Moravians?"

"No."

"Well, Zinzendorf is kinda starting a new church like the Reformed Church but with a heavy emphasis on mission work.

20

Moravians are good, pious people. They started a mission fer Christian Indians up north in the foothills called Bethlehem. I live there some."

"With the Indians?"

"Yeah."

"You a Moravian?"

"Not yet. I ain't actually joined the church. I just work fer brother Antes. But I'm good at listenin and watchin. They're good people."

Suddenly Knepp glanced toward the door of the courthouse. Two older men had emerged headed north a few dozen paces to a bench under the shade of a giant oak. They were heavy in conversation.

Knepp rose to his feet. Bending his head to the side he motioned Thomas to follow. Casually, the two young men sauntered over near the older men on the bench. One of the seated men nodded to Knepp, who sat down in the grass just inside the shade of the tree, a respectable distance not to intrude. Thomas followed his lead.

"John I'm not worried about the French out in the Ohio country. That's all about the fur trade. I don't care. I'm concerned about what is going on with the Lenape. You know as well as I that Logan was more concerned about land deals than he was about buying fur regardless of who his business partners might be. He didn't care so much about the French as they pretend. He was all about that iron works of his up north and how he was going to protect that lousy walking treaty he got done in 37. That was his future. Now that he is dead I can still see what is going on."

"Henry I know you think the Delaware Indians got a raw deal. But that's done now."

"It may not be as done as you think John. The Lenape know what happened to em. Even, if others don't want to see it. They were showed a map that was miss-labeled. Logan handed it to them. They expected the walkers to follow the paths normally traveled. He knew that's what they thought. They expected walkers not runners and they expected the line that was to be drawn back to the river to go toward the sun as it rises in the east, not in a northeasterly direction. That little direction trick included their most sacred lands into the deal. They sure didn't expect that. They may not all speak proper English but they are not stupid people. I find many to be smarter than a whole lot of the white people right there in this Courthouse. They protested at the time."

"But they signed the document Henry."

"It was mislabeled John. It didn't show the area they were giving up; it just called it out in writing. They mostly don't *read* English. They didn't think they were selling anything above Tohiccon Creek. That's what the map *showed*. Logan knew what he was doing. He was stealing the land around his iron works for the timber he needed to keep his smelter fired. He just stole enough extra land so he could buy off other white men by promising a big piece of the pie for them.

Some people will go along with anything so they can sell cheap land to new immigrants for a tidy profit. The big sellers will go on living here in their brick houses with their fruit trees and tea parties. We'll see them in church dressed in their finery, every Sunday.

It's the poor Germans and Irish who will go up above Tohiccon creek someday to hack little farms out of the forest. They're the ones who will pay the price for this swindle.

Antes paused watching the crowd shuffle around one of the windows. Two men were lifting up a little boy so he could see inside. They were all laughing.

"I tell you John, the Lenape are not over this yet. They have been pushed for a hundred years. They're pushed clear out of southern New Jersey now. They say they will not move again. The Schwampp area is starting to get settled. Those land prices are rising. Folks are starting to look up river toward the forks of the Delaware for cheap land even though they know the Lenape claim the land as their own. The Iroquois pushed most of them to move to the Wyoming valley on the Susquehanna River but they haven't made them like it. It's going to get ugly again."

"Well if you could get 'em civilized they could stay."

22

"The Indians or the Irish?" said the man named Henry, smiling.

" Good point," responded his friend. "Glad to see you still have a sense of humor."

"We're trying to civilize them John but it takes time," said Henry. He sighed. "They're good people, John, like us but they don't see things the same as we do."

"Well teach 'em to grow corn."

"John do you hear what you're saying. They taught white people how to grow corn. The old countries had never seen corn before folks started coming to America. We learned about it here. Now people say to me, all the time, teach 'em how to be farmers Reverend. That isn't the problem. They can grow corn just fine."

"Well I don't know what can be done Henry. Logan's partners and supporters are going to use the Iroquois to push 'em again. You heard them inside just now setting it up. The Iroquois want to stay on the good side of *Brother Onas*. When the Schwampp lands get expensive, white-folks are going to start buying that other land, up river, for their farms. Too many rich men here in Philadelphia have already invested in large tracts of that land to parcel off. Too much money stands to be made to stop it now. They'll say it's progress. Once they convince people of that there will be no stopping it."

"Well it ain't right, John."

"Maybe. Maybe not. I'm sorry my good friend but I don't see it being different any time soon. It's the way things are set. You must change people's heart before you can modify their behavior and as a minister of the gospels you know better than most the devil is always at work trying to steal a man's soul." He hesitated and looked at a man who had just emerged from the courthouse and was striding off across the commons. "There goes Mr. Franklin, Henry, let's go see what he thinks."

The older men rose from the bench, rushing off across the common, to catch their friend, leaving Thomas and Elias sitting in the shade.

"That's your boss?" asked Thomas.

"Yeah, Reverend Henry Antes."

"He was talkin about the Indians where you're livin."

"Yeah. The Delaware Indians, they call themselves the Lenni Lenape it means the real people."

"Where exactly is this place?"

"North of here, up toward the forks of the Delaware River near where the Lehigh River branches off to the west. But I guess that don't tell you much."

"No, It don't. I just came off the ship today like you said."

"It's a few days up river from here near where the Delaware River flows through the big mountains at what they call the Water Gap. Then inland into the foothills a day's walk. That's Indian country up north till you get farther on into the Minisink area. At Minisink there are mostly Dutchmen settled that have been living there for a long while. Them folks are mostly connected to the Hudson River-trade though some are beginning to float logs and such down the Delaware through Indian country to sell here at the sawmills."

Knepp looked Shirby over again.

"Would you like to come to Bethlehem? See for yourself? It's an interesting place, Thomas, the Moravians are educated people. You can learn a lot. I'm learning to play a clarinet."

"The what?"

"Clarinet. It's a musical instrument. Music is a big part of the Moravian church service. They play all kinds of instruments. It's a lively service every day. Indians love it. It's safe there. Everybody is friendly."

"Don't sound like it's always going to be safe from what Brother Henry was sayin. Thanks, all the same. I think I'll stick to my original plan, and go visit my cousins on the Juniata."

Chapter 6

Crows cawed as the sun rose over the mountain beyond the river. The birds perched on the highest branches of an ancient hackberry tree. This particular tree reached toward the sun three hundred yards from any other tree. For some unknown reason, it grew far out into a field of dark green corn. No one knew why it had been left growing here but it provided shade for farmers on hot summer days so no one had bothered to girdle it. Instead they named this place "The-tree-field" and gratefully sat in the shade of the big hackberry when resting from their work.

It was early July, the year of our lord 1746, according to the Moravian Missionaries. The corn reached, like the tree, to greet Father-Sun. Slender stalks stood the height of a mallard, elevated slightly higher because the corn grew on small hills. Using their hoes the Munsee women built these mounds at planting-time. It was called a cornfield but it will be a growing place for all the Three-sisters—corn, bean, and squash.

The corn-seed saved over winter was planted, five or six seeds to each hill, early in spring. The women then left their plot for many days. After corn planting, mornings came when fog hugged the earth so tightly that it mystically transformed the flat ground into a huge shadowy pond with fanciful beaver lodges appearing to rise above the surface of the imaginary water.

Days lengthened becoming warmer and dryer. Corn sprouts broke through the soil adding green leaves, as it grew. Munsee women returned to their growing area to hoe weeds and plant beans. A bean plant is a sister to the corn. Certain varieties grow thick bushy leaves, which shade and cool the roots of the corn, others have long vines which wind and climb slowly up the cornstalks so they can better see Father-sun. Beans and corn grow well together if the Munsee women and children guard the area to keep out the sisters' many enemies.

After bean-planting the women left their field again for many days. The children however continued to visit from dawn to dusk, guarding the crop from birds, squirrels, woodchucks and other varmints who love to eat the precious seeds and young sprouts. Each day the children of the village spread out over the field and fought off these predators in a great epic battle, to keep the plants safe. They were protecting their families and the village from starvation in winter. It was a serious fight and no one took his or her responsibility lightly. Everyone enjoyed the pudding, bread, porridge, mush and other delicacies provided by the crops. Like newborn babes the two sisters growing now needed protection.

Munsee women, today, are back in the Tree-field with the children. Presently, dozens of them, work at the east end of the cleared land, near the river. In small groups they are spread out across the entire width of the field. The women have brought their hoes. These are steel hoes acquired from the white traders of *Brother Onas*. Only a few of the grandmothers remember the stone tools used in the old times. These hoes are better. The women busily grub out the grasses and weeds, which have sprouted following their last working. The grass and weeds are enemies, who if left unchallenged will overtake the slow growing sisters stealing from them life sustaining moisture and nutrients. These Munsee farmers do not intend to let that happen. When the Father-of-life placed the Lenni Lenape (the real people) on the land he taught them how to care for the Three-sisters so that the sisters could feed the Lenape.

The women understood that the two sisters growing here today were lonely. They miss the third sister—the squash. Munsee women have been keeping the squash seed safe in storage containers within their lodges. Squash seeds come in many varieties, but all are delicate when first planted. They do not like cold. To grow well they need hot sun in the daytime and warm nights. It is such a time now. Once growing these squash will develop the most extensive and fastest growing vines of any of the sisters. The largest of all squash, called pumpkins, can, with their immense leaves, crowd out and smother some of the threatening weeds and grass. The squash and pumpkins will rapidly catch up with the growing corn and beans. Together, allied with a few of the Munsee boy's, they will defend themselves late in summer allowing the women and most of the children to tend other tasks.

Today, it is light work with the steel hoes, cutting off weeds and grass, grubbing up roots, breaking the soil, carefully piling

26

some of that soil at the base of corn and beanstalks. Older children carry squash seed in gourd containers held round their necks by leather thongs. Using a dibble stick (which is nothing more than a sharpened hickory stick, long as your arm and thick enough not to break) they punched holes in the loosened soil dropping in squash seed one or two at a time then covering them with soil. Carefully they planted squash in any open area where corn or bean leaves did not already shade the ground.

The sun was warm but not terribly hot. A gentle breeze rippled the corn and bean leaves, which were not yet developed or dry enough to produce the rustling sounds so prominent near a cornfield in late summer.

These farmers were in their field today soon after the grey light of dawn. They will leave before the heat becomes uncomfortable. For now they chat quietly as they work carefully. Birds sing to them. The sweet smell of freshly turned Mother- earth rises to greet them, mixed with the innumerable scents of near-by forest, river, meadow and mountain. It is a pleasant day in the Wyoming Valley of the Susquehanna River.

Stands-often a Munsi boy of eight winters is here but he is not standing. He is flat on his belly near the hackberry tree. He has crawled out like a snake through the corn and bean plants to put the sneak on the crows. His bow is strung and ready, an arrow already nocked in its string. Two more arrows with sharp bird points are in his quiver. He will defend his people. He is close, but not yet close enough.

Chapter 7

*I*t was Spring. The year was 1750. The Wyoming valley on the Susquehanna River in Pennsylvania has become the adopted home to the Munsee Indians who have been displaced from their homes on the Delaware River farther to the east.

A bay colored horse with a dark mane stood with his head down, ears twitching, munching sweet meadow-grass. The rest of the small herd is several yards upslope. A twig snapped over by the river. The horse raised his head high but saw nothing. He shuddered as if sheading flies. But there were no flies. Just in case, he trotted a few paces back toward the herd. Nothing followed. Wolves would have followed. He situated himself sidewise to the river, lowered his head, and went back to munching grass.

Something moved. The bay's head snapped up with his tail. His ears already up, he stood at attention, perfectly still.

He could see something over by the river. Whatever it was it was just standing, not moving.

The boy took two steps, along the river, but no closer to the bay with the dark mane. The boy halted, remaining quiet for more than a minute. The horse went back to feeding, taking a slow, measured step, now and again, as horses do when grazing.

Slowly the boy walked a few more paces, but not far, and not exactly in the direction of the horse. But he was closer this time. He came now toward the horse a few steps but then turned more parallel to the river, and then sauntered, back, a few feet. Predators never move away. Who was this? What was this? The boy paused again but he was closer than last time he halted.

They faced one another for a long moment, the horse and the boy. The bay took another couple strides and the boy came along this time but not directly at the horse. It appeared to the horse they were just traveling the same direction—slowly. A panther would never let herself be seen until pouncing, then, she would come straight on and lightning quick.

The boy and horse were aware of one another now. Birds sang. The grass was good. The horse was hungry after the long winter. Gradually the bay with the dark colored mane became aware that the boy was standing right beside him, only inches from his head. The boy's hand was out-stretched. There was something in the hand.

Horses are curious animals. The bay stretched his neck closer with his head slightly turned focusing on what was in the outstretched hand. It was just more grass but he took it.

The horse did not notice the slow movement of the other hand—the hand with the rope. He felt the ropes' pressure now. Too late, he was already caught.

The bay tried to pull away but the boy stood firm griping the rope, and the noose tightened. The boy pulled gently turning the bay as he spoke softly. The horse did not understand the words but the tone was soothing. The hand that had held the grass now patted his neck. It felt reassuring. It was honest. There was no tension in it. There was no fear. It all seemed familiar and natural. The bay colored horse with the dark mane had known this experience before. He would go along with this boy now. He could eat grass later.

Chapter 8

Stands-often led the bay colored horse with the dark mane along the Susquehanna. The river's water ran bank-full today, swollen by spring rains and snowmelt from farther north off Catskill mountainsides. The snow cover here had been gone weeks ago. Geese honked, the willows were yellow-green, the earth solidifying. Munsee women would soon plant this year's corn.

The Wyoming Valley was the only home Stands-often remembered. Almost all his twelve winters had been lived here. It was a pleasant valley.

Frequently the boy had heard his elders speak, in longing terms, of the old lands on the Fishkill. Mother said he had been born there but he did not remember those times or that place.

He knew only his home here. These forests, these meadows, these mountains and this river, were his world. For Stands-often it was enough.

The Munsee village was situated on the west bank of the Susquehanna, facing the river and the big mountain to the east. The Shawnee lived a days' hard walk down stream on the opposing bank. Upstream another day's walk brought you to a village of Mohicans and Naticokes living together on the east bank in much fewer numbers than they had known in earlier times. All were refugees. All had been pushed here by the Iroquois at behest of *Brother Onas*. All had been moved here to make room for white men and their farms.

The fields here were high enough above the river to avoid floods and the crops grew well. Tribes in the Wyoming Valley lived at peace with one another. Hunting nearby was becoming difficult but plenty of game still could be found in the surrounding mountains. Stands-often thought it was a good place for the Munsee to live.

More stragglers came every summer, Lenape Indians who had stayed behind, taken up ways of the whites, tried to live among them, failing for one reason or another, come home to live as cousins. They were welcome. But Stands-often noticed these relatives seldom smiled.

The bay colored horse with the dark mane had settled. The boy halted turning to face the big animal. With the noose still around the horse's neck he formed another loop in the standing part of the rope, slipped it over the horses muzzle and pulled it tight. Holding the rest of the lead rope in his right hand he grabbed the horses mane at its withers, with his left, and swung himself onto the back of the bay. The boy patted the bay's neck and gently nudged the horse into a trot along the river.

The sun had still not appeared over the ridge when Otter returned to the longhouse. A bay colored horse with a dark mane was tied to a post in front. Stands-often leaned against a little river-birch growing nearby.

"Did you bring me this horse nephew."

"Yes Uncle."

"Thank you."

Otter gazed at the boy for a long moment.

"I know you wish to come with us to visit the Moravians. I am sorry you cannot."

The boy did not respond. Otter saw the sun begin to peek over the ridge. He decided then.

"It is time nephew, for you to go out and seek your vision. There will be no moon tonight. You will leave in the morning. You will not return until the moon is full or you have found what you seek. Take little so you are not distracted."

"Yes Uncle. Thank you."

"You are welcome, nephew. Go, be calm, search with a pure heart, do not be discouraged by the evil ones, your Manitou *will find you.*"

"Yes Uncle."

31

Next morning Stands-often emerged from the longhouse early. His mother had prepared his favorite morning food, a cornmeal mush with maple sugar and dried berries. He had eaten two bowls-full as he blackened his face with the paint she had prepared for him last evening.

He wore a breach cloth covering his manhood and backside, moccasins on his feet, a deerskin shirt. He carried a small leather pouch around his neck on a leather thong and another slightly bigger one on his belt with his knife in a sheath and a big bright silver buckle. He carried a five-foot long hickory lance with a sharp copper metal point.

Early as it was others were up and about as he walked through the village. Uncles carving wooden bowls, cousins bringing wood or carrying water, mothers pounding grain, fathers patching canoes. They spoke quietly among themselves but none spoke to Stands-often or paid him any attention as he walked past with his blackened face. After his passing, however, their eyes all seemed to follow.

He walked briskly that morning, north along the river, then turning west he followed a feeder-stream as it meandered up into the mountains. It was a pretty little *run* about fifteen feet wide, but by afternoon it had narrowed to ten feet, and by evening Stands-often could jump across it in many places. He found a hollowed out log, filled it with the driest leaves he could find and spent a very long night beneath it waiting for dawn.

He slept little. He was already hungry. He rose with the first light and followed the stream higher up the mountain.

By noon he was weaker. Uncle had told him fasting did not mean starving. He knew he could not live a month roaming these mountains without eating something. But fasting did mean cleansing the bad spirits by controlling the appetite. He could wait.

He would rest. Maybe his Manitou would come and he could go home. But Uncle said an easily found vision was often not seen clearly. Such visions did not produce a strong guardian spirit. To be a good warrior or a good hunter required a strong vision.

Stands-often did not want to disappoint his family. He wished to be a great hunter and a great warrior. Likely he would not have his vision for many days. He was hungry and tired but he would wait. His Manitou would come to him when he had prepared himself to receive it.

Stands-often had wandered for days. He sat now next to a small fire. A fire, which he had sparked and lit using his flint and the steel blade of his knife. The firelight dancing in the darkness created strange shadows in his hidden lair. Smoke from his fire rose only a few feet before encountering and following the underside of the overhanging rock, finally rising out into the night sky. The air was cold, the moon not yet risen, the stars bright.

He could not remember how many days he had been here. He did not remember other camps. He did remember walking. He remembered walking a lot. He had dreamed many dreams but he did not feel he had seen a vision.

He worried he was not worthy. Maybe he had not prepared properly. Maybe he had not walked far enough. Maybe he should not have weakened, and eaten the parched corn, maybe he should not have eaten the mushrooms.

He was tired. He wondered if he had the strength to return home. Maybe he would die in the forest. He knew he was sick. His skin felt hot. He had found no Manitou to be his Guardian Spirit.

Stands-often passed out before the three-quarter moon rose spreading a silver light through the forest.

When dawn came Stands-often did not stir. The birds sang. The west-wind set the leaves to palpitating. The boy remained motionless.

Night came and another dawn.

A shadow passed in front of the small cave. Something scratched in the leaves outside. The boy's eyes opened. He saw the face of a cat. He shook himself awake and grabbed his spear. When he turned back he saw nothing.

Something still scratched in the leaves outside. He dragged himself out of his lair only to see a few turkeys running away through the trees making a terrible racket in the leaves.

He was done. He wanted to go home. His dreams did not matter. No vision had come. He had failed.

He looked up into the treetops and saw father sun. Something moved. He looked again. Still, there was nothing.

He felt faint. He remembered having set a snare near the little pond sometime in the past. He went to check it. There was a rabbit caught and hanging. He reached for the rabbit and almost touched the bobcat. For a second he stared into two big eyes the color of dark urine. Without a sound it bounded away vanishing in three long leaps. Then, It was gone.

Chapter 9

Wood smoke came carried on a breeze. Otter smelled it. A fire burned somewhere in the valley ahead. The bay with the dark colored mane shook his head and the horse behind stumbled coming down the slope. Otter turned to look back at Red-corn riding the black horse. Red-corn nodded. He smelled the smoke.

Gnandenhutton was up ahead. Moravians were friendly white men. Like the Munsee they valued hospitality. As did the Lenape they welcomed immigrants from Indian nations who had been displaced. It would hurt nothing to learn what could be learned about *Brother Onas* and others. The Moravians would have news.

Otter thought a moment about his nephew "Stands-often". *The boy learns quickly, and possesses a good memory. He is strong and has an honest spirit. He will find his Manitou.*

Otter heard an ax bite into a tree. It sounded close but he knew it wasn't.

The trail continued down a steep grade for more than an hour and then up for half an hour and then down again for another half hour. They heard no more of the ax. The wood smoke dissipated. They started up again. As they topped the little ridge in front of them, both the axman and the wood smoke came back to their consciousness, stronger, and closer this time.

Otter saw the light of a clearing in the forest ahead, down the slope. A thin ribbon of smoke rose into the sky. They started down again. After a short way a man with an ax appeared working off to the edge of that clearing. Otter saw a rooftop, then a cabin wall, and then another log wall, with a window opening, peaking through the trees.

Here came a man walking the trail ahead of them. The man stopped when he saw the horsemen. He yelled something back behind him. Otter pulled up his mount and to his rear he heard Red-corn's mount slide to a halt, stamp his hooves and shake his head. Another horse, from somewhere beyond the clearing, whinnied.

They waited—facing the man on the trail. Soon two other men joined the first. Only one carried a weapon, a musket, held under his arm. The man, they had first seen, motioned them to come on. Otter released his taught rein and nudged his mount ahead at a walk.

"Welcome Friends. Welcome to Gnandenhutton," said Elias Knepp.

"Thank you," said Otter. "Reverend Antes here?"

"No he's not." Said Elias " He went yesterday with some of the brethren to float a raft of lumber down to Bethlehem. Be back tomorrow or the day after. Come far?"

"Wyoming," said Otter.

"Brother James, will you show our friends to the chapel and see they receive some refreshments.   Samuel and I will find the goat," said Elias.

Brother's James and Samuel were dressed like Elias but they were obviously closer to being brothers to Otter and Red-corn—Christian Indians. There were far more of them living at Gnandenhutton than there were white missionaries. The Christian Indians talked less but they dressed and believed, as did the missionaries. Otter had met many in the last few years.

More Indians seemed to be joining the Moravians every month and not always just those who had been displaced. Otter did not understand why any Munsee person would leave their family, but he had stopped trying to convince them to come home.

The Moravians were good neighbors like the Shawnee, Mohican and Nanticoke. They were honest, hospitable, and courteous.   They lived in many ways similar to Lenape, sharing ownership of the land and resources as a community.

Like Munsee men and women Moravians prayed to a Manitou who they called Jesus. Their Jesus god had sought his strength in the wilderness just as Otter's nephew did now.

Moravians sometimes allied with Lenape in arguments with "*Brother Onas.*" They were not like other white men. They did not drink liquor or sell it to Indians. At times they suffered the scorn of the other white people. Otter had decided— *they* could be trusted.

Otter had not come to Gnandenhutton for over a year. As he rode in, following Brother James, he could see the Moravians had been busy. The chapel, two cabins, and a sawmill were finished on the west side of the creek. On the east side of Mahoning creek, spreading out in a semi-circle up the hillside, were thirty-or-so cabins, where Christian Indians lived. Beside each cabin grew a small garden of corn beans and squash. Beyond the cabins higher up the hill were orchards of young fruit trees traded to them by the Munsee women of Wyoming. It was a good town.

A few hundred yards downstream Mahoning creek fed its water into Lehigh River, which rushed on down passed the Moravian town of Bethlehem and then on to meet the Delaware near the small but growing town of Easton.

Otter and Red-corn would wait and seek council with Henry Antes when he returned.

Elias heard the bell tinkle just now somewhere ahead. He saw nothing but laurel thicket. Then he saw long tracks, stretched out in the mud, sliding down into the ravine.

This goat was a real pain in the neck. She was too smart to keep penned or tied and two dumb to find her way home. Still she produced well, and he liked the cheese made from her milk.

He looked over the ledge carefully not wanting to slide in himself. She was at the bottom with her rope caught above her on a tree root. Lucky it was not a deep gorge or the goat would have hanged herself.

There was no water running in the ravine today. He walked a few strides down slope where he could climb into the ravine without falling. He slogged back up to the goat. The ground was muddy at the bottom. She stood with her head pulled back the way she had come down. The rope was taut above her. He had to climb up a little to free the tangle from the root but he kept a good hold on the rope so she could not run away again.

It was almost noon when Elias got back on the trail, along the Lehigh, about two miles below the village. He started back but soon heard horses coming from behind. He stopped, tied the goat to a tree on the left side of the trail and slipped across and out into the brush on the right side.

Soon the horses appeared plodding along. It was Henry Antes and Brother John a Christian Indian. Elias walked back to the trail arriving by the goat about the same time as the two mounted men.

"Elias Knepp, good morning to you sir," said Reverend Antes.

"Good morning sir. Have a good trip?"

"That we did. The lumber was needed. They will be wanting more. Bethlehem is bustling with people, Elias, both coming and going. The land trouble is starting again. The whole countryside seems to be shifting populations. Any Indians south or east of us will finally be squeezed out.

I saw old acquaintances of mine from over on Perkiomen creek near Schwampp. Three of the Feagley brothers a couple of the Grub families and Obidia Rauch, were passing through Bethlehem. They're on their way to settle up north in New Jersey's Valley of the Paulinskill. Some Lenape stragglers who had been living on the Paulinskill are moved in near Bethlehem—for now. They came to Moravian Church Services.

A man named Fredrick Hoeth and his sons have taken up land near Poco-Poco. He claims he bought his land legal and I'm sure he did. He says others are coming soon. The Indians of Poco-Poco know they can't stay on their lands. They will join us here by fall," said Antes.

I see the goat is up to her usual ramblings."

"Yeah, she almost hung herself with her own rope this time." Said Elias.

"Luckily she has a good shepherd like you," said Brother John.

Henry Antes and Brother John chuckled a moment while Elias untied the goat. When they were all moving up the trail, toward town, Henry pick up the conversation where he had left off:

"I hope we can hold some kind of line here so the Indians won't have to move again. They've moved enough."

A hawk screamed somewhere off in the distance, and crows called nearby.

"The biggest news is from New York," said Antes. "Ten families, almost fifty people came from Shekomeko last week. They were exhausted. They're Mohican converts, driven out by their white neighbors. Governor Clinton was unwilling to protect them. He blamed the missionaries. We Moravians it seems are not long welcomed anywhere we go. Some of those Mohican families may join us in a few weeks here at Gnandenhutton. Looks like we're going to see big growth in our congregation. We'll have much work to get done, if we are to be ready."

"I forgot to mention Reverend, two travelers showed up from the Wyoming Valley day before yesterday. They're waiting for a council."

It was cloudy and still when the two Munsee riders topped the ridge where they had first smelled the smoke of Gnandenhutton a week ago. They were heading home to the Wyoming Valley. Otter was thinking about his nephew Stands-often when Red Corn turned back to say:

"I saw Willow in the town this morning while you and Henry Antes were catching the speckled trout for breakfast. Calls herself Mary."

Otter said nothing. Willow was a childhood friend. She had joined the Moravians over a year ago.

"She said she had been back through the Minisink all the way to the village the white men call Marbletown. She went with the missionaries. Munsee fields are now plowed in the white way. The Dutchmen are building more stone barns and cutting more trees. A few strangers have moved in but not many. She says New York and New Jersey still fight among themselves concerning who has the right to sell our lands."

Otter said nothing. An hour passed and they stopped beside a little run to let the horses catch their wind and drink. It was a dark, quiet place of tall beech trees, big rocks and green moss. The water babbled along as water does in such places.

"Did Mary see any of our old friends?"

Otter had used Willow's Christian name. Red corn noticed that and wondered about it. But he did not ask why. He knew what Otter was seeking.

"Your friend Joris lives with a growing family in a cabin still at Kendiamong. His bother Solomon married John Decker's daughter. They built a mill on Machackemack branch across the river from Decker's place. They too have many children. We get old my friend."

It was true. It had been over thirty years since they had learned to hunt and fish there, together with the two white boys, near Minisink Island. It had been many years since the Iroquois and Brother Onas had demanded the Munsee leave their homes on the Fishkill and move to the Susquehanna. Since that time he had not returned.

But Otter had wondered about his old friend Joris Davids. He wished now they could hunt together a few days like in the old times. He knew Joris would welcome him home, but he knew also, many of the other white men would not.

Chapter 10

(1751)

$\mathcal{H}$arness leather squeaked and hardware jingled. Heavy hooves clomped as the big team trotted past, pulling the empty wagon bouncing along the cobbled street. Elias was back on High-street in Philadelphia. In fact he had just bought a peach from the farmer who had sold one to Thomas Shirby a few years before but he had no way to know that. Anyway, Elias Knepp had forgotten who Thomas Shirby was. He remembered the encounter at the courthouse when the Iroquois were in town but not the name of the boy heading out to the Juniata River to find his cousins.

"Ain't you one of them Moravians that lives up north with the Christian Injuns?" asked the peach seller."

It was a slow day at market. Elias didn't feel any threat in the question. Just seeking conversation seemed the man's intent.

"Sort of," he answered. "I live with 'em. I ain't joined their church but I work for Brother Antes."

He wondered to himself a moment why that was. Why he hadn't joined the church? Why hadn't Brother Antes pushed him more to join?

"Well I heard about the massacre up that way," said the farmer. "Why wasn't you killed."

"What massacre are you talking about?"

"The one up at Poco Poco."

"I don't know what you are talking about. I know nothing about a massacre at Poco Poco. Who got killed?"

"I don't know the names," said the farmer. "I just heard they was burning and killing all over up there."

"Who?"

"The Savages."

"Which ones?"

"Hell I don't know which ones. Delaware, Shawnee, Iroquois, Wapinger, one's same as another as far as I'm concerned. Just Injuns that's all. You're lucky you got back here with your hair young man."

"When? When was this so called massacre?"

"Sometime back a couple weeks ago I think it was."

"There weren't no massacre," said Elias.

"Ain't what I heard."

"I just came down river last week heard nothing of it," said Elias.

"Maybe it wasn't where you was at, or maybe it happened after you left. But everybody knows about it. The Injuns are murdering white folks all over up near the forks of the Delaware."

"Who says?"

"Ever body. They was a trader feller came through yesterday he knew all about it. He said he talked to a feller had been shot at hisself. It's bad up there all right. You best stay away from there fer a spell.

Excuse me. Can I help you missy?"

The farmer turned to sell his peaches to a young black woman with a big basket in her arms.

Elias walked away. He learned long ago, you can't argue with ignorance. It was hard to tell folks about Indians unless they knew some personally. Most people didn't know any Indians. What's more, they didn't care to know any.

Rumors were always flying. They even had a name for it. People called it the flying news. It came carried one man to another, one place to another usually added to as it went along. He would probably read about the massacre in Mr. Franklin's newspaper tomorrow.

42

Still, often times, there was a grain of truth somewhere in the stories. Maybe someone had been murdered near Poco Poco. It happened from time to time on the frontiers and sometimes here in town too. It wasn't always Indians who did the killing but if there were no witnesses they usually got the blame.

He ate his peach as he walked back to John Branch's business. Henry Antes and John were seated on a bench outside the apothecary shop. It really was a slow market day for July. No Immigrant ships were docked presently at the wharfs, and many farmers still were busy working their fields following a month of very late rains.

Have you heard the flying news about the big massacre up at Poco Poco he asked?

Yes, John has told me all about it. Strange we didn't hear earlier about it since we just came from up that way," said Antes. "I doubt anything at all really happened. I suspect it's the burned out cabins and barns Brother William's family left behind. They had three cabins at Poco Poco and three barns. They were angry when they left. I'm guessing they didn't intend to leave their work for someone else to enjoy. That was selfish I know but as I said they were angry when they came to us.

Some new immigrant family likely came along saw the burned out shell of a cabin and barn. They didn't suspect Indians built it so they figured Indians killed the settlers who had, and then burned their houses and barns."

"They're half right anyway. Indians did burn the buildings."

He chuckled. John and Elias joined in. It was funny when you thought about it, if, you didn't think about it too long.

A dog down the street started barking and snapping at a big draft horse. There were a hundred other horses tied up or moving down High street this very moment. What this particular animal had done to offend that dog did not seem apparent.

"No massacre this time, I'm betting," said Henry Antes, "but it will take a month before Brother Onas bothers to send someone to be sure. By then the story will be so widespread it will never be tamped back down completely. That's my guess."

"Likely you're right," said John Branch, "but I think there really are problems out west. The French for a fact are on the move. They've built a new fort at Presque Isle up on Lake Erie and they are supposed to be building one now at Venango on the Allegheny River. The Virginians are all upset about it. They say the French are on their land. Brother Onas says it's his land. Everyone is trying to line up tribes to help them one way or another. It looks like some bad sign to me. There was a big discussion about it all up at the courthouse day before yesterday. The authorities are concerned."

"If the French are serious John there will be trouble," said Henry. "The Ohio Indians are dependent on them. They have been trading partners for years now. Plenty of Frenchmen are already married into those tribes out there in the Ohio Country. My Indians have told me about it. You know how loyal Indians are to family. The question is how much do the French want a fight with King George and what will the Indians north of here decide to do."

"I suspect the Lenape from the Ohio country will come visiting their cousins along the Susquehanna. They'll ask them to join their fight. I don't think they will but I'm not certain. Brother Onas needs to give them good reasons to stay loyal instead of using the Iroquois to kick them further away. Even a family dog will bite if it gets kicked often enough," said Antes.

"Well you can't make that argument Henry. People don't trust you folks. They think Moravians may be papists in disguise. I've heard the talk. Some are beginning to question me because I'm your friend. But I tell them it's just business. I hope that's all right with you?"

"You're a good friend John. I trust you not to get yourself in trouble on my behalf. We need you in good stead with the authorities. We may need your representation and it's not a lie we do business together."

"I wonder how much the Iroquois themselves can be trusted?" asked Elias. He had learned much in the past couple years living at the Forks. "They have brothers of their own living among the French up north. The Seneca and even a lot of

44

Mohawks have left their homes to move north. I hope Johnson knows what he is doing with those boys. Lots of Palatine Germans have been moving into the Schoharie Valley I hear. I wonder what the Mohawk think about that? Will they fight for us or against us."

"Well *we* are not fighting anyone said Antes. You know that Elias. If you want to fight you will have to leave us. The church's teaching is very clear on that point. Thou shalt not kill. *We* will stay neutral. We will do our work to promote peace and God will be our guardian. The Quakers will want peace. I'm sure the Amish will. Others in Pennsylvania will clamor for war. But war is never the answer."

Elias was quiet. He was thinking. *Maybe that's why I never joined. War may not be the answer but maybe the French won't give us a choice.* He said nothing.

Chapter 11

Sixteen–year-old Beletje Davids stood over the crock churn.

She could hear the cream splash under the lid with each downward strokes of the dasher held in her hand. She was a long way yet from having butter.

Churning was a daily chore. She knew its sounds. Like so many things she did, progress was gauged by sound, feel, or smell. After you did a thing often enough you just knew where you were in the process. Any shortcuts would have already been taken. She knew there weren't any more. It would be ready when it was ready.

There was no reason to rush. *Things just take time*, she thought, *it's the way things are. Good butter takes effort, but not as much as spinning.* She made good butter. Her sister liked to spin.

"Glad we're here cozy by the fire," she said, to Lea standing across the room at the spinning wheel, "the boys will have trouble breaking that ice this morning."

"Yeah, I'm glad too. Daniel and Jakey have had a tough time since Pa was killed."

" They're doing their best," said Beletje.

"I know. They're doing fine. They will get the animals to water. I wish Ma could get well and notice everything the boys are doing."

The elder Lea Davids, their mother, still lay in her bed. Lea of the spinning wheel, the oldest daughter, glanced at the door to the other downstairs room. *Mourning takes time*, she thought, *like anything.* But people were beginning to talk. Ma had ten children. She couldn't mope under the covers or in the shadows forever?

"I guess she will know when she is ready to face life again," said Lea to her sister, "She can't be rushed."

Lea knew of other women and men too who had lost a spouse. Death was part of life In the Minisink Valley. Second marriages were common in the neighborhood. Most people got over their loss after a time and went on with their lives. But she was also aware of others who never came out of mourning. Some died themselves; others were never the same afterward.

Lea stared into the fire burning in the stone fireplace for a few moments. A tall hickory flame licked at the chimney flue with little sound save the rush of hot air rising. It was a good winter fire—dry hickory burning hot with almost no popping or crackling. The room was warm.

The hum of the spinning wheel and the thump of the churn battled the sounds of a cold wind blowing outside the stone house.

"You think Pa was killed over the border fight between the Jersey's and New York?"asked Beletje.

"I know Uncle Joris and the boys think so."

"Who was grandfather Solomon's father?"

"Joris—Uncle Joris was named for him don't you remember."

"Yes, I do," said Beletje, "now that you remind me."

"What was his father's name?

"Christoffel I think," said Lea.

"No that was the old Uncle burned up at Schenectady with his family by the French and their Indians. Remember?"

"Yeah I know about him," said Lea, "but he was named after his father who was the Christoffel they used to talk about, who came down from Fort Orange in the old Dutch times to live at Kingston, called Esopus then. Remember? The one granddad Decker's family talked about too. The one everybody was scared of. The one that lived sometimes among the Indians, and the one who disappeared somewhere on the Hudson River on a trip to the Manhattans."

"That's right," said Beletje, "I wonder who his Pa was?"

"I don't know. Someone somewhere in the old countries I guess. Maybe Domini Freyenmoet might know. Maybe it would be somewhere in the church records."

"Why do you care?" asked Lea.

Just interested I guess. Never thought about it much before Pa died. Guess it don't matter but a person should know where she comes from," said Beletje.

"We know. We come from right here in the Minisink. Our families have been here for generations. Fort Orange is far enough ago to know who you are. The rest don't matter," said Lea.

"Guess not' but do you ever think about who your kids and grandkids will be."

"Not much. I just wonder who my husband might be. I'm kinda partial right now to that Westbrook boy," said Lea.

Beletje smiled. She couldn't hear a big splash in the churn now. The paddle was getting heavier.

Chapter 12

Stands-often was happy to be alone. He preferred to hunt unaccompanied. He enjoyed the solitude.

The wind still had a bite to it. Winter was not entirely gone from the Wyoming Valley. He thought he might smell snow.

It was early for spring, but there had been some warm days. The sap was running in the trees. The women went out daily to gather it in old bark buckets or new metal ones bought from the white traders. There was always a shortage of buckets this time of year. Soon the boiling would begin.

Lenape women loved to sweeten their foods with maple sugar. Munsee people had a sweet tooth. Christian Indians who spent time among the whites said they never could get accustomed to the salty taste of white man's food.

A few of the Christian Indians had moved home from Gnandenhutton. They said it was crowded now with almost 500 Indians living at the mission. They still worshiped their Manitou Jesus but they had come home to Wyoming to be near their families and relearn some of the old traditions.

The Christians and the white missionaries said it was the year of their lord seventeen hundred and fifty three. Stands-often knew that was important to them, somehow. He did not understand why.

He knew that the old ways of his people were changing fast and the new white ways were not always better. The new buckets were nice though.

He hunted today with his bow and arrows. He preferred the feel. He thought guns cost too much and took too long to reload. He could shoot three or four arrows to every shot with a musket. It was true the musket was deadly at a greater distance, but how often was a long shot really necessary. In the thickets where deer were hunted 30 or 40 yards was often as far as you could see anyway.

It was late in the day. He had traveled a long way from the village. He studied the tracks on the ground. There were many deer tracks in the mud around a little pool of water fed by a tiny run coming in from above and then flowing out to continue its journey toward the river. It was obvious the animals were frequenting this watering hole as they moved from the thick brush up the hillside, where they bedded down in daytime, before moving at night—out to feed in a small meadow down the slope.

He pulled his bow and slipped it over his shoulder to ride on his back with his quiver containing the four hunting arrows. He climbed a nearby cluster of big rocks to a fallen log where he had a clear shot over the outgoing deer trail, which meandered off through the brush toward the meadow.

I got here just in time he thought; *the sun will soon sink. The deer will come.* He took the bow from his back and settled himself on the log to wait.

Daylight faded. The crow made its final caw. Night hawks swooped above. Owls began to call.

The brush rustled and suddenly a deer appeared near the pool ... not the whole deer just its back, front shoulder and leg. That was all he could see. It was quiet for a long time. The deer's head was down at the water. Its back shivered once.

The brush obscured the hunter's view of the water hole. A few minutes passed and the daylight continued to fade. Stands-often was aware now of a second deer near the pool because occasionally it flipped its white tail. It was smaller than the first, *maybe this year's fawn.*

Then he saw the antlered deer raising its head sniffing the air. The buck smelled something amiss. *Danger perhaps?* What it was he was not sure, but he kept his muzzle up sniffing. He stamped his hoof and snorted. Nothing moved. Finally satisfied, he lowered his head to drink.

There were other deer nearby. Stands often could see an ear twitch or hear a hoof scratch. He wasn't sure how many. And then the doe trotted down the trail. He let her pass and then the fawn and then another doe. But as the buck came into the open he drew his bow. The arrow he had already knocked into his bowstring. He let it fly and it sang through the air to its target down just behind the shoulder of the deer. The buck stumbled and then bolted ahead. He was out of sight but Stands- often knew he would not go far. He waited for the deer's life to bleed out.

The antlered dear lay down in the brush to rest and died. The young hunter offered a prayer for the spirit of the deer and a prayer of thanks to his Manitou—the bobcat—for guiding him to this kill.

The remaining deer of the little herd trotted down the trail passed the buck and out into the meadow. Bats came to swirl and dart in the open air. Night frogs began their chorus.

Chapter 13

*T*he wood cracked and popped as it split. Zack Miller twisted the froe in his left hand and the wood split more. He let it drop into the crevice created. Twisting again he split off the shingle with a final clean *snap*. It toppled then into the pile at his feet. He set the froe back onto the wooden block gauging the three/quarter inch thickness with his eye. He struck the froe with the beadle he held in his right hand and started the process over. Twist and drop twist and drop until another shingle fell away. The oak blank had two more shingles left before he reached for another round to lift onto the splitting stump.

The barn would require many shingles. Jesse and William were busy with the cross- cut sawing the rounds. Little Johnny would be back soon to stack the shingles near the barn, or more precisely, near the pile of squared logs which would soon become a barn when enough timbers were hued square and enough neighbors came over to help raise them.

Old-man Meeks and his family would come to help. They lived in the cabin at the mouth of this hollow near the river. That was a couple miles away. Close neighbors out here. Miller liked this location up West Licking Creek. Life on the Juniata had been peaceful. Never the less, Zack preferred the security he felt a little distance away from the river traffic. *All kinds of folks travel the bigger water*.

This was the far western frontier of the colony. Only trappers and traders had any reason to travel further, through the mountains, west of the Juniata watershed. Indians came through to trade further east. Some followed the river downstream to the Susquehanna. From the confluence there, they could travel upstream into Indian country, Shamokin, Wyoming and other points north, or they might turn downstream to visit the world of white men, farms, and Philadelphia.

Miller wondered about Philadelphia. *I sure would enjoy another fine meal at the Town Tavern* he thought. *There is no fine dining here on the Juniata*. He had enjoyed his last meal in Philadelphia with the old German fresh off the boat. He had forgotten the man's name but he remembered he was set for the Schwampp with his family. *Likely had more money to invest than I did,* thought Miller. *I wonder how he's doing.*

Heinrich Feagley took another bite of the gooseberry pie. *I love gooseberry. Come to tink of it,* Heinrich thought, *I pretty much like all kinds of pie. 'Tis is all good so long as tis sweet.* Heinrich had a sweet tooth he couldn't deny it.

The day was bright and the white clouds were puffy little ones which seemed to hang in the same place like in a painting he had seen once back in the old country. The corn in the field across the road was about a foot high; the wheat up the hill was still green though beginning to turn yellow.

"vhat you think, Ezekiel, will you think about it."

"I don't know, Heinrich, It's only six acres but it's good ground. I hadn't thought about selling land. I'm like most everyone else... always looking to expand."

They sat on the ground, in the shade of the big sugar maple, settled with their backs against the tree neither facing the other, each one looking out across Ezekiel Graber's farm studying a slightly different slice of the panoramic view determined by the circumference of the tree. They were neighbors. They often worked their fields together. Still, this was business Heinrich had proposed.

Heinrich's wooden bowl was empty. Ezekiel knew... not because he turned his head to see but because he hadn't heard Heinrich's wooden spoon scraping the bowl in a while. Half Ezekiel's pie was still in his bowl.

"Go on and have yer second piece, that's why Anna brought two extra. Ones fer you ones fer me. Don't wait on me. I like to savor my food fer a spell. You go ahead," said Ezekiel.

Heinrich took his second piece into his bowl. Quiet settled around the two for a while except for the sounds of pie eating and a very gentle breeze in the leaves at the top of the maple. They were comfortable with quiet.

In a bit they became aware of a horse-team and wagon approaching. It came over the hill from the north. Soon they could make out a farmer they recognized but neither knew by name. That was more common these days on Swamp Creek. The empty wooden wagon bounced along, rattling. The two-horse team had barely broken a sweat. The farmer waved as he passed but he didn't turn in at the drive.

"What do you know about the Indian troubles... anything new?" asked Ezekiel.

"Nutting new. De drei younger boy's de movf up in New Jerseh auf de Paulinskill,"said Heinrich, "ve vorry."

"I'd worry too," said Ezekiel, " but, I'm sure your boys will do fine. There are lots of folks starting to move up past the forks of the Delaware. As long as they are In New Jersey they should be okay. It's the Pennsylvania side of the river and up in the Minisink area that might see trouble, and out west on the Juniata."

He sighed.

"I tell you what Heinrich I'll think about sellin the six acres but not this year."

"Danken." Heinrich said, as he rose to leave.

When he stood he looked back down. Thank Anna for de Pie. He noticed Ezekiel's second piece of pie sat untouched not counting the three horse flies perched on its thick brown crust.

"Das goot pie," Heinrich said, as he walked slowly away toward home leaving Ezekiel Graber in the shade under the tree.

54

Chapter 14

$\mathcal{T}$he horses were skittish coming down the trail. Yesterday's rain had been a refreshing break from summer drought. Today's temperature was cold for early Fall.

Reverend Antes rode the lead animal. Brother William and sister Elizabeth followed on their mounts riding abreast of one another. Elias Knepp followed the others on his big boned black horse almost fifty yards behind.

The Kings Road, as it was called, by some, really seemed to be a road through the Minisink area not a game trail as they usually encountered in northern Pennsylvania. They were not used to such roads until you got south nearer Philadelphia. Still as wide as the road was it did not seem heavily traveled. The grass and weeds were growing tall in it and little saplings were taking root some places. Elias had not seen sign of a single wagon track south of Minisink Island.

They had come down from Kingston a week ago where Brother Antes had met with the Elders of the Dutch Reformed Church. Yesterday, being the Sabbath, they had stopped for services at the Machackemack Dutch Reformed Church. Domini Freyenmoet had preached a long sermon and then talked at length with Reverend Antes before they could get away. Reverend Antes said he liked the young man, though they disagreed on doctrine.

It had been a long trip. It was Elias's first travel into the Colony of New York. Kingston was a nice enough town but certainly no city like Philadelphia. He wondered what Albany and New York were like.

The country was much as he expected but more pine forest, less hardwoods than at the Forks. Marbletown was the only village of any size south of Kingston. Otherwise it was just forest and road, hills and valleys, with an occasional isolated house and farm established along that road. He had noticed a few clusters of two or three farms together in a little valley, like at Machackemack, but not many.

There must be other folks in those hills, he thought, *because just in the fifty miles through the Minisink Valley there are three churches we heard about. They're small but they must have individual congregations? Though Domini Freyenmoet is their only traveling minister.*

Elias's horse balked and put its head down to sniff the trail. Elias noticed the bear tracks in the wet mud. *Looks to be three. Two are smaller than the other.* He wondered if his companions ahead had noticed. He figured one had. William was a hunter. But when Elias looked up the other riders were moving steadily away toward high mountains visible to the south.

The road grew steadily steeper as they traveled south. He knew they were nearing the water gap where the river cuts through the Kittatinny Mountains. On the west shore of the river was Lower Smithfield Township, Pennsylvania, at least according to the white folks. Although everyone was aware the Lenape still claimed the land.

Across the Delaware River, in Pennsylvania, the Kittatinnys were sometimes called the Blue Mountains but that depended on who you asked. Those high ridges stretching away to the southwest were fast becoming the new boundary separating the white farmers from the red ones. Most of the Indians were moving north and west. Soon the whites would occupy everything south of the Blue Mountains except for the area where Moravian Christian Indians lived in the forks area.

Elias noticed a narrow trail from the east merging into the road. They were getting close to Dupui's. Samual Dupui was an Indian Trader whose father Nicholas had taken up land on the West side of the river decades earlier. He had maintained good relations with the Munsee. He traded fair and was respectful.

But the fur trade was not what it once had been. Samual Dupui found his business more and more depended on trade of a different sort. He had new customers, immigrant settlers moving into the area to take up land and build homes. His trading post was becoming a cross road for German and Scotch-Irish immigrants moving between Philadelphia and the valley of the Paulinskill in New Jersey. Thus he had begun a

56

ferry business and started stocking different items for his trade.

Other tracks were on the trail now. *Looks like three other horses had come through from the east since yesterday, thought Elias.* The Mountains ahead looked steep. Elias knew they weren't planning to fight their way through that rough terrain. Soon they would cross Dupui's ferry to the west side. The trails through the foothills over there would take them home. Had they arrived a few days ago the ferry ride would not have been necessary. The horses could have forded the river on Saturday but today the river was higher, not near bank full but too high to wade.

The big boned black stumbled coming off the ferry and shied away from the rope coiled on the ground. Elias kept a tight rein and led him up the muddy bank. He and his horse were last on and last off the ferryboat so the others were already moving toward the trading post.

Dupui had several buildings but the main house was the trading business and there were six other horses tethered near the front door. His party of four more horses crowded the little yard. A boy came forward from near the barn.

"I'll water and feed 'em if you like".

Reverend Antes looked back at Elias.

"I'll stay with the horses," said Elias.

Reverend Antes smiled turned back and handed the boy his reins as did Brother William. Elizabeth gave charge of her animal to Elias.

The boy led the two horses toward a water trough and Elias followed. While the animals slurped up the mossy green water, the boy brought over a handcart loaded with hay and forked off a little of it for each animal.

Elias stepped to the top end of the trough. A small wooden sluice brought a steady flow of water in from a little run somewhere up the slope. He noticed a similar sluice took any overflow back beyond the barn and dumped it into a ditch directed toward the pig lot.

"Always got a flow?"

"Most times," said the boy, "there's a gristmill further up the hill and a sawmill closer to the river. The stream is spring fed from the big mountains. Had some water even this summer when it was plenty dry if you recall."

The boy was seated on a large stone which had been cut square for some purpose not presently apparent and dropped here to await it's future. The boy had put it to use in the meanwhile as a place of rest. Elias leaned up against the water trough to wait.

"Staying the night?" The boy asked."

"Doubt it," said Elias, looks like you have a full house and the Reverend prefers to make his own camp in decent weather." He nodded toward the house and asked, "strangers?"

"Yeah, never seen 'em before, not like you folks. You passed through with the Reverend last week and I seen the Reverend a couple times before that, going up to Kingston I bet. These folks I never seen before. They look like gentlemen. I was in there a while ago heard 'em tell ol Nicholas they was from Connecticut."

"Why they here?"

"Couldn't tell you.

They had been back on the trail for an hour. Henry Antes had said little. They rode abreast of one another right now and Elias was curious.

"Who were them folks at Dupui's?"

"I don't know for sure who they were," said Henry. "They said they were here to look at some land over in the Wyoming Valley."

"Did they look crazy?"

"They looked like strangers—but they weren't new immigrants or farmers. I told 'em anything north of the Blue Mountains was Indian land. They said Indians had sold some of it. When I asked which Indians they couldn't say. Said they were sent to map the rivers. I told them only the Pennsylvania government could legally buy land from Indians, *Brother Onas* had a law. They didn't say much after that. They weren't rude … just evasive and quiet.

"The boy said he heard 'em tell Dupui they was from Connecticut," said Elias.

"I figured that. They have tried before. They lay a claim overlapping *"Brother Onas*. There's been trouble over it for years. Some say their claim precedes; others say they have no claim at all. Until the kings ministers in London figure out how they can best make money on the dealings no one will decide the matter. I guess whom ever has people living there first will have a leg up on that argument."

"Well the Lenape and the Shawnee been livin' there fer years," said Elias.

"I know son. I didn't say it was right I just said that's what's going to happen. It always does. We came to the new world thinking it would be different here, but other men came with us and more are coming after. Some are good pious folks but not all. The Devil is at work wherever we go.

We are charged by the Good Lord to fight the good fight, but we don't always win in this life."

The frost crunched quietly under his moccasins; a crow cawed from across the river; water gurgled its way down stream toward the Chesapeake. The day was cloudless the sun had not yet toped the big ridge to the east. Squirrels chattered at Stands-often from a tall river bottom hickory off to his right.

The little spotted mare was almost caught. She was reaching out with her head low to take the grass in his outstretched left hand. The rope held by the boys right hand— the rope sliding over her neck—was not yet known to her. Then she felt it and pulled back, cinching the rope tight. The boy spoke some reassuring words and soon swung himself onto her back. It was then that the boy noticed the smoke.

A thin grey-blue ribbon rose from the trees down river. *Maybe a mile away.*

Stands-often hadn't smelled the smoke. He wondered who it might be. He was only five mile below the village.

Too close for a hunting party to need a camp. Shawnee from down river never hunt this way. Why would anyone need a big fire here on such a fine morning?

He climbed off the spotted mare, tied her to a nearby willow, and trotted off to investigate.

An hour later he squatted in front of the cattails among the reed grasses. Normally he could have stood here and not be seen but it had been a terrible dry summer. The grass was short. The grass no longer sparkled with frost but it glistened now with the welcomed moisture.

He could see three white men who would soon be ready to mount their saddled horses. A pack-horse stood mostly loaded. Two of the men were cinching up ropes on opposing sides of the animal. The third man was making water standing beside their fire. When the man finished, he turned and mounted his horse. The other two men tied off their ropes with a flurry and a slap. They too mounted, turned their horses and trotted away downstream the last man pulling the pack-horse behind on a long lead.

Stands-often watched them go. Finally he saw the pack animal's tail swished high in the air just as it topped a little rise and then the party of white men dropped down out of sight beyond. Quickly he turned and began running back toward the spotted mare tied to the willow a mile away.

The tracks led back toward Dupuis. Otter could tell the white men were pushing hard. He wondered why they were in such a hurry. They had only found one other horse handy when Stands-often brought the news. Therefore the boy now rode double behind Red-corn on the spotted mare. They had not come prepared for a chase. It would soon be dark.

60

Is that them coming back, he wondered. Someone had just topped the rise ahead walking the trail toward them. The man was dressed like a white man but he walked in the Indian way. *It's brother Joseph.* Otter recognized him now.

They waited for Joseph to come on.

"Welcome brother."

"Do you seek the white men I have passed."

"Yes."

"Don't bother. They are rude men. They have told me why they are here. They said they have ownership of land in the valley of Wyoming and they plan to return in the spring with a thousand other white men from Connecticut. They will build houses and farms. They say there is enough for all, and Indians do not make good use of the land anyway. They say we Indians can stay or leave it is of no matter to them. They plan to build a block house for defense and said they will deal harshly with trouble makers, or any types of thievery."

They call us thieves, thought Otter, *maybe we should pursue these white men and kill them tonight as they sleep.* But he did not voice his thoughts.

"The people will need to discuss this matter in council," he said.

Otter offered his hand to Brother Joseph who took it and swung himself up behind Otter onto the back of the bay colored horse with the dark mane. The daylight dimmed as they all turned back toward home.

Two little boys scudded up High-street chasing a wooden hoop. The markets were busy. Butternut squash, brightly colored gourds and huge dark orange pumpkins— the kind with big brown wart-like growths on their skin—were displayed everywhere. Mothers had their babies bundled up in little quilts. Everyone it seemed was trying to keep some kind of hat from blowing off in the breeze.

There were all kinds of hats and bonnets. Sailors caps, top hats, broad brimmed ones (almost always colored black) and short brimmed hats (usually the same color). There were even sock hats, which came in more various coloration... common preference today being red.

Josh Broadhead was not used to so many people. He didn't come to the city often. He was out of his element. But today he was a young man on a mission. Six foot tall and broad in the shoulders people stepped aside as he came stomping up the street.

There ahead of him was the sign with the paint beginning to fade and chip but still very legible if Josh could have read the words. He could not read, but he knew what the sign said. The bold, black, block, letters proclaimed: *The Pennsylvania Gazette*. Josh might not read but his cousin Daniel did. Josh had seen this heading often on the papers cousin Daniel read to folks at home anytime a newspaper could be had.

This was the place all right. Just as he was arriving a big black cur came running out of the ally-way and latched onto his left legging at his heel. Josh sidestepped like a rattler and kicked the dog viciously into a wooden barrel a few paces away. He thought about following up and stomping it to death but there were folks in the street watching. He smiled and trotted ahead to the doorway.

Mr. Franklin wasn't in. The big German lad operating the press said he was down at the Town Tavern. Josh knew where that was but he had never been inside the place. *Too rich fer me,* he thought. *I like the bars on Front street which is where I plan to be tonight.* Right now he had a message to deliver and if Franklin was in the Town Tavern, that's where he intended to go.

Franklin was not in the Town Tavern. He had left. A man inside told Josh he overheard Franklin say he had a meeting with Mr. Stretch and Mr. Harding over at the new Statehouse building, something about the giant clock being installed.

Josh bounded down the back steps and headed for the Statehouse. Everyone knew where that was. It had been under construction for over a decade. *They better stop worrying about clocks and fancy new buildings,* he thought, *and start worrying about the damn Connecticut trespassers.*

He had seen Franklin before. Late thirties, stocky build like Josh, strong looking (but likely not as strong as Josh), well dressed, and there he was standing out in front of the building under a big oak tree which had most of its reddish/brown leaves still attached while other trees' leaves blew away in today's breeze. Franklin was obviously in discussion with two other men both holding their hat on with one hand while pointing out various features of the building with the other.

Josh was no longer in a rush. He wasn't a foolish boy. He knew he was not in the backcountry. While he did not understand etiquette, he knew there was such a thing. He had been told people did not like their important conversations interrupted. So he stopped to wait.

Josh had done his best but he had miscalculated. He was standing to close. He had invaded their space. They were all staring at him and for a moment he was embarrassed. It was a feeling he did not remember having before and it was uncomfortable.

"Can we help you young man?" asked Franklin.

"Yes Sir. I brung a message for you sir, from my cousin Daniel Broadhead up near the Forks of the Delaware."

He hesitated.

"Well son what is it. The message I mean."

"He says to tell you that the Connecticut Company has sent three more men to map the way to Wyoming. They been through up home and he run 'em off fer now but they told others up that way that they're coming back this spring a thousand strong and they aim to settle Wyoming. He says to tell you Ol Dupui has been tradin with 'em and may be encouraging 'em. They's something going on fer sure this time Mr. Franklin and he said to tell you *Brother Onas* better get his head outen his ass and get some settlers up that way afore the Connecticut farmers get started. Once they get a blockhouse built it may be hard to get em dislodged."

He paused again. They were still staring. But Josh was no longer embarrassed. He could see they were interested in his message.

"That's all. That's what he said I was to tell you. He said you'd know what to do to get the ignorant Quakers to movin."

"I'll be on my way now."

"Wait a minute son. When? When were the Connecticut men through your area."

"About three weeks ago. Daniel set 'em packing, but he's worried."

Josh headed off toward Front street and the river.

Mr. Franklin watched him walk away then turned to his friends.

"Gentlemen I may need your help."

The men listened.

"*Brother Onas* as that young man so eloquently stated has for certain had his head in his ass for a while now. With the Quakers and the Moravians and the Amish all wanting to avoid violence nobody is facing facts. The French are stirring things up out in the Ohio country. The Indians north of us are upset. The Iroquois are afraid but won't admit it to anybody they keep trying to get more Indians to move in to Wyoming as a buffer for their southern boundary and to top it off these damn Connecticut people claim they own our land. Land we been promising and in some cases selling to new immigrants."

"Well Ben we ain't in the land business."

"Yes. Yes. I know neither am I, but Philadelphia and Pennsylvania is our business and we have to get the council to face some facts. We need a plan and we need to get prepared for what is coming. These next few years are going to set our future for generations. We have to get ready to meet the challenges. That young man and his cousin aren't the only ones who are worried. I am too. Brother Onas has to start moving or he is going to be run over by those who do."

64

Chapter 15

Otter looked back over his shoulder. People were still crowding into the longhouse. A hum of quiet conversation hung over the crowd. Young men jostled each other as they squeezed together with the others: grandmothers, aunts, uncles, mothers, fathers, sisters, grandfathers, wives, brothers—all cousins and members of the Munsee tribe living at Wyoming.

It was a cold day outside. The fire inside the big Longhouse was built tall. Its flames leapt high warming the people as it illuminated the proceedings. Smoke soared upwards with a tight spiral of gleaming sparks rising within it through the square hole in the roof, out into the crisp blue sky.

This would be a long council. It might take several days. There was much to discuss. People would come and go. Some would hang about the door if they couldn't fit themselves inside. Everyone would have a chance to speak what was in his heart.

Duck-woman sat near the central fire. Mother and grandmother to many in the crowd, she was industrious, amiable, and much loved. She rose. A hush rolled over the crowd like a wave in a pond when a stone is thrown. She did not have to bang a wooden mallet on a table or a spoon on a metal pan as Otter had seen white men do to gain attention in their councils. She was esteemed by all and drew attention naturally when she stood.

She spoke firmly but not loudly. In simple words she stated what everyone already knew about the Connecticut men who Stands-often had seen in the valley. The same men who had spoken to Brother Joseph on the trail. She recounted the details, as she understood them. Finally she asked the question. What shall we do? She sat back down.

Bowl-woman stood next. She was another grandmother, a good farmer, a virtuous person. She started off restating what she had heard Duck-woman just say. It would be repeated many times during the council. Everyone would understand the question. But from the second speaker onward each would say also if he or she had an opinion of what should be done and then state his or her proposal.

Honest John, a Christian Indian, was in the longhouse, today, sitting not far behind Otter. He had lived most of his life near white men. He had taken on white ways even before joining the Moravians. Honest John had seen many conferences among the white's and only a few among his own people. He was always impressed with Munsee council meetings.

Our deliberations are more civilized, he thought. The white men always talk so loud as if that will make them right in their thinking. They never agree because they never listen to one another. They constantly interrupt their speaker and sound much like hogs around a feeding trough, squealing and jostling for position to get more of the slop.

This is better. It takes longer but each will be heard. Everyone will understand the decision when it is reached.

All watched and listened. Bowl woman finished her statements and sat down. Little Raven stood up but it was not clear for the moment, Little Raven being very small in stature. Gray moon started to stand, noticed Little Raven and sat himself promptly back on the floor. Little Raven spoke loudly but did not realize how her voice boomed. Had she been aware she would have been embarrassed. She was a grizzled, hard faced, grandmother of many winters, few children, and even fewer grandchildren. But, she made the best corn pudding with bear meat, and when she did she was everyone's special grandmother.

"I have been told of the white men," She began, "they are bad men. The corn has not grown well this summer. The ears are very short and stubby like my first husband." No one chuckled out loud. "The summer has been too dry," she said, hesitating, "very, very dry. The corn will not ... much pudding." She paused and started to sit but stopped, tottering on her old legs for a moment. "I think we should move where the rain will come, the corn will grow better there." She hesitated again and everyone listened respectfully. "We can leave this land to the white people. I have been told that they farm poorly. Their men do women's work. The winters here are always cold. Maybe, the white people will starve."

Just after sundown Otter pushed the door flap open stepping out of the long house into a cold clear twilight. He needed fresh air. There had been much discussion. Opinions were mixed as they often were when serious matters were being decided.

This was a very complicated puzzle. What really were the intentions of the Connecticut white men? Would they come a thousand strong this Spring or was that boastful talk? Would *Brother Onas* allow these white men to invade Munsee lands?

Did *Bother Onas* himself have designs on the Wyoming Valley? Would he use the Iroquois again to push the Munsee west? Would the Iroquois allow any white men to live at Wyoming?

Have the Lenape in the Ohio country allied themselves completely with the French? What will the Virginians do? What about the Quakers, and the Amish? Can the Moravians be trusted? Do the other whites trust the Moravians?

Where will we buy blankets, copper kettles, muskets and powder? What prices do the French pay for fur. How much do they charge for steel knives, axes and hoes?

Will it rain next summer? Who will share food this winter? Are the forests here hunted out or will the game return?

Should we count on our treaty with Brother Onas? Will more immigrants forever come off the big ships which dock in Philadelphia? Will those immigrants be pious men like the Quakers, and Amish, or will they be dishonest white men who ply Indians with rum to steal their land?

Alliances were like sticks in a beaver dam holding back the water. Together, with attention from the beaver everything worked. But if the beaver left his damn unattended, failed to repair it, allowed sticks to float away the damn could be washed out by the pressures of a flood. All who depended on the beaver pond: the muskrat, the mink, the turtle and the beaver, might die.

Our lives depend on these decisions, thought Otter. *It is wise to take long to ponder such things. Everyone must have a part in this decision. Everyone's future hangs in the balance. We are Munsee of the Lenape,* he thought, *we live or die together, on land The Most High God provided for us.*

I think we must stay. If it becomes necessary we will fight.

But the question Otter could not yet answer was *who? Who* would they fight? *Who* could they trust. *Who?*

Otter spoke his mind on the second day, as did others. But there remained many questions which, begged answers.

On the third day Duck-woman rose to summarize their plan. Emissaries would be sent to all their neighbors, but none to the French or the Connecticut People. The Munsee would seek reassurance and assistance. They would stand by old alliances with Brother Onas, the Iroquois and the Shawnee. They would ask for support from the Lenape of the Ohio valley. They would stand ready to resist the Connecticut People or the French if their neighbors would stand with them. They needed to know *who* was their true friend? They needed answers. They needed them soon.

Chapter 16

Rocks fell above and rolled. Not big rocks maybe but big enough. *Likely something started them to rolling. Maybe it was a bear, or a man. A panther or bobcat would be too careful. Deer? Maybe, but why would deer be so high this time of year.* Red-corn could see nothing upslope. He just knew what he had heard. He crouched beside the fire listening. *Why would any animal be up that high today?*

It was cold. A drizzly, misty rain fell with a constant patter on the ground outside. A thousand tiny rivulets rushed along beginning their journey down to the sea. *I wish it were colder,* he thought, *cold enough to snow. Snow would be better.*

They were dry. Rock ledges above kept off the rain, which drained away to the side, or showered down, as a thin waterfall, twenty feet in front of them. It was a good camp well used by ancient men who had blackened the rock overhead with the smoke of their fires eons before the oldest living grandfather was born.

Rain loosed the falling rocks. That was probably it. They just fell of their own weight. The Father of Life sent the rain to tell the rocks it is time to move. Now they have found a new place where they will be happy for a long time.

Was this also why the Most High God sent the white farmers like a flood? Was it to tell the Munsee it was time for them to move? Red corn knew brothers and sisters who thought that was the way of it. A never-ending deluge of new white men arrived on the ships and flowed out from Philadelphia into the countryside.

He shivered sitting by the fire.

"Will the rain stop today?" asked Stands-often, who lay beneath the elk robe, on the far side of their fire, his young face peering out?

"I think it will—or tomorrow."

It had rained since noon the day before. They had been lucky to find such a place to den-up. They were finally dry again.

"It is too cold, or not yet cold enough, for us to move further. We will wait here for it to stop raining. I do not believe the snow is coming," said Red-corn. "We are almost through the big mountains. This rain will find its way to streams flowing west. The trail will follow those runs toward Kittanning on the Allegheny and down the Allegheny to Logs-town. We will soon feast with our Munsee brothers of the Ohio country. They will tell us of Frenchmen."

Red-corn wondered about the Frenchmen. White men had their tribes just as the Indian did. English, Dutch, French, Swedes. They fought among themselves just as did the Lenape, Iroquois, Cherokee, and Huron. *It is the way things are. We must not be caught unaware. We must find how hot the winds of war blow so we will see the storm as it approaches.*

Red-corn thought of Solomon Davids, his childhood friend from the Minisink. He remembered how Solomon's Father had hated Frenchmen and French-Indians. As boys, he and Solomon and Twisted-stalk had planned many war parties against the French of the North and the Cherokee in the South. Many a rotting pumpkin or old cornstalk had fallen to their tomahawks.

Twisted-stalk, his friend, was on his way now with a delegation to treat with the Iroquois. The two Munsee boys and the white boy had grown up together almost like brothers. Solomon's father had been a white trader living in a cabin at Kendiamong just north of the old Munsee village at Minisink Island on the Fishkill—the river the whites now called Delaware.

Twisted-stalk had told him at the council meeting that their old friend Solomon was dead. Other white men in a fight had killed him over a boundary line the whites were establishing between New Jersey and New York. Murdered on a trail. There had been no war. No fight with honor. The white men still argued among themselves and his friend was dead. Twisted-stalk had learned of the killing from Elizabeth a Christian Indian who had traveled through the Minisink with the Moravians.

I would avenge Solomon's death if I knew who to kill, thought Red-corn. *He was a good friend. He loved the Fishkill. We hunted well together. I will hunt with him again, someday.*
70

"Is that it up ahead," asked Thomas Shirby.

"No. Just a farmstead. New since we was last through. Couple more bends in the river afore we get to Harris' ferry," answered his cousin John Shirby.

"Well I'll be glad to get there. We gonna wait a day or so fer the water to go down afore we head back."

"Probably take a couple. Hope it don't rain no more."

" You better worry about cold. If it comes a real cold snap this river could ice up this time of year and we'll be walking home.

"Well walking would be a damn sight warmer and easier."

"Trouble is we can't carry everything we need. I guess we could buy a mule or horse at Harris's to pack the stuff back home."

"I'm not sure what Pa was thinking sending us down here this time of year."

"You know what he was thinking same as me. He wants to know what Harris has heard from them that know. What's going on with the French and the Virginians? What do the Lenape say from up north? What is Brother Onas prepared to do? Stuff like that. You know well as I do that's why we've come. He was pretty clear about the questions we're to be askin."

"Well Pa's a worrier, that's fer sure. Except he needs to worry more about us freezing to death on our way home. Them Frenchmen aren't going to want a fight. They're too busy buying up all the furs out west. I don't give a damn about fur trading. I think the Juniata is a fine place fer farmin. I got no reason to want to go over them mountains. They's plenty of land right here fer me."

The cousins dug deep with their paddles. The rain had stopped yesterday. The sky was bright and Harris would have a good supply of rum.

John Harris was on the west bank when the Shirby cousins arrived at his trading post on the east bank of the Susquehanna. They had barely touched shore when John Shirby said, "I'll see to some tradin'," jumped from the canoe, and headed up toward the trading post. That left Thomas to do the unloading.

That's okay, thought Thomas, *I'll have a pint later. I don't crave it like John does. Besides, there aint that much to unload.*

A few early skins, some tobacco, an old broken musket and a teapot, were not much to trade. *Maybe we can get some credit. The real business is news. Will it be safe this winter? What about next Spring?*

A boy came down to help Shirby unload.

"You one of the Harris boys?"

"Samuel."

"How long your Pa had this place?"

"Long before I was born. Granddad came over 40 years ago. He died a few years back. Left the place to Pa."

"Always get along with the Indians up river?"

"So far. They trade here all the time. Granddad always said you treat 'em right they're loyal as an old dog. Treat 'em bad, once, they don't ever forget. He said they may not kill you the day you do 'em wrong but they will sooner or later. Sometimes they go back home, think about it, and talk it over before they decide."

"That so. Guess I may need to remember that."

"Here at the Post we treat everybody fair. Got a good spot here. Good business, we do alright. We ain't never had no trouble with local Indians. Others have but we haven't. Pa says its cause we follow granddads rules."

"What's that? What rules?"

"Always look 'em in the eye, always trade right, never have too much rum on hand. Come to think about it, we follow those rules fer white men too. Pretty much works fer all kinds.

Some fellers leave angry but they don't cut you up in a drunken rage. That happened to some traders north of here a few years back. I found one of their bodies when I was fishin. Pa went up river to check on 'em said it was a real mess."

The boy glanced across the river.

"Looks like pa's ready to head back. I got to go work the mule."

Later that evening Thomas pushed the wooden trencher across the table so his cousin John could finish the beans in the bottom. His cousin was sulking because Harris had cut off his rum.

Hickory logs ablaze in the big fireplace radiated summer warmth across the room. Harris and his two older sons flanked the fire rocking in their chairs and smoking their long stemmed clay pipes. They had left the center benches for guests.

Sweet smelling pipe smoke hung in the air. Lazily the haze meandered nearer the fireplace, pulled along by the suction of the flue. It gather finally into a stream, picked up speed as it got closer, disappearing under the mantle-piece, going up the flue with the smoke of the fire, out into the cold, starlit, winter sky.

Thomas took a bench. Cousin John took the other.

No one spoke for a while. Wind buffeted the house outside, whistling its way in through the few cracks it could find. The house was chinked tighter than many on the frontier this night. Finally John Harris broke the silence answering the question he knew was on their minds.

"I don't know what to tell folks this year. Everyone will have to make his own decision about his own women and children. The French are for sure doing something behind those mountains. Ohio Indians are not coming this way to trade much. All the traders who travel to the Ohio are coming back claiming they have been threatened either by Indians or Frenchmen. There is talk of French forts being built up north and west of here on Lake Erie and even one on the Allegheny.

There is trouble brewing I just don't know when it's comin. Neither do the local Indians. They been here askin the same questions your askin."

He paused to pop the bowl of his pipe on the palm of his hand emptying out the burned ash and dropping it on the hearth in front of him.

"I have been to Philadelphia myself. The Pennsylvania Gazette is all riled up but no one in the government is taking it serious enough I'm afraid. I just don't know what to tell you boys. You have reason to worry. Everyone on this frontier is getting worried."

Harris took a breath as he thought about the situation.

"The Pennsylvania Council just doesn't want to levy any taxes to pay fer militia costs till they see the trouble. If trouble comes we'll be on our own fer a while. Gather your neighbors. Keep scouts out. Watch and listen. It's all we can do unless you want to pack up and leave."

Chapter 17

*I*n March 1753 Post Vincennes was a small French trading post on the Ouabache (Wabash) River. The Ouabache was a key trading and communications route. Via a short portage at its' headwaters over to the St. Mary's River Frenchmen in New Orleans were connected to Lake Erie and the Frenchmen of New France.

"Jacque, you waiting to see Father Meurin?" asked the corporal as he passed.

"Yes," answered the boy.

"He's visiting ol' Trattier. He should return soon."

Post Vincennes had been established in1732 by Francis-Marie Bissot, Sieur de Vincennes who, four years later, was burned at the stake by Chickasaw Indians in Tennessee.

Sixteen-year-old Jacque Ravelette had been born at Post Vincennes a year after Sieur de Vincennes was killed. It was the only home Jacque knew. He had heard the old stories about the war with the Chickasaw. He knew men who had fought in that war to keep the Mississippi River open to New Orleans for Frenchmen and France.

The river remained open but the Chickasaw had never totally been defeated. They traded now with the English, the natural enemy of Frenchmen everywhere.

As Jacque had grown to manhood in Vincennes there had been much concern about English traders. The English encroached more each year into French territories on the west side of the Appalachian Mountains. They came down the Bella Rivere *the beautiful River* (called the Ohio by the English)—to open illegal trade with the Indians.

These were rough boarder men who did not bring their families. They did not intend to live here. They just came to steal the trade from honest Frenchmen who made their homes here among the savages.

In recent years more and more Frenchmen had gone missing in the forests. The Indians had become sour to French trade items and prices. The English were rousing some of the natives against their French Brothers. It had become a constant fear stalking the Ouabache country.

Even the Piankashaw Indians, who had moved their village to live near Vincennes, were split on the question of trade with the English. Many of their Miami Brothers had been trading openly with the British traders at Pickawillany, at the headwaters of the Miami River, until last summer.

Last June, the hero Charles Langlade had led an Indian force from up north, which destroyed Pickawillany. They killed many of the traitorous Indians and most of the English Traders.

Since the Pickawillany success no more Frenchman had gone missing on the Ouabache this fall and winter. Local tribes found people were coming home to trade with their natural brothers, Frenchmen, who lived and worked among them. People in Vincennes felt safer, but they feared the English would return.

"Thank you for coming, Jacque," said Father Meurin, as he walked up.

"Yes Father."

"Have you seen her again?"

"Yes Father."

"Same result?"

"Yes Father."

"Did you say your Hail Marys as I suggested?"

"Yes Father, I did."

"Did it help?"

"Only a little Father. I still lust after her."

"Well today you will be leaving. I think that is good. If you feel the same when you return we will talk again. You will be gone a long time my son I have grown fond of you. Since your mother and father died I have felt it important we talk often. I 've tried to advise you, as they would if they were alive."

Jacque's parents had died of the small pox, which had swept all along the Ouabache last year, killing many French and even more Piankashaw people. Jacque had caught the pox himself with only slight affect. Father Meurin had told him it was a very good sign he had little to fear from the dreaded disease in the future. He was glad of that, but he missed his parents sorely.

"Lieutenant de St. Ange is a good Commandant and a good man. He would prefer to keep all the men at home to defend Post Vincennes. But, he has his orders. I will not speak against them." Said Meurin who glanced toward the blockhouse . "The King needs soldiers to oppose the English who threaten our way of life. It is important that we keep the Ouabache and the Bella Rivere open for Frenchmen to travel safely. We cannot let the English cut us off from New France in the North or New Orleans in the south. This is all French territory. We have been trading in these valleys for generations. Celoron marked our claim clearly in '49'. The English have been warned. We must defend what our forefathers fought so hard to win.

You know our fort at De Chartres on the Mississippi and Ouiatenon, north of here, up the Ouabache and further north Ft. Miami. You have been to these places I know. It was an adventure for you."

"Yes Father."

"Well now you will have an even greater adventure. You will help build and defend new forts on Lake Erie and down the Allegheny River all the way to the forks where it meets the Monongahela to form the Bella Rivere. You will join soldiers Coming from Fort Niagara and all over New France to achieve these goals.

It will be a great force but there will be great danger as well. The English are a strong and warlike people. France has fought them many times in the past. They are vicious people in wartime."

"Will there *be* a war Father?"

"I fear there will be my son. British soldiers sometimes give no quarter. If you battle with them, you will need to fight viciously to survive.

I am a simple Priest. I am ordained to teach the love of our Dear Savior.

But, I speak now as your surrogate parents not as your Parrish Priest."

He removed his cap.

"Do what you must Jacque to live. Return to the Ouabache. Your father and mother wanted you to make a life here at Post Vincennes. Do your duty to king and country but fight however you must. Come home to us. Marry the Piankashaw girl. Raise children in our Holy Church. Grow old here."

"Yes Father, thank you."

The Priest put his cap back on his head.

"The canoes will be heading north soon. Go with God. Be safe. Know you will be in our prayers. God will watch over you."

Jacque walked off toward three large canoes that had been hauled up at the tiny landing on the Ouabache. A small group of men stood at a fire near the boats. Dogs barked in the village. Geese honked above the river. The smell of frying bacon came on the air. The muffled pops from two different muskets drifted back over the distance from unseen hunters in the field. Across the river, tall prairie grass rippled in the fall breeze.

Chapter 18

$\mathcal{T}$he canoes left Vincennes mid-morning. Ducks and coots scudded away ahead of the bark transports as they proceeded upriver. Jacque soon saw the big rock landing where he had spent many hours fishing. *That hillside under the big beech will soon be covered with mushrooms. I guess the Trattiers will find them first this season.*

Soon Jacque lost himself in his paddling. One bend in the river gave way to another. At noon they stopped for a short respite on a sand bar jutting out from the east bank in a wide bend. At dusk they set camp on the west bank.

First light found the party back on the river. The sights were becoming less familiar to Jacque as they proceeded north. The second night they camped beneath high sandstone bluffs on the eastern bank. Jacque had been here before but not often. He couldn't remember any landmarks further north.

I guess I'll have to pay more attention this time.

Paddling canoes up the Ouabache with light loads was surprisingly swift work for this time of year. The spring rains had been light so far this season. The voyagers were strong experienced men. This was their business. They knew it well. Travel was unimpeded except a portage around rapids above the mouth of Eel River. Days passed in the familiar way.

Jacque's party stayed only a day at Fort Ouiatenon. A few more days paddling brought them to the headwaters of the Ouabache where they floated into the tiny Rivere Petite paddling on northeast toward Lake Erie. It would have taken longer if not for the beaver community left unmolested, by common agreement, on this waterway.

Everyone understood the important contribution to French and Indian transportation made by these particular creatures. Their dams kept important water contained in the headwaters floating these loaded canoes north and east ever closer toward Fort Miami. With the beaver's help, even in dry weather you could paddle all the way to the great swamp.

Before reaching the swamp, however, the voyagers came to a landing on the right bank with a well-traveled trailhead leading east. Without the beaver and their dam it would have been a twenty-seven mile haul from the forks of the Ouabache. From here, however, it was only a nine-mile portage to the St Mary's River, which flowed north to meet the St. Josephs River coming south. The confluence of these two streams formed then the Maumee River flowing eastward.

Finishing the carry they arrived on the banks of the north flowing St Mary's. Jacque knew that Jean Baptiste Bissot de Vincennes, father of Francis-Marie Bissot de Vincennes had, many years ago, built a French fort here called Fort Miami. British Indians had destroyed that fort a few years back in 1747. The charred remnants stood as clear reminder. A new French Fort to replace it had been built three years ago relocated, down the St Mary's to the fork, and upstream a couple miles on the St Joseph's River. The new fort was called also Fort Miami.

Jacque's party proceeded to the new fort and rested for two days. It felt good not to be paddling. On the third morning they launched the canoes again. Soon they picked up speed riding the freshet from the St Joseph's and St. Mary's Rivers working to their favor pushing them downstream on the Maumee at a rapid pace through greening forests toward Lake Erie.

Flat water and gentle breezes from the west help move them along the edges of the Lake. Ten days after leaving Fort Miami and thirty-two days after leaving Post Vincennes they approached a large natural harbor on the south shore of Lake Erie.

"Presque Isle is just around that point," said the corporal, his paddle indicating direction for a moment between strokes. "The Captain will want us looking sharp as we come in. Stay alert. Put your backs into it."

Jacque looked ahead. The point jutting out into the lake was still over a mile away. In a few minutes more they were nearing the landmark and preparing to turn into the small bay. Jacque heard pounding off in the distance.

When they rounded the point they could see the worksite across the bay a quarter mile away. A new French fort was presently under construction. The mingled sounds of hammers, axes and adzes, the jangle of harness chain, the shouts of laboring men gradually became clear to the ear. As they drew closer Jacque could distinguish the sounds of saws and sweet smells of fresh cut lumber.

At Fort Presque Isle the seven men transported from Vincennes were put quickly to work. There was much to be done.

Early the next morning Jacque came to the water's edge as the voyagers who had brought him boarded their canoes silently and shoved off. Without a word of goodbye they paddled east toward Fort Niagara.

Good luck my friends. And good luck to me. We may all need it.

As Jacque watched, the canoes gradually disappeared one after another into a fog bank which this morning hugged the surface of the Lake.

Jacque had never been to Niagara but he knew it was an old French Fort below a great waterfall protecting the passageway between Lake Erie and Lake Ontario. For New France to survive these waterways must be secured. That would be difficult with the new influx of Englishmen. It would require more forts, more French soldiers and more workmen.

Jacque was a good listener. He quickly learned that the French commanders intended to build four new forts this year protecting what they called the Venango pathway. Essentially that meant travel overland from Presque Isle down to French Creek, onward via water to the confluence with the Allegheny River, then down that river to the fork with the Monongahela River, where the two waterways converged forming the Bella Rivere.

Frenchmen considered the Bella Rivere a southern branch of the Ouabache. It meandered slowly southwest to meet the important trade route. It was a second pathway to Post Vincennes and Fort De Chartres. From the Illinois country the Mississippi River was open to French travel all the way south to New Orleans—where the ports yearlong remained free of ice.

Completion of the French strongholds they were now building would secure Frenchmen in their homes and trade. The work was hard but the spirit of the men was high. Finally King Louis was sending necessary resources for them to secure their future here in America. The English traders would soon be forced to remain on their side of the mountains.

But haste was called for, before the English discovered their intentions. The British would not be happy to see Frenchmen preparing such defenses. If possible they would stop this construction before it could be completed.

A year past, and then a month and another. Late July, 1754 was hotter than normal.

Jacque rolled over and grunted. His blanket was twisted again. It was under his thighs. A depression in the earth, beneath him, had not been dug deep enough. He was uncomfortable sleeping on the ground.

He'd been trying to improve his sleeping arrangement, when time permitted. He hadn't got it right yet. The ground was rocky and uneven.

But, it wasn't just rocky ground keeping him awake.

Jacque missed Post Vincennes. He was homesick. He knew every one of the thirty French families living at the Post and most of the hundred Piakashaw families living nearby. He missed his talks with Father Meurin. He missed the Piakashaw girl. He missed familiar faces.

The last sixteen months had been exciting, as Father Meurin said they would be. The Fort at Presque Isle was complete. A fort called Le Boeuf had been erected near the head of French Creek. Fort Machault was finished at the confluence of French Creek and the Allegheny River.

Jacque had helped build them all. He had gone back and forth between the three forts several times. Each time he noticed other crews working at Fort Le Boeuf building canoes and bateaux's. More of both than Jacque had ever expected to see in a lifetime.

In April, Jacque along with twelve hundred other Frenchmen boarded one of the three hundred canoes or sixty bateaux. Swiftly they paddled down French Creek into the Allegheny heading for the Forks of the Ohio where Englishmen had recently and arrogantly built a fort. Each canoe carried four men and the bateaux were loaded with more men, supplies and most importantly, eighteen cannon, something never before seen on this waterway. It was a great force intended to expel the English from French territory and keep them out.

No epic battle followed. Jacque had actually felt sorry for the Englishmen huddled in their little wooden stockade, forty-one defenders looking out upon such a grand French force finally disembarked and drawn up in battle lines before them. *Holy Mother of God!* they must be thinking, *where have all these Frenchmen come from.* There were actually a few chuckles down the French Line when two of their officers approached the gate of the little fort under a white flag of truce.

The English were given one hour to surrender. They could hope to do nothing else. That evening they dined with the French Commanders who the following morning sent them sadly on their way, toward their Virginia homes with all their supplies and arms. If they learned their lesson, there need not be a war.

That had been a few weeks ago. The English had learned little. Much had happened since.

Jacque could lie on the ground no longer. He got up and stepped away from his tent. He stretched his arms above his head and yawned. A fire burned brightly close by. Two other soldiers sat beside it smoking their pipes. Last night's rainstorm had cooled the temperatures. Gusts of wind ruffled loose canvas throughout the camp and fanned the flames of a dozen tiny soldier fires sending sparks from each up into the night sky. Theirs was a small fire but its warmth was welcome in the dampness. Jacque sat himself down wrapping his wool blanket around his shoulders.

Stars shined brightly in the west, above the darker than night forms of high wooded ridges across the Monongahela. Cloud cover blowing east, revealed more stars as it traveled. It was still a few hours before dawn.

"Couldn't sleep?"

"No," Jacque answered."

"Us neither."

"Edouard is still upset."

"Shut up Pierre."

"I agree, no one should be left in the woods to rot like that," said Pierre.

After the English had been expelled from their little stockade at the forks they had joined forces with other Englishmen further south. There had been skirmishes with French forces. Frenchmen had been killed.

Edouard had been with a platoon, which had discovered the bodies of a Captain Jumonville and his men. The English and their Indians had slaughtered them in the woods mutilating their bodies and leaving them lay. Edouard said nothing now. He just puffed on his pipe and stared into the fire.

"Yeah. We taught them Virginians a thing or two when we caught them at Great Meadows," said Pierre.

(After Jumonville and his men had been found, French commanders sent out a larger force which overtook the English at a place called Great Meadows. There had been a battle.)

"you should have seen Edouard fighting," said Pierre. "He must have killed more than a few. He was like a mad man taking chances to kill the English."

Edouard still said nothing. Jacque had been left behind at fort Duquesne when the others had left to catch the English. Duquesne was the name of the French fort they were building here at the forks of the Bella Rivere. It was to be a serious fort not a pitiful stockade as the English had constructed. There were to be regular troops stationed here not just a trading post with a few soldiers attached. The French commanders were building a large fortification with cannon to control the river and impress the Indians.

"Well there may be a war now," said Jacque

"A war? Maybe," said Pierre, "But if so the Englishman, Washington, has started it. I was at Fort Machault last December when it was still just the old cabin left by the English blacksmith. I was in the room when that Colonel Washington showed up and was entertained. Him having the nerve to tell us we shouldn't be here in our own country. He had sand I'll say that for him. Coming all the way from Williamsburg in winter to tell us we're in the wrong valley and should get out.

I heard the officers talking later, they said when he got to Fort De Bouef the commander told him we intended to build these forts and defend them and by-god we would do just that. They sent him packing for home in the snow.

Should've killed him then. He came back with more Englishmen. Should have let our Indians have him the other day when he surrendered that little fort they threw up in Great Meadows. He was out-numbered, still, he made us fight to take it. Too many good Frenchmen have died. But the officers once more let him pack his people back to Virginia.

He's an arrogant son-of-a-bitch. He'll be back. When he comes again someone needs to put his head on a stick and let the Indians dance round it for a day or two," said Pierre

Edouard grunted, stared into the fire and muttered: "I might dance around that."

Chapter 19

*T*here is a time just preceding a great storm when animals sense its approach. Birds stop singing, horses and cattle herd together, deer seek thickets, dogs lie down near the door.

Wind blows. Lightening flashes. Thunder rumbles. Rain begins.

You never know how fierce a storm will be until it is upon you. How well you weather the storm depends upon your preparations, its' severity, and sometimes the actions you take.

During spring and early summer of 1754 the storm clouds of a war were building. People on the frontier were scurrying about trying to read its' approach. Everyone could feel it coming. No one yet knew how big a storm it would be but everyone in the boarder country knew something was about to happen. No one wanted to be directly in its path.

Alliances were being questioned. Could old friendships be trusted? Was power shifting in the world across the big waters?

The French were building new forts... big forts ... many of them... with cannon. The English weren't building forts but their farmers were settling land further west and north each year, crowding and pushing the Lenape, the Shawnee and even the Iroquois.

Both English and French were courting the Indians again. New promises were being made and assurances sought. Some of the far western tribes had made their choice already, allying with the French.

Most Native Americans in Pennsylvania and New York waited and watched. The French and the English were going to fight. *Which side shall we support? Who is our friend?*

"We don't get much company", said John Decker, standing in the doorway of his stone farmhouse near the Machackemack River.

"Well I've passed this way twice in the past two years," said Elias, "once with Brother Henry Antes and this time with John.

John Branch and Elias Knepp had just returned from the conference with the Indians at Albany, New York, June 19 through July 11, 1754. They were returning, now, down the Kings road through Machacemack toward Dupui's trading post and ferry just north of the water gap. From there they would proceed to Bethlehem where they would meet with the Moravians. They had stopped here at John Decker's farm on the Machackemack Branch for the night. Dinner was over. The evening was warm, though the sun had dipped behind the mountains. Summer afterglow would brighten the blue sky for a spell. The cool evening breeze had not yet come down the valley.

They sat outside on old stools and benches made from split logs hued flat, held up by rough cut wooden legs. Their long stemmed pipes were lit. Smoke hung about their heads.

"I remember now," said Decker. "You came to services at the church. You were with the Moravian and them two Indians."

"That was me."

"Well you mentioned you was comin from Albany this time. Tell me more about what this Pennsylvania fellow was proposing at the big Indian Congress?"

"It was Mr. Franklin," said John Branch "he's a printer by trade but was a representative of Pennsylvania to the conference. He suggested the colonies need to be bound together under the crown but with one grand council here in the colonies administered by a single President General. He compared it to how the Iroquois have bound themselves together and run their affairs representing the good of the whole rather than each separate part."

"Wouldn't that be something," said Elias, "If we start doing things like the Indians stead of the other way round."

"It was the big talk of the conference," continued Branch, "other than the Iroquois demanding to get William Johnson back as the Indian agent of the Crown." Branch thought about that for a moment and puffed his pipe a couple times. "The

Governor better give them what they want on that score. If he don't they could switch over and join the French themselves. They love Johnson. He's the only one who can keep them loyal. The Governors cronies be damned. We need the Iroquois on our side or at the very least neutral and out of the fight. Johnsons the only white man they trust"

"Will they stay Loyal?" Asked Decker.

"They claim they want to stay neutral. The Seneca and Cayuga out west trade with the French. Some Mohawk up north do too. They wish to stay out of the fight unless old enemies like Huron and Ottawa invade their territory to get at us. If that happens they claim they will fight *with* us," said Branch.

"Well what are New York and New Jersey planning?"

"I can't tell you. And I don't know what Pennsylvania will do either. That's the problem Franklin was getting at. Hell, Virginia didn't even send representatives to the congress. Then, the Connecticut people are all sneaking around, behind everybody's back. Trying to make new land deals with the Indians. Every colony and every tribe has its own agenda. We talked for weeks. They will take weeks more to print the results. After everything, said and done, no one will really know how the various governors will react. I doubt seriously they will like Mr. Franklin's idea much.

When the shooting starts no one is going to be certain who will be fighting who. It's a mess as far as I can tell."

Decker looked west toward the mountain ridges across the river. "Do you have any idea about the Delaware in Wyoming?"

"Well not from this congress. Last November I was at the Indian congress in Carlisle (Pennsylvania). That included mostly Ohio Indians but some of the Lenape from Wyoming were present. The Ohio Indians we spoke with claimed to be siding with the Virginians and us. They claim they don't like the French building forts in their area on the Allegheny. But I don't know that they speak for all the Indians out there or even all those in their own tribe. My sense of it is that they may be playing both sides trying to decide who really is serious and who may be strongest. Right now it's the French building forts and bringing cannon.

The Indians ain't too happy either about how Brother Onas or the Virginians control their own traders. The Indian leaders claim the traders sell too much liquor and cheat their people.

We have been warning the governor ourselves about that. But, no officials want to regulate the fur trade in a serious manner. Too much money being made. Too many bribes being paid."

He let that thought settle in to see if Decker would respond. He didn't. So Branch let it go and went on.

"When the bullets start flying I guess we will worry about it then. I tell you Mr. Decker, this little valley may not be safe if war comes. You might want to make plans to move east of the mountains. I wouldn't go north or south if I was you. And I sure wouldn't encourage anyone to move to the west bank of the Fishkill. Too many folks living over there already I think."

"Well we aint planning on goin nowhere," said Decker, "been here a long time. Known a lot of Munsee. Done nothing to offend any of them. Personally never had any trouble with 'em. Don't expect none now. If they come east of that river looking for trouble I guess they might find it. I expect they know that.

Frenchmen are another matter. But, I see little reason for the French to come here. They'll more likely go after Albany or Philadelphia and we ain't on the path to either place. We may be safe here I reckon."

"Well the Minisink is a pretty little valley. You folks have been here for generations. You probably know best. Maybe you're right. I hope so. The Moravians south of you treat the Indians fairly. Maybe you all can stay out of a fight if it comes. If the Lenape in Wyoming and the Iroquois up north stay neutral that may be the buffer you need. Lets pray that's the way of it."

"Where you going, Beletje?" Decker called, to a young girl mounting a bay horse near his barn.

"Home," she called back, trotting the horse northeast toward the Machackemack River.

"Well hurry up girl its getting dark!" he called after her.

She kicked the horse into a gallop and rode away along the edge of a big cornfield.

"Granddaughter," he said to the others. "Her uncles are still working the other end of that field and her brothers will be across the river, on the other side, not far. She lives with her Ma at the mill across the river another mile. Her Pa was killed a few years back. Visits her grandma a lot. Wish she had started home sooner though."

Chapter 20

*L*ast fall, white men had built a cluster of new cabins downstream on the Lehigh between Gnandenhutton and Bethlehem. John Branch and Elias Knapp approached those cabins now. They were riding their horses down a little slope through open understory beneath giant beech trees. There was almost no underbrush. The leaf canopy high above filtered thin shafts of light, casting a dappled green shadow on the ground. It was a charming location for half a dozen small well-built cabins. Brighter daylight beyond indicated where the cabin-logs had originated and where the fields would be planted. There was the crack of an axe thinly audible from off in that direction.

It's getting warm today. Elias wiped his shirted forearm across his brow and brushed a horsefly from the back of his neck with his hand.

The horses plodded along, picking their way, at a walk, down the path, hoof-beats softened and quieted by thick forest duff except occasionally when they clicked upon solid underlying rock exposed in the trail. Those clicks of hoof, the squeak of saddle leather, the occasional swishing of a tail melded together with the gentle tapping of little downy woodpeckers and chattering chipmunks. It made for a peaceful ride into the new community.

Ahead they could see two men mounted horseback in front of one of the cabins with another man standing at the doorway. All were armed with muskets at rest. Each warily studying John and Elias as they ride in.

"Morning gentlemen," said John, as they neared the cabin.

There was a pause. A nuthatch called from a tree above. Fly's hummed in the air around the horses.

"I'm Jeremiah Tincher," said the man standing, "This here is Daniel Broadhead and that's Josh Broadhead," he said nodding toward each of the mounted men, "are you Moravians?"

"No, not exactly but we just came from Gnandenhutton." Said John.

" Well you don't sound like Yankees. Thought I saw you young feller with Brother Antes before," said Tincher, eyeing the pistol Elias had tucked in his belt.

" That's right. I work fer Brother Antes. Live in Bethlehem some. Some in Philadelphia," answered Elias.

"You armed?" Broadhead asked, looking at John.

"I have a pistol in my saddlebag. Don't wear it."

"Humm!" grunted Josh, "maybe you ought to start."

There was another awkward pause and then Tincher said.

"Get off and sit if you like. You can water your horses at the creek. These boys are telling me about the big battle in Virginia. You might want to hear about it if your going to be travelin' the backcountry much.

"What battle?"

"Some Virginia Colonel got into it with Frenchmen near the Forks of the Ohio. The French had thrown out the Virginia traders who had set up there and started building themselves a fort."

"Who threw 'em out," asked John?

"The Frenchmen like I said. Wasn't you listenin'." Said Daniel Broadhead. "It ain't good fer nobody. Then this Colonel and his men was at a place called Great Meadows in Virginia and the French came on to that place and attacked 'em. Philadelphia is all whipped up over it. Everyone is all concerned the Indians in our own country may start being influenced by Frenchmen livin' right at their back door."

"We just came from the Albany Congress with the Indians." Said John.

"Yeah. I heard all about that Congress with the Indians when I was in Philadelphia," said Josh Broadhead. Little late gettin' home ain't you?

92

Franklin has it all over his Pennsylvania Gazette. He has that snake picture on the top of the page again. Show 'em Jeremiah. Jeremiah can read. I bring him the newspaper to show people.

I don't need to read it, myself," Josh continued, "I heard all about it in town. Franklin's preachin' unity again. *Join or die* ain't that what it says Jeremiah?

Ain't likely to happen though, according to what I hear. None of the colonies trust each other enough to unite under one government."

He is right about that snake though, said Daniel Broadhead, "we all got to join together 'er die. I ain't countin' on Virginia 'er New York to come to my aid but I am countin' on my neighbors.

The Moravians had better quit their preachin' and get them selves armed. We all need to stick together. Show them savages we mean business. If the Frenchies get 'em stirred up they need to know they can't push us 'er we'll kill 'em all."

"Well I think the Iroquois are going to stay out of any fight between French and English," said John, "You may have more to fear from Connecticut."

"Yeah, well I sent them fellers packing before," said Broadhead, "I'll do it again if I have to. This is Pennsylvania by-god. We ain't going to be pushed off our land by nobody. What we need is some more neighbors settled here afore them Connecticut fellers show up next year or whenever they come. Probably all talk anyhow. We're here first. We ain't likely to be leavin."

"What we need is a few more boat loads of good Scotts/Irish or Palatine Germans livin up in Wyoming 'stead of Munsee or Yankees from Connecticut or Moravians," said Tincher.

He smiled at Elias. "No offense young man."

"None taken," said Elias.

But he was a little offended and a little ashamed at not having stood up for his friends in Gnandenhutton and Bethlehem. Maybe pacifism wasn't going to be possible, here in the Quaker Colony. It seems wherever pious men try to draw themselves apart (from the world), sinners follow, even here in the wilderness of America. Elias wondered if the great armies of France and England would fight each other here in the forests of Pennsylvania. If they did what would it mean for the people living here.

Chapter 21

*I*t was planting time in the Perkiomen Valley. Two big draft horses stood beside the water trough where they were tied during lunch. They had shed their shaggy winter coat and were shiny damp with this morning's sweat. Heinrich was sitting on a bench outside under the big sugar maple picking his teeth with a sliver of wood he had cut from a stick.

"I don't know Ezekiel. I use dat wagon too. Me and de boys really need all tree."

"Well Heinrich, the advertisement says they will pay fifteen shillings a day for a wagon and four horse team."

"Can't spare no horse, narry a one."

Ezekiel sighed, looking up into the leaves.

"I know. You told me that already. I can provide the horses and the driver. But I need your wagon to make the deal." He hesitated. "You get a third I get a third. My boy Ben will drive and he gets a third. It's a lot of the King's money. They are to pay in silver or gold, not credit. It's a big opportunity for us all. Five shillings a-day hard money, think about that?"

"How long dey need my wagon?"

"I guess as long as it takes fer Braddock to march his army out to the Forks and run them Frenchmen out of there. Maybe all summer, time they get back. Who knows, could be longer if they have to keep the army resupplied?

We need to get in while we can. You can bet others will be building new wagons and trying to cut us out soon as they get the chance. Everyone who has a wagon is gonna want in."

"Why Virginians not usin' der wagons," asked Heinrich?

One of the big horses snorted and shifted his weight jangling his harness hardware. Their big tails intermittently swished at a fly.

"There ain't a decent wagon in Virginia," said Ezekiel. "They don't have good roads to run 'em on if they had 'em. Which they don't.   Everything in Virginia moves by boat or pack-horse. They got damn few wagons and none to spare. That's why they're advertising in Pennsylvania. Every farm here has a wagon or two or three.

"No good roads?   How dey gonna use my wagon if dey got no roads?

The army's going to build a good road as they go, bridges and everything."

Maybe dey tear up my wagon.

Maybe. Probably not. Ben will take good care of it. But even if they do you can buy a new one with the money your making. Maybe two. It's a good deal. But, we got to move on it now. It won't be here next week. The opportunity is now.

"How big dis army King George send?"

"Over two thousand men I hear.   Going to send another thousand colonial troops mostly Virginian, Maryland and Pennsylvania men.

We got to get in on this.   It's a big opportunity. It's our duty to our neighbors. Hell, everyone is sending something. You remember that Quaker named Boone used to live over on Owatin Creek.   The one that got in a huff with the other Quakers few years back and moved to Carolina."

"I tink so."

"Well his boy, Daniel, was through here yesterday talking to some of the neighbors, getting re-acquainted, trying to get more wagons. He's a teamster for the army. He's goin along. Benjamin remembered him. They're about the same age. All the boys want to go with this army. The French won't stand a chance when Braddock gets all them cannon in place. Should be quite a show.   He'll blow em right out of that Fort Duquesne.

They'll build a good road. Got to, in order to get the cannon there and keep the fort supplied once it's ours. Got to feed all them soldiers, keep 'em in ammunition."

"I don't know? Maybe ve not get paid?" said Heinrich.

"It's the King not the colonial councils. He's good fer it. Besides how often do they offer to pay. If we don't supply enough wagons fer em to rent they may just send some soldiers to take 'em. If they do that they might take all three of your wagons. This way we all make out. Wha-do-ya-say?"

Heinrich sat silent for a moment rolling those last comments over in his mind. He shook his head. Then he rose to his feet with a groan and stretched his stiff back.

"I'll get de axles greased tonight, when I come in from de field. Benjamin kin pick up my wagon in de morgen.

Chapter 22

*T*here was no rain. General Braddock's army moved toward the forks of the Ohio in June. He had all the wagons he needed.

A huge wagon-train of men and material inched its way along as engineers built road ahead of it. It was a winding road over rough mountainous country. It was an arduous, dusty, professional, advance. Reports of it's progress kept coming to the settlements. By the eighth of July The Kings Army neared the forks of the Ohio where Fort Duquesne had been built by the Frenchmen.

The British and French Empires were about to clash again in the American Wilderness. This time the Frenchmen were outnumbered and the English had brought bigger cannons. And they had more of them.

By mid-July there was still no rain.

"We'll I'm glad that paddle is over." Said Thomas Shirby as they beached their canoe on the banks of the Susquehanna at Harris's Ferry.

"Sure never had that much carryin' and draggin' before on these rivers," said John Shirby.

"It's the driest year I ever remember. God must have it out fer farmers this year. I bet we won't get enough corn to feed ourselves this winter let alone the horse and cow."

The ferry was tied up, to a long rope, water being so low. The rivers' normal muddy bottom was dried and cracked thirty yards out from where it rose sharply at its normal bank. John Harris was sitting now on the porch of his cabin talking to another man when the Shirby cousins walked up the bank. Neither Harris nor the other man seemed happy to see the cousins.

"You boys might as well hear what I been tellin' James," said Harris.

"Fella came through here a couple days back who had been to Carlisle. He says General Braddock has been done in."

"What about the army?"

"That's what I'm telling you. It's all destroyed. Defeated. Been slaughtered by the French and Indians at the Forks of the Ohio."

"All of 'em?"

"Most of 'em according to this fella."

"How did he know? Was he there?"

"No. Three Pennsylvania boys that was there, got away, made it through the mountains to Carlisle to warn people. Most folks now are pullin' up stakes and heading east."

"The whole army's destroyed?"

"Far as these boys knew they might be the only ones that made it back alive. They were teamsters. They said the soldiers were runnin' through the woods everywhere with Indians on their heels. They were lucky enough to get some horses cut out of their harness and get mounted. Rode them old horses hard for twenty miles abandoned 'em on the road, fearing another ambush. Then headed north through the woods being careful about their tracks. Smart young fellers I think."

"Maybe just deserters makin' up a story?"

" I thought about that. Didn't sound that way. Sent one of my boys to Lancaster, to see what can be learned. He ain't back yet. You boys might as well stay a day er two see what news comes back up that river."

Everyone who heard the story in late July or early August, 1755 would first question it. Could it really have happened? Could General Braddocks' army have been slaughtered.

Elias Knepp heard it on High Street in Philadelphia from a farmer   He told John Branch who went straight to the print shop where he found the people at the Gazette had gone off to locate someone official to ask about it.

A week later Henry Antes heard the story in Bethlehem from Josh Broadhead who had come with the warning. Josh suggested again that the Moravians needed to get them-selves better armed.

Samuel Dupui was told first by an old trader named Jake Kuckendal who had heard the story in Easton. Kuckendal was heading north to the Minisink area to warn people there. Dupui gave him a fresh horse and started warning the few settlers in his immediate vicinity.

Ezekiel Graber told Heinrich Feagley. Heinrich put an arm around his old neighbor and asked no questions about his wagon.

Red Corn brought the news to Otter and Duck-woman. Duck-woman sent out a call for the Munsee of Wyoming to gather at the central longhouse. They talked for two days.

Beletje Davids joined grandfather Decker and the rest of her family and neighbors of Machachemack in the Church to hear old Jake Kuckendal make his announcement from the pulpit.

"The General is dead. Most of his officers are dead. Over a thousand of his soldiers are dead. The supplies and camp followers including women and children have been drug off. The French have loosed their devils on our frontier. Everyone needs to make preparations to defend themselves." That was the gist of what he said. It wasn't pretty to think about.

Obadiah Rauch told the Feagley brothers living in the Valley of the Paulinskill. They thought they were safe here for now but they worried about their family out on Perkiomen Creek.

The bay with the dark colored mane cropped at the dry grass in the meadow near Wyoming and had no thoughts of war. The bear and the bobcat continued hunting. Bee's made their honey in the tree just like any summer.

After the battle of Monongahela Jacque Ravelette was tormented. He'd never seen Ottawa, Huron, Shawnee drunk on victory and captured rum. It would take a long time to get the screams of Englishmen out of his head.

The battle had been exhilarating. He had fought, faced death and killed. He was not ashamed of what he had done. It was his duty. But the two day drunken debauchery of torture and death, which followed, had been horrifying. French officers had saved some of the English captives, others had been marked for adoption into the tribes but many were killed—in terrible ways.

Jacque worried the truth of this would be learned. The English would seek retribution for the killing of the wounded and the torture of captives. The War might never end. And it would consume more than just Englishmen.

Jacque wanted to go home. He wanted to talk with Father Meurin. He wanted to fish, eat cornbread, and hunt grouse in the prairie across the Ouabache. But he could not leave. Every Frenchman would be needed.

Chapter 23

$\mathcal{A}$ late spring frost came to Wyoming. The green corn leaves turned black and the crop died in the field. It was too late to replant.

In July news came of the defeat of Braddock's grand army. Munsee from the Ohio had been near Fort Duquesne to witness the slaughter of the British and colonial forces. The Lenape had not taken part in the battle but they had remained close enough to know the truth and see the result. English red-coated soldiers were not invincible no matter how impressive they looked on the march. Their big cannon were useless in the forest. Their generals were arrogant men who would not take advice from their Indian brothers. They could be beaten.

Following Braddock's defeat, Lenape and Shawnee warriors from the Ohio Valley joined the French in huge numbers. They were closest to the flames of war beginning to rage. They did not wish to be burned, and they, themselves, had some old scores to settle with the English.

Representatives of the Ohio Munsee visited Wyoming often in July, August, and September requesting the Susquehanna Munsee join with them, ally with the French, and destroy the English.

Severe summer drought damaged the beans and squash. Leaves turned yellow then brown, seed-pods and blossoms shriveled, fruit failed to develop. The harvest would be meager. The three sisters were hurt. Even nuts and berries of the forest were sparse. Councils were held with much dancing and prayer.

Emissaries were sent to Brother Onas in September requesting he share food supplies so that the Munsee might survive the approaching winter. No food had come except for a five-horse pack train from the Moravians who had little to spare. The lack of response from Brother Onas puzzled the Munsee.

Otter thought about these questions now as he squatted beside a fire outside Duck-woman's longhouse. He was building a new mortar with which she would grind what little corn or acorns they might find. He worked a four foot walnut log, as big around as he could reach with both arms. It stood upright, now, near the fire, with two foot of its length buried in the ground. The top had been flattened with a white-man's crosscut saw. Presently Otter chipped away the center with a steel hatchet leaving undisturbed about four inches of solid wood banding around the outside edge.

The most recent Ohio Munsee who had visited were very insistent. They warned that fifteen hundred French Indians were preparing to attack the English. Ottawa, Huron, Potawatomy, Miami, Shawnee, would all be coming. No one would be allowed to stand in their way. The Wyoming Munsee must choose sides.

After those cousins left, Duck-woman selected spokesmen for the people sending them south with another plea to Brother Onas. Support and supplies were essential. Brother Onas must tell the Munsee of Wyoming how he intended to help them to expel these invaders.

A few more Indians from Wyoming moved west or north. Some joined the French, others simply moved further away from the troubles they feared were coming.

Every few days Christian Indians returned home, from Gnandenhutton to Wyoming, even though there was little food. Fear grew on the Frontier. Families split apart and, or pulled closer together.

Otter thought about all this now. He stopped chipping with his hatchet. He sat it aside and pick up a white-man's metal fireplace shovel. He shoveled orange and red coals from the fire into the center depression he had formed in the top of the log. The coals would burn down into the log for an hour or more. Each shovel-full popped and sparked, then settled to burn and smoke as they did their work. Otter would return when these coals had cooled to chip out the charred wood and repeat the process until the depression was deep enough. *This will be a good mortar, when Duck- woman is ready to grind corn or acorns. If any can be found.*

In October, two French Indians came to Wyoming. They asked the Munsee living here if they were preparing to join the fight. The French Indians brought no wampum. They asked for no council meeting. They spoke quietly to a few cousins known to them, ate what food was offered them as guests, boasted of great success against the English and departed the following morning. Everyone noticed the fresh scalps carried on their belts but no one asked and the cousins offered no explanation concerning where they had been taken.

Two days later Red-corn retuned from a scout to the south. He did not bring good news.

"I saw three cabins burned on Penn's creek," he explained to the people gathered in the Longhouse. "I counted seven bodies I think. It happened before the quarter moon. Body parts were scattered by the wolves and scavengers. Hard to tell for sure.

I did not go on upstream to the other cabins. Buzzards circled off in the sky that way. Likely more of the same.

White men are coming up the Susquehanna. I saw their canoes. Maybe forty men. They will find what I found. John Harris leads them."

By the time Harris' party approached Wyoming, two days later, other scouts had come in with reports of French Indians all about in the woods to the west of the river.

Otter met Harris and his party at the river's edge. There were only ten men. The others remained down river a couple hundred yards on the east bank. Otter noticed rifles in the canoes were close to hand. His warriors came to greet their guests with only a few tomahawks and knives in their belts.

"Welcome John Harris," said Otter. "Why do your other men not come in?"

"They needed a rest. We're heading back right away. Just wanted to inform you of the war being made against our people on Penn's creek. You wouldn't know about that would you?"

" We know," said Otter. "Our own scouts have been down river. They brought back the news. It was French Indians not Munsee from Wyoming who did the killing. They are all about on the west side of the river. When you return stay to the east side. Our scouts say that side is free of the troublemakers for now. We have asked for help from Brother Onas but he has sent none. We need arms and powder if we are to repel the invaders."

"I'll take that word back to Brother Onas," said Harris. "I'm pleased to know the Munsee of Wyoming are still looking to Pennsylvania for protection. That's good. Together we'll hunt the French and their red brothers who have come into our country. Together we will kill them. Their women will cry and their children will go hungry. I think we may need a fort near here. We will return soon with many soldiers."

Harris turned and seated himself in his canoe. His party floated downriver to those white men left behind. Then the entire party paddled down river hugging the West bank.

"They stay to the west bank." noted Red-corn.

"Yes," said Otter, "you cross to the east side, follow behind them to Penn's Creek. See if they continue to hug that bank."

They did hug the west bank as far as Red-corn followed. But at the bend of the river just before the confluence of Penn's Creek he stopped following.

Pop, pop, pop came the report of rifles being fired from the west bank. In a moment he saw the powder-smoke rising from the brush along the shoreline. Continued firing became a steady barrage from behind the trees on shore and from the men in the canoes shooting back. Soon the battle swept with the canoes floating in the current around the bend in the river. Sounds of intermittently discharging muskets receded down the Susquehanna. Red-corn turned back toward Wyoming. John Harris had distrusted the word of the Wyoming Munsee. Now he was paying the price in lives.

On November 8, 1755 John Branch was in the Pennsylvania House Assembly listening to a meeting mostly controlled by

Quakers. The big room was crowded with assembly members and spectators. The fireplaces at either end of the room burned brightly and those closest to the flames had removed their coats.

Branch heard the appeal made by the Delaware spokesmen from Wyoming. They were eloquent and honest. The Indians said clearly that with some small effort Brother Onas could reassure the Munsee of Wyoming and keep them loyal to the English. With some food, arms, gunpowder and a simple promise to keep whites from settling their land the Munsee would fight the French and help keep them out of Pennsylvania.

The Quaker statesmen passed several embarrassed glances back and forth. There was some whispered consultation. They thanked the Munsee for coming. They presented the Lenape with a few presents, mostly silver trinkets and clay pipes. They talked long and made some vague assurances that the whites would soon decide how to best defeat the French. They were busy now gathering a great army somewhere to the east. They did not mention where. Soon they would notify the Munsee how the Lenape would be asked to help in the grand victory. Go home and wait until that time was the only direction they were ready to provide for now.

When the white men finally finished talking there was a long silence in the room while everyone waited to see how the Indians would respond. The Munsee sat quiet waiting to see if the conference had ended.

Finally the taller of the two Munsee rose to his feet.

"Is this all Brother Onas has to tell his friends in Wyoming?"

The white men said nothing but nodded their heads as they glanced back and forth among themselves.

Suddenly, the Munsee gathered their gifts and left. Branch watched them shuffle through the crowd inside, out the door and down the steps, then walk north toward High-street, their heads held aloof and solemn. It was late in the afternoon and the sun would soon drop over the western horizon.

"What's goin on?" asked Elias as he walked up.

"Nothing good," said John.

"The Quakers and the Penn family still can't decide who will pay for the war preparations. Their waiting on the Crown and the King's representatives are still adding up the financial losses of Braddock's debacle. The result is nothing getting done. Meantime reports keep coming in that the French and their savages are burning our frontier, killing and carrying off more people every day. The gentlemen in here," he said, nodding toward the front door of the Assembly which had closed behind him, "ain't likely to do much of anything until they smell smoke. By then I'm afraid it will be too late for many of our people. We may need to get the news to Brother Antes. Can you ride in the morning?"

"I'll get ready." Said Elias.

On 9 November, 1755 the two Munsee spokesmen left Philadelphia for home. Elias Knepp rode along the trail heading north through Bucks and Northampton counties toward the Forks of the Delaware, Bethlehem and Gnandenhutton. The sun was warm the sky clear. A steady breeze brought red, orange and yellow leaves flying on the air. Geese honked high above as they flew south to avoid the cold they knew was coming.

Away to the northwest in Wyoming the river was rising slowly from heavy rains north in the Catskill Mountains. No one at the village had noticed yet. The valley remained dry. Geese honked here too, gathering by the thousands on the river, due to dryness in the normal wetlands. Stands-often was returning from a hunt along the water. He carried a dead goose on his belt and his bow in his hand. He saw the two white men approaching from the Warriors Path through the Blue Mountains. They came from the direction of Gnanadenhutton on the Lehigh. They rode in, their horses at a walk, their rifles pointed toward the blue sky for all to see.

Stands-often was cutting an angle across the meadow toward the crossing near the village moving the same direction as the riders. The river was yet an easy ford. He removed his moccasins and waded the river ahead of the two mounted men.

The strangers hesitated as a crowd began to gather on the opposing bank to greet them. Then they waded their horses over with water barely above the fetlock as they came.

The white men were grim faced when they rode their mounts up the west bank. The bigger of the two men spoke:

"Im Charles Broadhead. Cousin Josh and I are here to talk to yer head sachem"

The closest thing they had to a chief was Otter but he really was only a warrior. The other leaders were away to the north meeting with the Nanticoke's. One of the Christian Indians spoke up and said they would fetch Otter but it would take a little while.

The two white men were invited to sit which they declined to do, preferring to stay mounted. They declined the food that was offered also but did drink some water from a gourd dipper and thanked the woman who had brought it. It was no more insulting than many white men who had visited the village. The thank-you was noted by the Christian Indians who understood its meaning.

Thirty minutes or so passed and the Broadhead cousins were beginning to sense some kind of treachery. Sweat was beginning to trickle under Josh's deerskin shirt. Rifles had gotten heavy and both men had lowered them to lie at rest across the pommel of their saddles.

Otter came through the camp then with a small entourage. There were about forty people here now listening. Hoping to hear a message about Brother Onas sending them help.

" You the head man."

"No, but I can hear your words for the Lenape here at Wyoming."

"Well, we've come to tell you that it's well known you people have been murdering settlers all over the frontier. Our Pennsylvanians are coming in a great army soon. Those guilty Injins will be dragged away in chains and thrown in prison. Any who resist will have their heads chopped off. So stop the killing now or when the army gets here nothing in this valley will live when we get done."

Otter said nothing.

The Broadhead cousins had delivered their message. They backed their horses to the river turned and splashed across the Susquehanna. Water was now knee deep on the horses.

A month passed. Elias Knepp rode a borrowed horse with a rough gate. He was one of those animals who never seemed comfortable with a rider and tried to share his discomfort. The borrowed saddle also left much to be desired including the lack of a stirrup on the right side, which had been replaced long ago with a loop in the end of a rope—a rope that looked now to be rotten from age and exposure. Elias tried mightily to ride without putting any pressure on the right side, but it proved hard to stay balanced in anything more than a walk.

He was mounted though and he wasn't complaining. Most of the men were afoot. The column of a hundred men moved slowly with scouts ahead on the trail and flankers out on either side watching for possible ambush.

They had left Bethlehem yesterday morning on a rescue mission. Christian Indians ... individuals and small family groups ... had come through the woods to Bethlehem all carrying the same frightening news ... Gnandenhutton attacked ... many French Indians ... the community burned ... missionaries killed ... Christians Indians scattering into the woods, running for their lives.

Buzzards were circling overhead. The sky was alive with migrating fowl. It was another bright fall day. The smell of charred wood and smoke lingered moment to moment in shifting breezes.

The column halted now as scouts scattered out to encircle the community ahead.

A year ago over five hundred people had been living here at Gnandenhutton. In the past twelve months most had drifted away a few at a time moving either south to Bethlehem or northwest to Wyoming. Last week a hundred or fewer

109

remained living here when the horrifying war cry had broken the stillness at dawn.

A few minutes passed. Elias dismounted, stretching his legs. He walked off the trail and urinated in the bushes. A ground squirrel jumped out to perch indignantly on a nearby log and scold him. *I wonder what the scouts have discovered. How long before we move ahead into the village. What are we gonna find.*

The column was relaxing. Some of the men had sat down on rocks and logs. A few had moved out toward the flankers who were visible off to the right and left fifty yards or so. They conversed back and forth in quiet tones across the distance. But everyone's eyes kept sweeping the surrounding forests.

These were not city men. Some were new immigrants but most had grown up in these or similar forests. They had volunteered to come along on this rescue mission though some speculated they would find more bodies to bury than enemies to fight. *Still,* thought Elias, *we're not sure how many Frenchmen or French savages are out in these woods today. Braddock certainly found more than he could handle and he had an army of three thousand men.*

Half an hour later two scouts came in within a few moments of one another... one from the right ... the other from the left. Then came the order to move forward.

The chapel, barns, mill, and dormitories, were all in charred ruins on the west bank of Mahoning Creek. The huts of the Christian Indians on the east bank were deserted and quiet except for a tin pan tied to a pole beside one of the near cabins, which kept flapping and rattling lightly in the breeze.

Elias had already noticed the body-parts. They were scattered about. A few men dismounted and began to gather them. It was a job no one wanted but it had to get done before they could leave. They all knew that. No one wished to remain here any longer than necessary. Soon everyone was busy or at least pretending to be busy doing something. The work was finished quickly. As always, a few did more than many but each did what he could bring himself to do and there was little discussion. The bodies got buried and the words said.

Eleven Moravian missionaries had been murdered here. They were all white men. The Indian huts were still standing empty but not burned. Most of the Christian Indians had not moved to Bethlehem, which caused some of the white-men to speculate that the Indians had been in on the attack or at least warned ahead of time.

It was a quiet ride back toward Bethlehem. Elias had seen more of war today than he ever wished to see. He was angry but more than that he was sick. Some of the men killed had been his friends. The rope stirrup broke as he rode along on his rough mount. He hardly noticed.

A day or so later an old Indian traveled through Gnandenhutton on his way home to Wyoming. He saw signs of the white man's visit. It had been a small army.

He had been told about the threats made by the Broadhead Cousins. He thought about those threats all the way back to Wyoming. He pondered what must have happened. He saw some evidence. He imagined much else. He arrived with exaggerated stories about white men rounding up Indians, and dragging they away in chains. He had seen headless bodies in the woods and witnessed white men on horseback carrying mysterious bags he supposed to be carrying the heads back to Pennsylvania.

This news spread like a wild fire through the longhouses. They were certain now. Harris had gone back thinking the Munsee had attacked him. Brodhead's threats were true and now they had come to pass. Their choice was clear. They could wait to starve this winter or be killed by the Pennsylvanians next Spring. Or they could join their cousins from the Ohio, ally with the French and possibly regain their old homelands.

All the uncertainty was swept away in one night of tribal council. There was no dissention. Their path was clear. They had made their decision.

All the insults were remembered. It was plain now why Brother Onas had been so coy. He intended to destroy them. It was a matter of survival. It was a matter of honor.

A great fire was kindled outside. The war dance begun under the night sky continued till dawn. Preparations for war began. Emissaries left traveling west. Weapons were gathered and readied. War leaders and captains were selected. Women began preparing war-paint. Prayers were offered.

The commitment had been long in coming but now that it was made nothing would be held in reserve. The English must pay for beheading and enslaving their Munsee brothers and for every indignity the Lenape had been forced to suffer in recent memory.

Now the world would be forced to see. Munsee men were not women as the Iroquois said. Munsee men were warriors.

Chapter 24

Christian Lapp swung the corn-knife in his right hand.

Almost effortlessly he cut the stalk held in his left, tossing it to the pile on the ground a few paces away. It was a frosty clear morning in Northkill Valley, Pennsylvania. Beyond him at a distance, the Blue Mountains rose steeply reaching toward a morning sky that brightened as the sun rose behind him.

Pausing a moment, his gaze passed along the mountain ridges stretching from the southwest, looming darkly over his log cabin which sat on the gentle rise in front of him, and faded away then into the distant horizon toward the north-east.

Ducks quacked down near the creek and winged away south, following the Norhtkill, on toward the Perkiomen, the Schuylkill and Delaware Bay.

Christian Lapp had come to this valley seven years ago with his new wife Delilah. It had been hard work but the farm was beginning to take shape. He could hear a cow lowing now from inside the barn and he heard the muffled scrape of a wooden bucket on stone. Delilah was milking.

The cabin was a small single-room log affair but the barn was substantial, built of field-stone with the help of neighbors—mostly other Amish farmers who had come to the area with the Lapps. Those people lived now in similar farms spread out over the landscape off toward Germantown and Philadelphia a few days travel south. It was good ground for farming. Even in this dry summer, Christian Lapp's farm would have a crop. His fields had fortunately caught two short summer rains just at the right time. He had been blessed. The drought had been severe, elsewhere. Many farmers would not be so lucky this fall.

Christian cut another cornstalk. He tossed it to the pile. He felt a crushing blow to his back, knocking him forward. He noted the pile of corn, aligned neatly waiting to be tied. Before his face hit the pile of stalks, he heard the loud report of the musket that had killed him. He died quickly his face buried in the pile of brown stalks. He did not feel the knife cut the scalp of blond hair from his head. He did not hear the triumphant war-cry of the brave who had shot him or the screams from the barn. His war was over. But for most people on this frontier it was just beginning.

Little Owen Creek lay east of South Mountain where the Blue Mountains of Pennsylvania fold into the back parts of Maryland. Waters of nearby streams run south toward the Potomac River and empty into the Chesapeake Bay instead of the Delaware. Still, most folk's hereabout looked to Lancaster and Philadelphia for trade goods and news. Valleys here have less flat ground and more hillside. There are Quaker families and other Pennsylvania Dutch but most folks are Scots/Irish Presbyterian. The Morrison's are one of those families and James Morrison is the second youngest son of eight boys and three girls born to Arthur and Blanch. James is nine and small for his age. He has been sent to the creek for water, the spring beside the house having stopped flowing in early August.

He saw two of his older brothers, Daniel and Joseph, were harvesting what little corn they could find in the field as he went behind the barn to the tree line. His sister Elizabeth waved at him from the barn door as he looked back just before the path he followed was swallowed by the shade of the big trees. It was a cold afternoon and many of the big oaks and beech trees had held their leaves long into fall.

Today James preferred the open field and having the bright sun on his back. The day was advanced. It would not warm any more. In fact it would most likely get back close to freezing just as soon as the sun dropped behind the mountains. Before entering the woods he had noted the orange globe beginning its daily decent behind the ridge. He needed to get his water and get back to the house where Ma was cooking supper. Little Owen Creek was a good quarter of a mile away.

James could never remember their spring failing to produce water before. Pa said it never had happened. Elizabeth was born the same summer the family moved to the farm on Little Owen Creek. She was twelve now. This summer had been the driest anyone could remember. Surely winter rain and snow would revive the spring, making these trips to the creek unnecessary. If not Ma said they might have to move the cabin.

114

James scurried along now like the squirrels he saw moving through the trees heading for nests. Soon he had two wooden buckets full of water balanced across his shoulders on a carry pole. He started back up the path. He heard the crack of a musket followed shortly by two other similar reports. He wondered about the three shots. Were all his brothers out hunting? Why did it take three shots to make a kill?

William missed again, he thought, smiling to himself. His sixteen-year-old brother William was the worst shot among his older brothers. They all teased him about it.

James was strong but the water buckets were heavy. He stopped twice to rest on his return trip. On his second rest, he heard people shouting from the direction of the cabin and he heard someone scream. *Jenny chasing Elizabeth with that snake again?* A bit further up the trail James smelled and saw the smoke. Too much smoke. It was rising up into the dark blue sky. *Something's wrong. The house or the barn is afire.*

He set his buckets down without spilling the water and ran up the path toward home. *I might be needed.* Without fully understanding what was happening some old instinct caused him not to follow the path any further, but instead to cut across though the trees and circle out around the clearing to the north and west side of the cabin. He stopped for a second beside a big beech tree before stepping out into the open.

He gasped! He slipped back further behind the tree. *Indians.* He ducked lower and slowly now stuck his head around the other side of the tree. Through the Jo-pye weed at the edge of the clearing he could still see, a little, and he was much better hidden from this position.

Indians were in the meadow above the cabin. They had Elizabeth, Mary and Jenny. They had Nathan too.

Mary and Jenny sobbed quietly, their heads down together. Elizabeth, her chin up, watched calmly back toward the cabin, beyond the barn, into the woods were James had gone to get the water. Nathan hung his head. Blood ran down from his hairline across his forehead. It dripped off his nose to the ground.

The enemy braves had tied the youngsters' hands and now were placing nooses about their necks connecting the Morrison siblings together in a human chain like horses in a pack-train. Something was said by one of the Indians. James could not hear what was said, but suddenly Nathan looked up, determined. Then one of the savages grabbed the lead rope and took off trotting up the slope toward the tree line above the farm leading them all away. James counted six Indians. Moving swiftly the hostiles were soon gone into the forest along with his brother and three sisters.

The barn was burning. Flames licked outside the loft door and through the shingled roof in several places. Smoke was coming out the cabin window but no flames were visible there yet.

Where are Ma, Pa and everyone else? James quickly shot downhill toward the cabin careful to run within the trees. Then he darted across the open field between the barn and the cabin. An eastward breeze blew keeping most of the heat and smoke from the barn fire away but still he felt the hair on the left side of his head suddenly bristle. He reached up to brush it back and forth with his hand. It had the stiff feel of a hogs hide.

The house was billowing smoke out the door opening and the window was belching flames by the time James got to the front step. He could not enter and no one could be left alive inside. There was no way he could save anything or anyone from the burning buildings.

He ran toward the cornfield. *Where are Daniel and Joseph?*

He found them. Dead! He couldn't look anymore. He ran... toward the path leading to the creek. Just as he arrived at the relative safety of the trees an Indian brave leaped up from the ground in front of him like the springing of a snare. The man grabbed James by the hair. Quickly the Indian slipped a looped rawhide rope about the boy's neck and with his fist full of rope and no small amount of James' hair began sprinting back up the hill past the burning cabin toward where the other Indians had disappeared a few minutes earlier.

James could do little but try to keep up. Tears stung his eyes. He feared his hair being ripped from his head. His lungs burned from smoke and exertion. His feet barely touched the

116

ground as they flew up the slope toward the trees. What was happening? What could he do? The man was huge and strong and fast. No one could stop him.

There was a sudden boom/flash and James was flying though the air. The savage still held on to his hair, the big man's legs still ran, but without their previous strength or purpose. Then James was suddenly smashed to the ground. He couldn't breathe. The big savage lay on top of him shuddering and then as still as a log.

James tried to breathe. He was dizzy and it was getting dark. Suddenly the big Indian was rolled off. James gasped for air, filling his lungs. It was his brother William who had him by the arm, now, lifting him to his feet, holding him up. His brother Patrick was by their side pounding the savage in the face with some kind of war club. The skull was being smashed. Blood and grey matter flew about them.

"He's dead! Let's go!" said William. They were all running again, back down the slope. Passed the burning buildings, through the corn patch, well out into the trees and up the next ridge before they stopped and collapsed beside a big boulder to catch their wind.

James stared at his sixteen–year-old brother William who held his musket close to his chest and thirteen- year-old Patrick who still gripped the club with white knuckles.

William began to reload his musket.

"Ma and Pa never came out of the cabin," said Patrick. "Me and little Johnny got away cause we was already in the woods when Daniel and Joseph got killed. Johnny is stashed down in the hollow log were I killed that doe last Spring. Remember?"

James nodded his head. Patrick nodded back and spat on the ground. "I came across William when he was sneaking in from the south. We saw them take Nathan and the girls. We were working our way around the left side of the farm to go after 'em'when we saw that big bastard grab you and take off coming back up the hill. We had to hurry to cut him off." Patrick paused suddenly to look at William. "Brother that was some damn good shootin. Hit that ugly son of a bitch right in the side of his head. About the onlyist place you could aim fer, to miss hittin James."

William was still shaking. He said nothing. "Let's get movin," said Patrick. "You boys get east of the creek and go to Hostetler's. I'll get Johnny and we'll stay west, go to old Ducker's place. Michael is still missing out there somewhere but he may be denned up. We ain't seen him since breakfast. He's always out runnin the woods. He ain't no fool. He may yet be livin. He may have already got help comin'. But we cain't count on it. Let's go."

Quickly the three boys separated heading off through the darkening woods two bearing left and one heading right. The Morrison farm grew quiet except for the popping and crackling of the two burning buildings, that lit the darkness now settling over Little Owen Creek Valley.

Chapter 25

*B*ehind the Blue Mountains, West Licking creek runs off Backlog Mountain. West Licking is a small creek little more than a dozen paces across. It flows west for about four mile in a narrow valley through rolling country before it cuts the last low ridge then flowing north into the Juniata. The mouth of the West Licking opens into the Juniata where the larger river bends back on itself, twice, in wide curves, traveling fifteen miles to make four, winding its way toward the Susquehanna. It's pretty country. All along the Juniata there were a scattering of homesteads. Mostly they were Scots Irish folks with a sprinkling of Pennsylvania Dutchmen. No one had been settled here a decade ago. Most settlers came three or four years back, but none came after Braddock's defeat at the Monongahela.

Zack Miller took a swing with his maul and almost missed the glut (wedge) entirely. It was a glancing blow at best and twisted the handle, which in turn twisted his shoulder. It didn't exactly hurt but it didn't feel comfortable either. He was tired.

He and Jesse had been splitting rails since soon after daylight. The sun now was high in the southern sky. It wasn't hot but it wasn't exactly cold. Splitting rails was good work for such a day. There was ice along the edges of the creek when they crossed this morning to split these logs for old man Meeks who needed a fence to keep hogs out of his garden patch next summer.

"Let's take a rest," said Zack.

He leaned the maul against the log he was working and sat down on a nearby stump. Jesse sat down on the log they had been attempting to split. He picked up a nearby stick, pulled his knife, and started shaving the bark.

Jesse was always cutting, shaving, or whittling something with that knife. He kept it sharp with a small whetstone. Handles, spoons, pegs, door latches, pitchforks, rake teeth were all quick work for him. He liked keeping busy. He was handy with the knife and he took pride in his work. It was a skill appreciated by his family and neighbors.

Someday Jesse hoped he might be able to acquire wood working tools beyond the ax, knife and froe. Unlike most folks he didn't want to be a farmer. It wasn't his 'calling'. He had seen men in Lancaster who made a good living working wood. That was his dream. Someday soon he hoped to float downriver to Lancaster and find a way to become an apprentice to one of the cabinetmakers or wheelwrights.

Zack uncorked a jug and took a swig. The water was good. He tipped the jug again as he watched a small bird scurry headfirst down the trunk of a big hickory a few paces to his left. The bird went around the tree as it came down. When it was behind the trunk Zack could still hear it's claws scraping the bark till it appeared again on his side of the tree. The bird stopped suddenly and stared toward Zack who had set the jug back on the ground. Neither moved. Then the bird cocked his head from side to side and let out his distinctive call. On the last note the nuthatch flew off with rapid wing beats up Backlog Mountain. Zack turned to smile at Jesse.

It was then he saw the Indians. There were four standing a few paces beyond Jesse, in front of an old rotten log. Out of the corner of his eye he saw two more enemy braves off to the left of the first bunch and another a bit further back standing next to a big oak.

No one move. Jesse hadn't seen them yet. He was still working on the stick.

Zack cast a quick glance right. There were the muskets, propped against the big sycamore, where he and Jesse had left them, now as close to the savages as to him. One of the Indians noticed his glance and locked eyes with Zack when his gaze turned back toward them. The Indian smiled, a knowing smile neither friendly nor evil. He shook his head slowly at Zack.

It wasn't possible. Zack knew it even before the next Indian stepped from behind the sycamore to take possession of the weapons. That move startled Jesse who spun around to face their predicament.

The fight was lost before it was begun. The adrenalin pumping now into Zack's legs made him shudder when more savages appeared suddenly in the forest around them. Even a run for freedom was now hopeless.

"We're caught," said Zack.

"Damn," said Jesse, as he dropped his stick and slipped the knife back into its sheath.

The braves smiled, looking from one to another. They said not a word but two stepped forward toward the Miller cousins. The first produced a leather rope and began tying Zack's hands behind him. The second stepped to Jesse and nodded his head looking at the knife in the sheath on Jess's belt.

"Damn!" said Jesse.

He knew what was expected. Slowly he removed the sheath and the knife from his belt and handed it over.

The young Indian quickly hung the sheath on a leather thong and slung it over his head and under an arm so that it rode just above his right shoulder where he could access the bone handle with his left hand.

Soon Jesse was tied also and the cousins were bound together on a tether with loops about their necks. At a trot they were led away. Not a word had passed between captives and captors but Zack knew his life and the life of his cousin hung by a thin thread and there was little either could do right now but try to keep up. Instinctively, he knew that was going to be important.

Within the hour they had waded the Juniata and were well up Jacks Mountain on the other side. Zack had seen the smoke from Meeks' cabin before they had gone far but he did not see smoke rising from the Miller homestead further inland. Maybe the rest of their family was safe. Maybe help would come. Both William and Johnny were good trackers ... if they were still alive.

An hour later the Indians and their captives entered a bald near the crest of Jack's Mountain. From here Zack could see down the Juniata around the two big bends. White wood smoke rose from no less than half a dozen big fires. They could be brush fires from clearing timber but somehow Zack didn't think so. His heart sank and he saw Jesse stumble ahead of him.

'*Don't fall*' he thought, though he didn't have breath enough to express it. On they trudged. Always up. Always it seemed going higher. *When will we stop*, he wondered and *what will happen when we do.*

What Zack didn't know was how widely those house fires were burning and how many families were dying or being torn apart that fall. For hundreds of miles in a huge arc from the southwest to the northeast through Virginia, Maryland, Pennsylvania, and into New Jersey from the forks of the Delaware up through the Minisink Valley homes were burning and people were fighting, dying or fleeing. The Lenape living along the Ohio had joined the Shawnee and the other tribes from the Illinois Country allying themselves with the Frenchmen and the French Indians (the Huron and Ottawa). Even the Munsee from the Wyoming valley had taken up the hatchet against the English. Each group had their own reasons but they were all determined and for now they were all in a common cause. They were winning and it was the English settlers who were dying. More precisely it was, for now, the Scots Irish and German settlers who were dying. Distinctive groups to some but all the same as far as the Indians were concerned.

Chapter 26

$\mathcal{H}$einrich Feagley had forgotten about Zack Miller until he arrived at the Town Tavern in Philadelphia. He had been back to the city only twice over the years and both times he had come to the tavern for a meal. Each time he remembered the young man who had joined him at his table years ago. He could not recall the name but he had not forgotten their talk. The young fellow had spoken of heading out toward the Juniata River where he had family.

Heinrich wondered about that now. He had heard a lot about the Juniata River in the past few weeks. Since the attack on the Northkill there had been hordes of families streaming down the road past his farm heading south and east toward Germantown. Some had their animals and themselves laden with heavy loads. Other families looked as if they had left with just the clothes on their backs. Swamp Creek Dutch Reformed Church was full of folks who had fled here hoping for security from Indian attack. Many of them were from out on the Juniata.

But folks were trudging in from the Northkill and from up toward the Lehigh as well. The men had a tight-lipped, confused look. Women's faces showed puffy red eyes. The children were quiet—too quiet—and they all had dirty, tearstained cheeks.

Shared stories of rape and murder were common, but few had actually witnessed any atrocities personally. All had seen burning fires or passed by the charred ruins of homesteads on their retreat. The whole countryside smelled of wood smoke when the wind was right. Some had seen bodies of the slain along their way, and a few had taken the time to bury the dead.

Many of the refugees had stories of family and animals who were missing. Some had left behind fathers, brothers, uncles to search for the lost. Those families watched the road behind continuously hoping soon to see their relatives catch up.

It was a sad procession. Heinrich had noticed that it continued all the way into Philadelphia though after Germantown the road was less crowded and there were at least a few people traveling against the tide—going home to farms not yet abandoned.

"Here you are," said Ezekiel. "Lost you in the crowd at the courthouse while I was talking. Ready to eat?"

"Ya. Might as vell get a goot meal out of de trip," Heinrich said, slowly climbing the stone steps into the tavern. He was tired and hungry. Something smelled good.

The food was soon ordered. A girl brought beer in pewter steins. Heinrich took a big swig. It was stout, just like he remembered.

"Vell? We going to get any-ting outen de gobermunt? Any forts? Any soldiers? Any money fer to oufit and pay militiamen?" asked Heinrich.

"I don't know," Ezekiel answered "The council is fighting with Governor Morris over how to raise the money, how to organize, and who will be in command. The council is controlled by rich men who have been here forever, mostly Quakers, and a few other folks like Mr. Franklin who ain't a Quaker at all but votes like he is. These days most of the Quakers believe they can fight in defensive wars but some of 'em still say turn the other cheek forever. They won't vote to fight for any reason. Those ones mostly live here in the city, and some of them are the rich men on the Council," said Ezekiel.

He let out a sigh and took a big gulp of his beer.

Heinrich leaned back in his chair.

"Maybe vhen more folks get here dey change der mind. Maybe Indians not the only problem dey got."

"Maybe. I hear talk there is a big group coming soon from Lancaster area to get the attention of the council or hang a few councilmen if that's what it takes, but that may just be talk," said Ezekiel. "I think the real obstacle is over who is going to pay. The Council is willing to levy a tax on property but the Governor is insisting the Penn Family's property must be exempt. The Council isn't willing to go along with that. It's the usual struggle for power. They did finally agree to spend some money on relief for the refugees. That will keep some folks from starving this winter I guess."

The girl brought the steaming hot stew in china bowls on a wooden tray. She sat it down in front of them. A serving boy in a white apron and a black felt hat brought fresh bread and butter to the table. The two old friends looked at each other and smiled for the first time today. The room buzzed with conversation but the two farmers ate in silence. There wasn't much more to be said.

Chapter 27

In late November, a group of angry German farmers from Berks County began a march on Philadelphia. Before they arrived the Pennsylvania Council passed a bill authorizing sixty thousand pounds for defense. A proposed compromise between the Governor and the Council had suddenly been adopted. The Penn Family agreed to make a one-time donation of five thousand pounds instead of paying a tax on their property, thereby avoiding bad precedent so far as the law was concerned. With hundreds of angry farmers on the roads to the city and enemy Indians raiding the frontier that was close enough to satisfy most of the Council. Only four of the pacifist Quakers voted against.

Benjamin Franklin, a member of the Quaker party, was appointed to a three man Committee of Defense tasked with planning and oversight of the Pennsylvania war effort. Forts would be built, arms would be acquired, militias would be raised and supported. Most of the angry German farmers went back home.

Christmas came and the Faulkner Swamp Dutch Reformed Church had a special service. People came from all around in spite of the six-inch snow, which had fallen over night drifting the roads, clinging to the trees and was still coming down. Heinrich was pleased to hitch his horses to the sleigh. The ride in was smooth over the fields and even on the roads, which for weeks had been cut with deep muddy ruts so as to be almost impassable, especially after those tracks froze hard as a rock.

Ezekiel Graber had returned from Germantown yesterday. This morning he was to give a report from Philadelphia regarding defensive preparations. He was late. The services were ending and he had not yet arrived. Then the door at the back of the church swung open, bringing a cold wind in with Ezekiel stomping snow from his boots.

Heinrich Feagley sat in the third pew with his wife Hilda where they always sat during church. He had arrived early. He could no longer see his breath; the stone building had warmed with all the people in attendance and the doors closed. Still he was happy for the tightly woven grey-wool scarf his

126

wife had presented him that morning. It was wrapped now about his neck. Hilda sat beside him smiling at Heinrich admiring her gift. She was getting on in years, like Heinrich, but she was still the young wife to him. He smiled back and admired her new bonnet.

Ezekiel strode up the center aisle finally stepping tentatively toward the pulpit. He tripped over something and lurched forward catching himself on Reverend Leydick. Several in the audience chuckled. Heinrich wasn't one of them. Ezekiel turned to face the crowd with a somber countenance.

"I have word from the War Committee. Our militia will be paid."

There was a collective sigh of relief from the crowd and heads nodded.

"But, we will have to reorganize into units of 60 men each. The men will elect their own officers. The officers will be required to send in weekly reports and keep record of all expenses for later reimbursement. The government will pay no clerks. The officers must keep their own records or pay a clerk themselves.

Powder and lead is on the way. More muskets are not yet available but should follow later. There will be no money for forts here on Swamp Creek, but further north there will be forts erected all along the edges of the Blue Mountains—In the gaps mostly where the trails come through. Some like the one at Wind Gap on the Lehigh are already being built. Others will get erected in spring when the ground thaws. Logs are being cut now for a fort behind the mountains, up river, on the Juniata by folks still living there. Some of our friends here today may be able to go back home."

A few visitors nodded. Others shook their head. Most looked at the floor.

" Except for the Juniata area, the forts will be on this side of the mountains all the way from the Maryland border to the Minisink Valley on the Delaware."

There were whispers in the crowd. Heinrich stood.

"Dat's a long way, Ezekiel. How far between forts?"

"No more than a days march; fifteen to twenty miles I've been told."

"How many forts dat be?" asked Heinrich.

"I don't know Heinrich, I did not ask that question. But it will get done. It has too."

The crowd nodded and whispered among themselves. A few like Heinrich shook their heads and stared at the floor— calculating.

"What about the French army setting up to come through those mountains next spring?" asked a voice from the back of the crowd.

Heinrich looked back but could not see who spoke and he did not recognize the voice. *Likely one of the strangers*, he thought.

"Those are just rumors," said Ezekiel. "No one has actually seen that army. The French would have to cut roads to get cannon here. We have scouts out. We would be alerted."

"What if they use the road Braddock himself cut? What then?"

"The British Regulars watch that road. If they come that way they will be seen. If that's the way the French army decides to travel it's a far distance south of here and not our immediate concern."

"What if they leave their cannon behind and just try to put the sneak on us. Come through the mountains somewhere else?" asked the voice. "That would be our concern quick enough."

"Well that's why we need the string of forts to support scouts ranging all over those mountains. We must know if that happens so we can muster our troops to counter their offensive," said Ezekiel. "The forts will at least provide a place of security from the small war-parties doing all the killing right now."

"Only if you got time to get in 'em or stay inside 'em all day every day. When you go out to work your fields or tend your animals they can still get you quick enough. My cabin is five miles from my nearest neighbor if it ain't burned down already. Even here farms are spread out a mile or two between and that's just in the flat areas. There's plenty of cover for a small war party. Ask the folks from up on the Northkill," said the voice.

"Listen I don't have all the answers," said Ezekiel. "I'm just telling you what I've been told. That's all I know to tell you. If you want more answers maybe you ought to go to Germantown or Philadelphia your own self next time".

Reverend Leydick stepped back in front of the pulpit.

"Thank You Ezekiel for that report. I'm sure our young men will want to talk about this some more after church. I suggest that you all think it over and meet here on Wednesday morning next, to organize our militia and elect our new officers to take command... Now, let us pray."

There was a shuffle through the crowd. Heads bowed. Whispering ceased.

"Almighty God," prayed the reverend, "your people beseech you now. Help us in our efforts to defeat these godless savages, who have attacked us. These devils, who are even now burning our barns and homes, killing our animals, ravaging innocent families throughout our countryside. Be with our militia and our leaders. Guide them to smite our enemies as you guided Joshua in times of old... Amen."

The crowd remained quiet for a moment—thinking. The wind could be heard, outside, blowing the snows into new drifts.

Chapter 28

$\mathcal{T}$he winter was long and cold. March came and brought some warm weather, which brought rain, which turned to ice, and sleet, and then snow again. April was dry until the last week. May was sunny and bright.

Today it was hot and dusty inside the mill. David Shultze was already waiting before Heinrich arrived. He was reading newspaper articles posted on the walls. He looked up as Heinrich walked in.

"I posted that one," he said, pointing to an article.

"What's dat bout?"

"An army of 30,000 Frenchmen invading the Island of Minorca."

"Yah, I heard bout dat. Where is dat Minorca."

"Somewhere in the Mediterranean Sea. This war is spreading. It's not just being fought here in the colonies. There are big armies fighting and the Navy's of France and Britain are going at it too."

"Yah," said Heinrich, but he really didn't care about the old countries anymore.

"Did you know 'Shoe' Bastel up at Chestnut Hill."

"Nein."

"He died. Last week. So did John Martin's son and Henry Riesse's wife."

"I know Henry Riesse but not dee frow (the wife)."

"Lots of sickness."

"Yah. To much dis year."

"I noticed your plowing," said Shultze.

From the 8th to the 19th Heinrich had plowed 12 and half acres.

"I plant most to buckwheat in a week or two, said Heinrich, I start cutting hay tomorrow. How's your wheat?"

"Looks good, should be ready early in July," said Shultze. "Frost hurt your corn much?"

There had been a late frost on the first day of June a couple weeks before.

"Yah. Tis damaged."

Heinrich studied the cracks in the floor for a moment, thinking about his corn—promising green leaves suddenly over a night and two days turned black. It represented a lot of work for naught. No time left to replant. A few shoots were beginning to sprout a second time from the seed still left in the ground. Something might grow from that but most plants would never come back.

"You're next Shultze," came a cry from the floor above.

After Shultze stomped up the steps Heinrich started reading the articles the best he could.

The Pennsylvania Gazette had published many stories about the war. The newspaper came from Philadelphia up the Germantown Road with the mail by dispatch rider weekly to Henry Antes' big house. In normal times, the mail continued on up the post road to Bethlehem in another day. But these days with the enemy raids the mail didn't always run on to Bethlehem, but instead went back to Germantown and Philadelphia.

The mill owner had articles posted all over the wall, grouped loosely into areas of interest, and separate from other local news. Heinrich Feagley read now as he waited. He could read—a little. He didn't get all the words and he had to work at it but he understood much of what was printed.

> *February The Quick family was attacked by a small war-party near Bushkill on the Pennsylvania side of the Delaware. The old man and two sons were out cutting hoop poles when the father was tomahawked and killed. Both sons unable to aid the father did witness the grizzly affair and made their own escapes through the woods.*

> *April 1 — The barn of one Simon Westfall, at Minisink, was burnt by the Indians, with 24 cows, 9 horses, and about 400 bushels of wheat.*

> *May 21 — We have advice from Sussex County, New Jersey that the house of Anthony Swartwout was attacked. The wife of said Swartwout was found shot dead with a bullet thro' the back and three children were found at a little distance from the house, with their heads split open with a hatchet, but none of them were scalped; and that Anthony Swartwout and his other children are missing, supposed to be carried off by the enemy.*

> *We have also advice that the house of Capt. Hunt in Hardwick Township in Sussex County, was burnt about the same time, and a white lad about 17 years of age, and a negro man, who had care of the house are both missing, and several Indian tracks were seen.*

Heinrich had sons living with their families in the Valley of the Paulinskill. That was in Sussex County New Jersey near the Minisink. He had a grandson named Jacob in the militia there… somewhere.

New Jersey was ahead of Pennsylvania in constructing forts up their side of the Delaware. According to Ezekiel those forts were planned to work in concert with the Pennsylvania forts along the Blue Mountains. The line of forts met together near the water gap where the river flowed through the mountains.

The Minisink valley was isolated from the rest of New Jersey between those Kitattinny Mountains and the River. The last of the Pennsylvania forts up that way was Fort Hyndshaw above Dupui's. There was only about ten miles between Fort Walpack on the New Jersey side of the Delaware and Fort Hyndshaw on the Pennsylvania side.

North of the Water Gap in Pennsylvania was called Upper Smithfield Township, Northampton County, Pennsylvania. It was the area directly across the river from the Minisink Valley and recently most of it had been abandoned to the savages.

Much of Northampton County, and all of Upper and Lower Smithfield Townships, had been acquired by Pennsylvania through The Walking Treaty. Everyone knew the Munsee living in the Wyoming Valley disputed that treaty and wanted that land returned to them. They had asked many times that it be restored to them. Those requests had fallen on deaf ears. Now, it appeared, they intended to take it.

Chapter 29

$\mathcal{F}$ort Allen was a solid stockade erected on the east side of the Lehigh River at Gnandenhutton upstream from the burned Moravian buildings. Elias Knepp had helped to construct it. He stood now at its gate, watching the sun fall behind the mountains closing out this warm June day with a cool breeze and a blushing sky.

This was high hill country. The fort was well situated in a wide gap between the tall ridges. The palisades were cleared for a distance all around making a good 'field of fire'. Mr. Young had commented about that.

Elias thought he understood. Most of the men with their muskets were pretty good shots out to about eighty or ninety yards. The ground around the fort was clear of obstruction well beyond that distance.

Mr. James Young was the Commissary General of the Pennsylvania Militia. He was here from Philadelphia to inspect the line of forts in the Lehigh country. He had arrived yesterday. He was a tall stout, middle-aged man with black hair that stuck out under the brim of his hat. He had come through Falkner Swamp last week traveling past Reverend Antes house. He had consulted with Conrad Wisner at his plantation near Reading. Continuing on he had begun his inspection at Fort Franklin, a few days ago before coming east to Fort Allen.

Tomorrow, Mr. Young and his escort party would travel to Fort Norris and then on toward the Minisink. Elias Knepp would show them the way. He wondered about that journey now as he watched the sunset fade to purple.

There was no light in the morning sky when Elias filled his cup from a pot, which sat on a bed of red/orange coals to one side of the fire. It was his second cup of coffee. He had finished his breakfast. His horse was saddled, and his gear tied on securely—what little gear he had.

They would be moving fast. Young's escort included a dozen handpicked, serious looking men all well-armed and well mounted. Quick movements left little time for the enemy to react or so said the discussions he had overheard last evening.

"Ready Private," asked Young.

"Yes sir," answered Elias, noticing the first sign of dim light in the east.

The first six miles was good wagon road following alongside a rushing stream at the foot of North Mountain. Dawn had arrived. They made quick time here and passed two plantations both with houses burned and no one seen about them. Then the road started up into the hillier country. The pathway narrowed becoming more stony and treacherous. The riders slowed, proceeding in single file with their eyes scanning the trees and rocks all about them. What little conversation there had been now lagged and then stopped altogether. Weapons were close to hand, primed and ready. The next seven miles passed slowly.

They witnessed another plantation in a high meadow with its cabin burned. Elias wondered about the people who had lived here. It was a new plantation of only a few acres. *No more than three years old* he thought.

Elias was relieved a couple miles further on, when another valley meadow opened in front of them revealing fort Norris ahead a quarter mile distant.

The wooden gates were closed. There was no activity that Elias could see as they approached—no sounds of people. Three milk cows and five sheep grazed on the grass beside the fort. A big woodpecker pounded on one of the palisade posts.

As they moved closer the woodpecker sounds became louder and Elias could hear the cows cropping the grass forty yards away. The only other sounds were the horses' hooves treading the ground.

Then there was the sound of heavy wood sliding over wood and the gates of the fort suddenly swung open.

"Sergeant where is everyone," asked Mr. Young.

Sergeant George Kline and six disheveled and tired looking privates stood before them. They were the only human beings in sight.

"There are fifteen other men here sir, but they're all trying to get some sleep. We were up most of last night and they will be needed on the walls tonight. Ensign Zimmerman is out ranging the woods toward Fort Allen with twelve other men."

"We just came from that way. Didn't see anyone."

"You must have passed them sir. They stay off the trail when they can. They may have seen you, maybe not, but they went out that way. They should be back before nightfall."

"Where's your captain?"

"He went to Philadelphia to see about out our pay. He left on the 16th. We ain't been paid sir. The other Sergeant, Sergeant Yerger, is gone to Easton on furlough since the 20th to get his family settled in. On account of them having to abandon their plantation. You passed his place on your way in."

"Any women or children here?"

"Not here sir. They're all moved elsewhere fer safety. The Ensign should be back before dark... sir."

"We won't be here that long Sergeant. We plan to stay at Bossert's if he is still forted up. Is he?"

"Yeah, he's still there with some other folks. Least they was there couple days ago. It's about 12 miles further on toward Dupui's."

"Well show me around a bit without wakin anyone who can sleep through this incursion. Elias you and the boys see to the horses while the Sergeant here shows me around. Then we'll be on our way. We need to get to Bossert's before we lose our light."

Philip Bossert's plantation was lightly stockaded but looked secure. Young and his escort found families here from six other plantations as well as the Bosserts themselves. These were big families and it appeared they had at least forty men among them of fighting age. Even the women and children looked menacing. They were hospitable but they didn't seem overly friendly. They appeared to be well supplied and well-armed. They didn't ask for anything. Everyone was soon settled in and Elias was quickly asleep.

Next morning as Young and his escort mounted their horses, a tall slender man stepped forward. *He was introduced as Tom something or another*, thought Elias.

"I got one last question fer you", he said.

"Sure," answered Young.

"Is there a bounty yet passed fer Injun scalps."

Not when I left Philadelphia said Young. He hesitated.

"It had been proposed," Young added.

It was clear to Elias that Young didn't want to have this conversation.

"How Much", asked the man.

"The proposal hasn't passed yet," said Young.

"How much, was proposed to be paid, if it does pass."

"Sixty dollars for braves", said Young.

"How much fer women and children?"

"Forty for women."

"And the young uns?"

"Twenty, said Young, in a whisper.

"We'll save 'em' up," said the man. "We won't be safe here till there ain't no more Indians.

Young spurred his mount and they all galloped off leaving the surly stranger where he stood.

Elias looked back before the Bossert place disappeared behind them. *I wonder how many they got stretched and drying out in the barn already.*

Chapter 30

*T*hey left Bossert's at first light. It was a good wagon road and the land lay well for later development when the area could really get settled. It was now six-of-the-clock, dawn had arrived, and they were approaching Fort Hamilton. This fort had been first in the line of forts built. It had been constructed in haste with limited materials and few tools while the enemy lurked about in the woods and the cries of alarm were frequent.

Fort Hamilton was situated well enough in a cornfield, next to a stone farmhouse, open all around for a good distance. But the palisades were, as Young wrote later in his report, *"all very ill contrived, posts not firm in the ground, some with six inches between them"*.

As they approached Young stopped his horse and studied the situation before him.

"Is this your post Mr. Knepp?" asked Young.

"No sir; I'm posted at Fort Hyndshaw at the end of the line upriver from Dupui's."

"Who built this one?"

"Captain Van Etten and Lieutenant Hyndshaw were put in charge of the construction by Mr. Franklin. But they built Fort Norris and Hyndshaw's Fort too. The other forts are better built, there was more time then. This one was all slapped together in a big hurry, due to us needing a place, quick, fer people to get into. There was little time then it seemed between actions. Everyone was desperate to get something up and ready before it might be too late. After this one was built and serviceable they were able to take a bit more time on the next. They learned some as they built this one. Better tools got found and brought in, and materials were acquired from better sources and…"

"Yes—well I guess I understand. It shows though doesn't it?"

"Yes sir."

"Well, we will have to take time now to fix a few things I think. Don't mention I asked. I wouldn't want the officers to think I don't appreciate their efforts. It was built under difficult circumstances."

"Yes sir. I mean no sir I won't say nothing."

They found Capitan Craig, of the Irish Settlement, north of Bethlehem, in charge of the fort. He had with him with only seven men. Six other men were away with a Sergeant escorting a prisoner to Easton. The Lieutenant, Captain Van Etten and the remainder of the men were at Hyndshaw's Fort, further north, on the Bushkill.

Young did a quick inventory of supplies, noting that evening in his report:

> "Provincial Stores: 1 wall piece, 14 muskets, 4 wants repair, 16 cartooch boxes, filled with powder and lead, 28 lb. powder, 30 lb. lead, 10 axes, 1 broad axe, 26 tomahawks, 28 blankets, 3 draw knives, 3 splitting knives, 2 adses, 2 saws, 1 brass kettle."

Commissary Young's party rode away from Fort Hamilton the next morning. By eleven of-the-clock they found themselves arriving at Samuel Dupui's plantation, which was a modest, two stories, stone house, well-fortified. People bustled about both inside the walls of the fort and outside in various surrounding buildings and tents. There was a sawmill and a gristmill situated not far away on a little stream flowing down from the hills above. It seemed the hub of great activity.

They dismounted. Young handed the reins of his mount to Elias and went inside the house. By the time the horses had finished watering he walked back out and down the steps.

"We aren't staying", he said, "the Lieutenant is not ready with his muster reports. Take me on to Hyndshaw's Fort".

The wagon road from Dupui's to Hyndshaw's began as a comfortable track with the river on its' right about a quarter mile distant, across well-drained bottom ground. Some of the fields between had been cleared years ago and were now planted for this season. The crops looked promising— corn-field growing green, wheat-field turning yellow, flax-field blooming blue, an orchard, bee hives, native meadow grass on toward the river, red tail hawk above in a sunny, summer sky—a pleasant landscape.

Then the road moved away from the river proceeding up toward higher ground.

"I thought Hyndshaw's Fort was on the river," said Young.

"It is," said Elias, "the river bends way out here. It will come back this way before we get to Hyndshaw. Hyndshaw's Fort is on the Bushkill bout a quarter mile from where it flows into the Delaware."

"How far from here?"

"It's about ten mile from Dupui's. Nine or so from here, I guess."

Young looked back toward the fields of Samuel Dupui.

"Dupui seems to have quite a place here."

"Yeah, the Dupui family have been here a long time. His Pa, Nicholas before him. He came almost 50 years ago, I guess."

"What kinda name is Dupui? Sounds French."

"They are French, so I been told. Huguenot. Not like other Frenchmen. Came down with the Old Dutch families from the Hudson Valley back around the turn of the century when Kingston was still called Esopus and Albany was Fort Orange. Actually the old time Dutch families across the river in the Minsink Valley still call it Esopus when they go, even though it's been Kingston fer seventy years or more. They don't get to the settlements much and things are backward here abouts."

"Well it's New Jersey across the river isn't it?"

"Sure, technically, but them mountains keep the people in the Minisink isolated from most of Jersey and more connected to Esopus—I mean Kingston . It's easier travel to the North. They even got em a pretty good road when it's dry or froze. It's closer and easier than going south to Philadelphia or over the mountains to Elizabethtown. No big rivers to cross either. They really are isolated over there, even more than parts of our own frontier. New York and New Jersey still can't settle the border issues between them. They fight each other over taxes and such. To the north and west are the Pocono's and the Catskills and Indian country, to the south and west is Pennsylvania but until this war came officials and businessmen in Philadelphia just worried about selling the land to German and Irish immigrants. Not many roads got developed."

Elias paused. *I been talking a lot. Maybe he don't want all this information. But he needs to know how things sit.* He went on:

"We're kinda new comers as fer as Dupui and them old Dutchmen are concerned. Besides that we got the damn Connecticut thieves claiming they have ownership of the land here too. I've been over there across the river several times. The Dutchmen have themselves some nice plantations—good stone houses, and barns and mills, even church buildings. Now that the war has come, the Jerseys' have cut em a new supply road through the Kittatinny Mountains, good enough at least fer horses and mules. They are busy building forts on their side of the Delaware like we're building ours southwest along the Blue Mountains."

"Yes, I read the reports," said Young. "I know the plan. I helped draft it. Remember private New Jersey just has this little fifty mile stretch of border along the river they have to cover. We have almost three hundred miles of Indian border through Pennsylvania all the way from here to Maryland". Young paused. "How far is it to the New Jersey Headquarters at Fort Johns?"

"Half a day after you get across the river."

"Tell me about Captain Van Etten and Lieutenant Hyndshaw. Where they from"?

"They're both from the Minisink Valley born and raised. Their families are from across the river originally but they moved over to Lower Smithfield Township a decade or so back after the Munsee sold this Land to Brother Onas and Brother Onas started offering cheap prices fer good acres. Like the Palatine Germans and the Scots Irish comin off the boats in Philadelphia them Dutchmen know a bargain land price when they see it. And In Pennsylvania they didn't have to worry so much about the border dispute between New York and the Jersey's."

As they rode along Young noticed a farmstead appearing on the right side of the road. It was abandoned, the house burned. It was the first since leaving Dupui's. There were a dozen more just like it—houses and sometimes barns too, burned— before they finally approached Hyndshaw's fort.

Young was quiet. *I guess we all got to worry now about our border dispute with Frenchmen and Munsee*, he thought.

Lieutenant James Hyndshaw met them at the open gates. Laundry hung from the stockades. An old lady stirred a pot heating on a smoky fire between the fort and a stream whose cascading waters shot past, on a bedrock bottom and flowed on toward the river. A group of five young girls sat under a canvas lean-to, carding wool from a small cart and placing the cleaned strands into baskets on the ground. It was a warm day.

"Lieutenant James Hyndshaw, Sir. How can I be of service".

"Lieutenant it is a pleasure to meet you. Are you in command of the fort?"

"I am Sir; Captain Van Etten has gone up river to the Jersey side with five men. Indian trouble up that way yesterday. Messenger came last night. Captain left this morning. Gone to Mashipacong Island, about eighteen miles north of here."

"What kind of trouble Lieutenant?"

"Folks on the Jorris Davids' Plantation at a place called Kendiamong fired on six Indians trying to steal horses yesterday morning just after dawn. The neighbors and the Jersey militia are on alert and everyone is on the scout to find the enemy. If there's six there may be more. We got scouts out here ranging the woods, north, but nothing has turned up yet."

Well, have you time to show me around, let me take stock of things, asked Young? Yes sir. My orders are to stay right here for now. It will be an honor to show you our fort.

By nightfall, Young was back at Dupui's. His men and horses were settled for the night. Young was in a small upstairs room in the stone house. He had positioned a small table near the open window and placed a candle upon it to best advantage. It burned brightly as he drafted his report. He paused, from time to time, leaning back in the ladder-backed chair, smoking a clay pipe, collecting his thoughts. The light flickered occasionally in the gentle breeze and moths circled to get their turn at the flame.

It was pleasant by the window. He could see the night sky bright with stars before the moonrise. He dipped his pen into the ink bottle and wrote on his paper:

> *Fort Hyndshaw, 70ft. square, clear all around for 300 yards, stands on banks of a large creek about ¼ mile from the River Delaware. I think a very important place for defense of the Frontier. Mustered the 25 troops present and found them all very agreeable men.'*

He paused yet again, rocking back. The breeze shuddered his tiny flame almost to extinction. Then it settled, came back to life, and once more spread light across his writing paper, just as the moon began to spread light across the fields. He sat his front chair legs back to the floorboards and wet the quill again in the ink.

> *'Leadership at Hyndshaw is good I think. They do however need powder, this fort being most distant on the frontier. I have written a letter to Captain Orudt at Fort Norris, where is a large Quantity of Powder, desiring he would deliver 30 LB. powder and 90LB. of lead to Fort Hyndshaw. I thought it very necessary for the good of the service. Left Hyndshaw's and arrived here (Dupui's) at 7 PM.'*

He held the paper to the table blowing on it gently to set the ink. He corked the inkwell and used it to weight the edge of the paper. He pushed the chair back, stood, licked his fingers, and pinched out the flame. He slid the table carefully away from the open window. He stretched his arms over his head, yawned quietly, lay down on the small bed, which accommodated the room, and fell asleep without another thought.

Chapter 31

Υoung woke in the cool, predawn darkness. He rose from the bed and walked to the corner of the room. He found the crock slop-jar on the floor. He picked it up and did his mornings business. He sat the jar down and reached for the candle. Finding it in its' holder on the table, he took it and felt his way out of the room and down through the near total blackness of the stairway to the kitchen below.

There he discovered three middle-aged women puttering over pots and pans scattered around two small fires ablaze in the large stone fireplace. Unconsciously he ran his fingers up through his black hair. He took a sliver of a stick off a stack of kindling, lit it in one of the fires and transferred the tiny blaze to his candle's wick. He nodded toward the women who watched him.

He was mindful of them now. All three had the same blond hair pulled back into a tight little bun. All were dressed in homespun. One was slimmer and younger than the others; but all had the same roundness of face—cheeks glowing moist from the heat of the fire. *Attractive women*, he thought, *without being pretty—sisters I bet.*

"Morning," he said.

"Morning sir," they responded quietly, in unison.

Without another word he left, finding his way by candlelight back to his room. He placed the candle in its' holder on a wooden candle-stand. He yawned, stretching his arms above his head, noting how his dark shadow spread its' way up the whitewashed walls and across the ceiling.

He thought about the War. He slid the table back to the still opened window. He retrieved the candle, placed it and its holder back on the table and then repositioned his writing materials as he had arranged them the night before.

James pulled the chair beneath him. He took a deep breath listening momentarily to the dueling of whippoorwill's down toward the river and mocking birds in the nearby orchard. There was yet no light in the east. The breeze had disappeared overnight; there was a slight dampness to the air. The candle flame reached toward the ceiling and did not flicker. The only sign of moths were the burned remains sticking to the tallow candle.

Young uncorked the ink well, pushing his pipe and tobacco across the table away from him and picked up his pen. Carefully, he produced another sheet of paper from his leather pouch. He wet his pen in the ink and began scratching words:

> "Fortifications at Dupui's are adequate and he is very well supplied. In fact his commerce meets most of the needs of his neighbors and he has yet more available for use of the Province. However his prices are high. More importantly he seems to think that Pennsylvania is indebted to him for housing our militia. He is agreeable enough in conversation but has many strong and negative opinions about the Council in Philadelphia, the governor and the Penn family.
>
> I hesitate to write this as I even now accept hospitality in the shelter of his home. I feel we must support this post for the good of the service. However I believe we must keep an eye out for the costs and the accounting thereof. Mr. Dupui is no doubt committed to our cause in support of his neighbors, but he sees himself first a trader and due to his long, well established, location and honest reputation seems quite independent of any control."

Later that morning, the summer sun peaked over the Kittatinny Mountains of New Jersey lighting the Minisink Valley, and lifting a hazy vapor from along the River Delaware. James Young and his party mounted their horses. They were about to depart south toward Wind Gap and on to Easton. His inspection of the forts near the Forks of the Delaware was almost complete.

Young hesitated and looked down at Elias Knepp who stood a few paces away.

"Private, I appreciate your service these past few days. You have been most helpful. Good luck."

With that comment James Young reined his mount out the gates at Dupui's Fort and rode off toward Wind Gap.

Elias soon had his gear gathered and on his back. The horse he had ridden for the past few days was now trotting south with Young's party. He picked up his musket and walked out the gate at Dupui's just as a team of draft horses pulled a wagon load of walnut boards in from the saw mill. Their harness chain jingling in time with the clomp of the horses hooves.

Turning north Elias began trotting along the river road toward Hyndshaw's Fort. He soon had set himself an easy pace he could keep up for a long way. His senses were returning to his time and place. He listened for the sounds of his world. He heard the sound of leather fringe softly slapping time as he jogged along but none of his gear jingled.

Chapter 32

$\mathcal{B}$eletje was surprised at the smell when she opened the door and entered the house. It was an acrid, musty odor.

"Oh", she said, "leave the door open we need to air things out".

"Oh," said her cousin Sara Decker, turning up her nose and entering behind Beletje, "Doesn't smell like Ma Decker's house does it? We need a fire. Rain the other day wet the chimney flue. Without a fire it's smelled up the whole house."

"Yes", agreed Beletje.

They left the door open behind them and walked through the main room of the small stone house to the kitchen. Beletje strode straight to the woodbox near the back door.

"There's kindling but we'll need wood".

Sara unlatched the back door, and stepped out into a warm sunny morning. A little wren in the grape-arbor greeted her with its' song; june-bugs and bees buzzed in the air above the herb garden. She drew in a deep breath smelling dried manure, growing grass, sage and wild onions. She looked across the fields. Her brothers were driving in a small herd of sheep, across the pasture, toward the big stone barn.

Sara walked to the woodpile, split and stacked a few paces away, retrieved an armload of medium size pieces and returned to the kitchen. Beletje was already striking steel to flint. Soon a spark glowed on the char cloth. She blew on it causing the hot glow to brighten. Beletje placed the cloth amidst the straw held in her left hand. She blew on it again gently. A tiny flame popped through the straw. Quickly the burning straw was placed under the kindling which waited, prearranged, on the hearth. Carefully, a few more tiny pieces of wood were set atop her small conflagration.

The kindling took the fire and smoke began to fill the room. The girls coughed smiling at one another as they stepped toward the door waiting for the smoke to find the flue. In a few moments Beletje returned to the hearth and placed larger pieces of wood on the burning fire.

The smoke found its way to the chimney and began to flow upward. Warmed by the hot air the chimney drew more efficiently. In a few minutes the atmosphere in the kitchen began to clear. Slowly the obtrusive smell, which had been so overpowering, began to dissipate up and out of the house.

The young women hardly noticed. They were busy already cleaning and readying pots, pans and utensils.

For months Beletje and Sara had been living with most of their neighbors at Coles' Fort two miles south. Normally Beletje lived in their own house at the Davids' Mill on the east side of Machachemack River, and two miles north of here. Sara normally lived with her family a mile north on this side of the river. This was their grandfather Decker's plantation on the west side of the Machachemack, closer to the fort.

They had come with brothers and cousins to care for animals. The Davids' family animals had been moved to this side of the river and were fed now together with granddads stock. There were cows, oxen, horses, sheep, goats, hogs, chickens and a small flock of domestic geese. All the farms near the fort had extra animals and yet other people were forced still to go several miles to care for their farmsteads.

No one enjoyed staying forted up but it was necessary most of the time. Still, work had to get done or next winter people might starve. Groups of men went out daily from the fort to work different plantations. Some were posted as guards while the others worked. There was a group out today south of the fort.

The families with close farms, however, sometimes chose not to wait. They took themselves to their farms allowing the guards to cover folks further removed. Grandfather Decker's place seemed safe enough today. Beletje's uncle, Jorris Davids, was scouting the woods northwest of the farm. There were three well-armed Decker cousins outside helping Daniel and Jakey care for the animals.

"Did you see the new horse?" asked Sara.

"Yes Daniel showed him to me," said Beletje. "He looks to be a good animal." Daniel was lucky to catch him.

Yes, well I'm happy Daniel and Jakey got back safe. They were gone a long time. I was worried. They didn't know many of those fellas they went with. Most of them were from over on the Paulinskill," said Sara.

"I'm glad they didn't run into any Indians. Burning their homes was important though, maybe that will drive them further away."

"Maybe, but Daniel said they had already abandoned those homes before the militia got there," said Sara.

"You know, maybe those were the homes of the Indians that tried to steal Uncle Jorris's horses last week just before the boys got back home. Wouldn't that be something? We steal their horses while they try to steal ours. Then when they get back to Wyoming their homes are burned and their families and horses are gone. Wonder why they didn't take their own horses when they abandoned their houses. That doesn't make sense."

"Lots of things don't make sense these days. Joris not going with the boys is one of them," said Sara.

"He won't go fight west of the river. He's got to many old Munsee friends. Still he killed that injin in March when they was burning Simon Westfall's barn and he shot to kill the other day. He just missed. He's all mixed up with his feelings like when Pa got killed over the border", said Beletje, "but I don't care what people say. He is still my uncle and I feel safe when he is around. I hope he stays right close by. Maybe he's got the right idea. If everyone stayed at home maybe there would be fewer problems".

Two weeks later and over a hundred mile south at Faulkner's swamp, Heinrich Feagley was reading newspaper articles about the war posted on the wall at the gristmill? One caught his eye.

> *"We hear from the Jersey's, that on the12th last month four officers, with 25 men set out from Paulinskill, towards Great*

Swamp, in search of Indians; and that they returned on the 19th, after burning four Indian towns, one of which was a Shawanese Town, over the Susquehanna: But that they all appeared to have been deserted some months past.   They brought in six horses with them."

Heinrich was happy to hear about Indian houses being burned. He wondered who were the men from the Paulinskill. He wondered about his grandson Jacob in the militia up that way. He wondered about the horses. Were they good horses?

He had no way of knowing about the new horse in the pasture at Decker's farm north of Coles Fort, an Indian horse, grazing with other horses but keeping itself slightly apart, a pretty bay colored horse with a dark mane.

Chapter 33

$\mathcal{T}$ he bow was rosined and the fiddler played a jaunty tune.

They kept the fire small. It was too hot this time of year for a big one. A few candle lanterns scattered about and three torches mounted and burning from a six-foot post provided plenty of light.

A long table sat in the middle of the parade ground at Coles's Fort. Actually, it was three tables arranged end-to-end. The table was covered with linen cloth, bowls platters and plates containing bread and jam, beef and pork, corn puddings, green beans, summer squash, pickles, and cooked cabbage, and there were pies— blackberry, peach, apple, and gooseberry. Much had been already eaten. The surrounding farms and orchards had produced well this summer. July was a good time for a party.

"Do you see what I see? "asked Lydia VanAken.

"Yes I see them," answered Sara Decker.

Lydia was the daughter of Abraham VanAken. The VanAkens were the neighbors living nearest to the Davids' mill. Lydia was a big-boned, young woman, still single and a bit of a gossip.

"Well?"

"I don't know. She looks pleased, and she is particularly pretty tonight. I guess she deserves to have a good time," said Sara.

"What do you think Jacob would say?"

"Well I don't know. I guess he should have stayed around for the summer instead of trotting himself back over to the Paulinskill. They haven't married or even gotten themselves engaged as far as I know. Besides Daniel Cole has always been sweet on Beletje since they were little."

"He does look handsome tonight."

"Yes he does," said Sara.

Across the fire at the edge of the light, her blond hair pulled back and tied with a ribbon and her blue eyes sparkling, eighteen-year-old Beletje Davids smiled and clapped to the music. Bouncing and swaying to the beat she occasionally brushed against the tall young man with a narrow waist, sandy hair, and particularly big smile, who clapped beside her.

"Why did that Fegley boy go back home, anyway?" asked Lydia.

"His enlistment was up and his Pa needed help is what Beletje said. She says he's coming back this fall."

"Well that may be too late from what I'm seeing."

"Maybe—we'll see."

The drums beat a steady rhythm and the people danced. It was the green corn festival. The best time of the year for the Munsee. The dancing would continue through the day and the night with old people and young people, men and women, participating as the mood struck them. But always with someone dancing and the drums resounding

There would be special treats, speeches, and sacred ceremony. It was a happy celebration.

Most times food was plentiful in this season. This year the fields had produced well enough but there were many more mouths to feed. The war had brought Munsee refugees from the Wyoming Valley and elsewhere from the east. From the west there were many visiting braves from the Ohio country, bringing with them Frenchmen, passing through to fight the English. Kittanning, the Munsee village on the Allegheny River was crowded with people bustling all about.

This was a time for hospitality. Everyone was welcome. It would be fun tonight. The war would wait until tomorrow. And so the people danced.

The dress and food requirements for this festival were formal and encouraged traditional ways. Bowl women had cooked her famous corn pudding. She had served it in a special bowl.

This earthen bowl she had made herself in the old way. She had dug the yellow clay from a bank beside the river. She had kneaded it and rolled it into coils and dug the hole in the ground where she formed the coils together shaping and smoothing and baking it repeatedly in her fire. It had taken much time. She was pleased with the result, especially the tiny mussel shells that decorated it's rim.

Trade goods from the French and English had replaced most of the old utensils but there were still a few things among the people made in the old ways. Some people like Bowl-woman still practiced the old crafts.

Such things came out of hiding during the Green Corn Festival and the people remembered a time when white men had not always been among them. The people celebrating here tonight could not personally remember those times. It was too long ago. But their storytellers told the history and they knew it was so.

Stands-often wondered about that olden time now as he stopped dancing and looked at the food around him. He had been on his feet a long time. He was hungry.

There were iron and copper pots and kettles, crock bowls and wooden bowls, large and small sitting all around several different cook fires spread throughout the village.

He walked about trying to decide where to start. He saw Dry-corn-soup sweetened with maple-syrup. There was a pot of three-sisters-soup made of corn, beans and squash. He watched a grandmother stir in several fresh squash blossoms to thicken and flavor.

There was crawfish-chowder and catfish-stew, kettle fried green-beans, corn roasted in the shuck, fried husk-bread, boiled chestnuts, wild-rice-with-blueberries. There was parched-corn-pudding seasoned with maple-syrup and bear-grease, hickory-nut-pudding, and corn-squash-pudding.

His favorite food was baked-squash with hickory-nuts and maple-sugar. It was here. There was the complete feast from forest and field provided by the Great Spirit. And Stands-often hadn't seen it all yet. Here was more: roasting venison, rabbit, and turkey; bowls of hominy, succotash, and baked-beans.

154

There were ashcakes, johnnycakes, cattail-root-and-corn-biscuits, acorn-and-corn fritters.

It was all here. It was good, and the people danced.

Chapter 34

"*H*ey shut it down Jakey. We heard something."

Three of the Davids' siblings were back in their gristmill near Machackemack.

"What was it?"

"Sounded like a musket shot over toward Abrahams. He and Lydia went home after one last load of wheat. They ain't back yet. Benjamin has gone to check," said Beletje.

"I'll tag along," said Daniel, picking up his musket and trotting down the road toward the VanAken farm.

"Beletje, let's you and I wait in the house," said Jake.

Jake was sliding down the wooden ladder from the second story of the mill his feet hardly hitting a rail. They had been grinding grain. Everyone else had gone back to the fort. Jake realized now as they ran that they should not be this far away from the fort. But it was a little late for that thought.

They were quick to the house, Beletje grabbing the ax from where Daniel had left it as she ran past the wood-stack. Inside, they closed the wooden shutters, which Beletje had opened earlier in the day. She positioned herself at the back door looking out across the fields toward the river. He peered out the front door where he could watch north and south up and down the road and east up slope past the mill toward the woods that bordered the little pasture above. Beletje could see a quarter mile downhill across the open fields. Jake had a good open view but only for a couple hundred yards.

If they come that way we'll have little time to decide what to do. He thought.

How did I get us in this situation? I hope the boys get back quick.

Time passed slowly and then Jake saw Daniel running up the road glancing back over his shoulder every few paces. Jake went out a little way to meet him. He saw so no one else.

Daniel, getting closer, called out: "Indians! Abrahams been shot. Benjamin ... taken them back to the fort. We need to move.

"Come on Beletje!" cried Jake.

They hurried out the front door to meet Daniel.

"The Indians went up in the woods," Daniel said, after he had caught a little breath. "There may be more of them. Benjamin saw three. I don't trust the road. Let's go to the river."

There was only one horse. A little spotted mare that Beletje had ridden out this morning.

"You and Beletje ride, I'll run," said Jake. "Forget the saddle." He took off as he said it, running out past the house and down the hill across the open fields. Beletje and Daniel quickly mounted, bare-back, and soon the little mare carrying them trotted alongside Jake as he ran. Jake handed Beletje his musket to lighten his load and they pushed hard to put distance between themselves and the line of trees upslope behind them.

The Davids siblings made it back to the fort having crossed the river above John Decker's farm and come down the road passed his house. It took about an hour. They stopped at the river and watch the open fields for a few minutes before committing themselves to the road.

It was a risk they took. It paid off. They were back, safe, inside the walls, with people all around them.

"Did you see any more?" someone asked.

"No—how is Abraham?"

"He's been shot in the arm and his hand."

"Is Lydia alright?"

"Just scared. She was almost killed. Abraham saved her."

"How many? Anyone else see them?"

"Don't know how many. Only the VanAken's seen any and they all agree there was but three they actually saw."

"Don't mean there ain't more waitin out there in the woods."

"No it don't."

"Got any water? I'm kinda thirsty," said Jake.

Jake was handed the water bucket with a dipper and the crowd began to drift away.

Uncle Joris stepped up and reach out his hand. Jake shook the offered hand. Joris leaned in close and said in a whisper:

"Three ain't come in yet. Gerardus, and Peter Westphalin went with Sam Finch out to his place to look after some horses. They may be holed up somewhere. I'll go out tomorrow early if they don't come in tonight."

Suddenly there was a large boom and then two more in quick succession. Swivel guns signaling down river. Cole's fort was under a threat.

The three men did not come in during the night and Joris Davids slipped out of the fort before first light the next morning. He did not come back until after dark.

He found them. Dead.

The next morning thirty men came up the road from the south. The New Jersey militia had arrived.

Scouting parties went out for a couple days. Nothing more was seen. Tracks disappeared in the mountains.

"They've moved on," said John Decker, "It's what they do. They'll be back."

Unfortunately, the relief column had its' own bad news. The British Fort Oswego on Lake Ontario had been taken by the French in a serious fight with many cannon. Over twenty five hundred men had been captured or killed no one knew for sure. Almost three hundred of those at Oswego were New Jersey boys. Some from Sussex County. It was said that a handful escaped. No one knew how many or who. It was bad news.

Oswego was on the passage between the Mohawk River and Lake Ontario. The French controlled the Lake with a fleet of ships. If the French had an army with cannon near the Mohawk River they could float down to attack Albany, bypassing the British forts on Lake George, William Henry and Fort Edward. If Albany fell the Hudson would provide an easy float to Esopus (Kingston) and finally New York. This was worse news than Braddock's defeat out at the Monongahela.

But the people at Cole's fort had little time to think about the French army at Oswego. Two days after the relief column left to return to headquarters, Simon Westfall and Gotleib Hess were shot at while hunting a strayed horse. They ran back to the fort to sound alarm. Death continued to stalk the settlers of the Minisink Valley

In church Heinrich Feagley heard about Oswego falling to the French. When he got to the mill that week he noticed another article from the newspaper.

> *"We have it from the Northern Frontiers of this province, That on Thursday last, Abraham VanAken, Esq; a Justice of the Peace in the county of Sussex; was shot through the left arm, and had one of the fingers of his hand shot off by an Indian, who had concealed himself in the cellar of an old house in one of VanAkens fields; and as he was driving his team with a load of grain. His Daughter who had been helping him being upon the top of the load. When the Indian fired on him, VanAken called to his daughter to jump off and run for her life. The girl in leaping down, happened to fall and the Indian was going to dispatch her with his tomahawk, which the father perceived, wounded as he was, made toward the Indian with his pitchfork, and saved his daughter from the stroke. And VanAken's son coming up with his gun at the same time, the Indian fled: and when he got to the end of the field he was joined by two companions, but they all ran away. This was done within a mile of Cole's Fort upon Mahackamack River, near the Delaware. Justice VanAken lay so ill of his wounds, that his life was in great danger.*

Heinrich studied the cracks in the floor again and shook his head. *I thought we were getting away from all this when we left the old country.* Then he read on:

> We have a further account from the same place, that on Friday last three men, to wit. Gerardus Swartwout, Samual Finch, and Peter Westfailin, were found Murdered, scalped and stripped quite naked."

Chapter 35

$\mathcal{T}$he day bloomed purple over the Kittatinnys. A few long cloud striations hung above the ridges reflecting variations of color. Closer, high over the river, the mists displayed as small puffs of light pink. Westward, the vapors cleared altogether revealing blue sky over the Poconos. It was a cool, September morning at Hyndshaw's Fort.

Captain Van Etten sat at a table he had moved into the light of the open doorway scribbling quickly with his quill. Mr. Franklin's orders called for a daily report. But, that didn't always get written. Van Etten had promised himself that he would never let more than a week pass without catching up. Paper work had to get done quick if men were heading south. The record in his journal must always match the messages flowing toward headquarters. No one had gone south in a while.

Lieutenant Hyndshaw snoozed, sitting upright on a slab-bench to the right of the doorway with his back against the log house. Elias Knepp sat on another bench left of the doorway. Instead of sleeping he was watching two young women puttering about a cook fire across the parade ground against the south stockade wall— shapely young gals, dresses tied above their ankles, hair hanging loose and falling about their faces as they bent to tend pots and pans. The smell of frying pork wafted through the air.

"What you looking at," asked Van Etten.

"Nothin."

"Sure."

"Finish your reports?"

"Mostly just about wood cutting and scouting, nothing too serious."

"Did you put in about those boys coming in up at Coles fort last week?" asked Elias.

"Yeah, I did, said the captain. "Wasn't that a story? Them fella's was lucky to make it back. The folks up at Machackemack said they looked more like starving Indians than white men They're lucky they didn't get shot approaching the fort. I can't believe they made it all the way across them mountains staying off the trails, nothing to eat, no weapons, no clothes."

Van Etten shook his head and reached up to grab the wooden trim above him. Holding tight he bent his knees to stretch his back. As he hung there he pretty much filled the doorway, his eyes studying the morning sky and the mountains.

Elias watched the cook fire where the dark haired gal was leaning over a fry pan from the far side of the blaze. The tops of her breasts showed clearly even at this distance.

"What do you think about the forts over in the Jersey's?" asked Hyndshaw. They getting them finished? They getting supplied better than us?"

The conversation had awakened the lieutenant. He had not opened his eyes yet, but he was listening.

"It's a good string of forts, far as I've seen," answered the captain, "some like ours some better."

Van Etten looked south, downriver. I ain't been to Fort Reading. It's eighteen miles south of Van Campen's. There is a fortified house called Ellison's somewhere between. Never seen it either. You've been to Van Campen's big stone house. They got a good stockade around it now."

Hyndshaw nodded his head, still not opening his eyes.

"Walpack across the river yonder is still not done," the captain continued. "We may have to go help them with that one. We need it done as much as they do. Fort Johns up the road is ready fer business. The supply road is good fer horses and mules bringing supplies through the Kittatinnys from Newton. They're planning to have a hundred frontier guards housed there. Only thirty arrived so far."

He paused to think. Then he went on:

"Nominack is still being built, but not much done since we was up that way. Carmer's, Westbrook's and Brink's are all fortified houses pretty well done, better than when you and I passed through. Cole's Fort at Machackemack is a good one cause John Decker and his neighbors have seen to it. I haven't yet had a reason to see Gardners on the road to Goshen. Did you hear about William Cooper's wife?"

"What about her."

"She died. She was livin across the mountains at Deckertown with a passel of her kids and grandkids."

"Lot of our old folks and kids livin over there."

"Yeah I know. People think it's safer and I guess it is. These forts may not stop all the raiding parties but if nothing else we seem to draw their fire. Not too many Indians see a need to pass over east of the Kittatinnys when there are plenty of good targets still living right here."

"You ever get the feeling we are just bait to draw the attacks."

"I've had that thought. It may be, but there are lots of good plantations that need our protection. And some folks got no place to go. I guess I'm happy to stay and lend a hand. We got to stop them devils somewhere. You thinking about goin east when your enlistment is up?"

Hyndshaw's eyes popped opened. He looked up at Van Etten who was smiling down at him.

"And the horse you rode in on too," he said, smiling back.

The single page newspaper had just come off the press in Philadelphia. John Branch had picked one up when he came by and now he was reading it aloud to Reverend Antes who was in town on business:

> *"We hear from New Jersey, that on Sunday Night, the 29th 3 men arrived at Elizabethtown in a poor, weak, and starving condition, to wit Thomas Shirby, Benjamin Springer, and John Denite, who had been prisoners among the Indians, and were almost naked, having only one Indian blanket about*

them to cover their nakedness. *They made their escape from the Indians at a place called Jenango or Venango, an Indian Town, situated on the head of the Susquehanna, and were 32 days in the woods, during which time they suffered great hardship, for want of food, and were obligated to eat rattlesnake, black-snakes, frogs and such vermin: and sometimes they could find nothing to eat for days together. The first settlements they made, where they found any inhabitants, was the upper fort, upon the Delaware River in New Jersey, called Coles Fort; and from thence they were sent under guard to Elizabeth-Town for fear the white people should annoy them, they looking more like Indians than Christians, being very swarthy, and their hair cut by the Savages after the Indian Fashion, and dressed only in Indian Blankets. Springer says, that he was taken prisoner on the 22ᵈ day of May last, when being at work at one Anthoney Swartwout's in Sussex county New Jersey, about Ten o' clock on the morning, two Indians attacked the house and shot Swartwout's wife dead upon the spot. They then seized Swartwout and Springer, and three Indians drove Springer away with a negro, who they had taken the night before at one Capt. Hunt's in said county making them run all the way, until they came to the River Delaware, which they crossed on a raft of rails, about 8 miles above Col. Van Campen's. When they were got about a mile and a half into Pennsylvania, they waited in the bushes for two Indians to catch up who were left behind with Swartwout and his children: and in about half an hour the said Indians came to them with only two of Swartwout's children a girl of about 12 years old and a boy about nine. These children told Springer, that the Indians had killed and scalped their father about seven miles from the house near a brook, where they likewise killed their little sister, and threw her into the brook. The Indians then carried Springer, Swartwouts two children, and the negro, to the Indian towns where they were disbursed about. Hunt's negro told Springer, that the young brother to Capt. Hunt, who was also taken prisoner with him, was killed by the Indians, in endeavoring to make his escape from them. This is the first intelligence we have had of Swartwout and his children, and of young Hunt and the negro, since they were missing in May last, when Hunt's house was burnt to the ground. Shirby says he was made prisoner at Juniata, in Pennsylvania, by six Indians at the house of Daniel Williams in December last when Williams himself was killed, and Shirby and Williams' wife carried into captivity, Denite was taken prisoner in the back parts of Maryland by 7 Indians, in May last as he and another were splitting rails, who were both carried into captivity. They were all three taken care of at Elizabeth-town, and a collection was made for them to clothe them, and enable them to travel to their several places of abode."*

Being at Hyndshaw's Fort, Elias Knepp never read the article and never knew the names of the men who had stumbled into Cole's Fort, alive, back from Indian captivity. If he had heard the names, it's doubtful he would have recognized the name of the young man he met only once in Philadelphia. Thomas Shirby had finally met the Indians he had asked about that day. But the ones he had met were not playing clarinets with Moravians.

Chapter 36

$\mathcal{T}$he hammer in his hand pounded hot iron against a sturdy anvil. It struck with a heavy thudding sound for three or four stokes punctuated by a sharp ring when he purposely missed bouncing the hammer off the anvil instead. On each missed stroke he deftly turned the steel bar he worked. It was graceful movement and a comfortable rhythm wasting neither time nor motion. He struck often and precisely while the iron he worked remained red-hot.

Johannas Stolting was good at his craft. He had a booming business all year long, especially in late Fall and early Winter. Wagon wheels, scythes, plowshares, saws, axes, hoes, harness chain, hinges of every size and shape, fireplace trammels, shovels, any tool or implement which might be made of steel, or iron, were strewn about, laying on the stone floor, leaning against the stone walls, or piled against one another, waiting their turn to be repaired by the smith. It was hard to find a place to sit or even stand.

Half an hour ago David Shultze had entered and found such a place near the forge where he would be out of the way and could still watch Johannas work. He nodded now as Heinrich Feagley opened the wooden door and entered with a cold wind blowing at his back.

Small paper tags and posters hanging about the place rattled in the breeze until the large door closed with a thump. Heinrich's eyes adjusted to the darkness of the interior. He found a place where he could drop the plowshares with others already chalk-marked. He nodded to Jahannas. The smith stopped hammering. The steel he worked was gripped in tongs, held in his left hand—the hand wearing the long heavy leather glove. The smith raised the tongs and inspected the metal. Then he shoved it back deep into the smoldering coke fire in the forge. Laying the togs aside Stolting reached up and pulled down slowly the handle of the big bellows attached to the forge supplying a rush of air to the base of his fire. The fresh draft brought the smoldering coke roaring back to life, burning red-hot, heating the iron.

Heinrich picked his way around a few piles until he stood beside Shultze. He removed his gloves and warmed his hands over the forge.

"Vee hear you went to 'de' big Indian Council over at Easton?"

"I did."

"See any savages?"

"Plenty of them."

"Any get shot?"

"Men were there who would have killed them had they thought it possible. But the new Governor kept the militia close. Everyone was careful. Most folks behaved. There were a few little tussles but the hotheads were kept under control. The savages didn't even notice."

"We get a peace?" asked Heinrich.

Depends on who you ask and what happens next. Lord Loudon put William Johnson back in charge of all Indian treaties. Weiser is out. He can't make peace agreements himself without approvals from Johnson."

"Dat may be goodt fer New York, but I tink not for us. Weiser knows our injins bedder den udders do," said Heinrich.

"Teedyuscung was at the council, like last time. Says he's been made King of the Indians. He was whining again about that damn Walking Treaty. Claims it was a fraud. Pemberton and his part of the Quakers, most of the Moravians and some of the Dunkers agree with him. The Penn Family and the others say it was a fair deal and the Indians just want to get paid a second time. Hell, the Governor has agreed to pay them more if that will make it right."

Stolting had clamped his tongs back onto the hot iron pulling it from the fire. Now it was as red-hot as the burning coke. He looked it over carefully waiting for a bit of sparking to stop. Then he placed it back on the anvil and picked up his hammer. The rhythmic dance between hot iron, heavy anvil and hammer resumed.

"Teedyuscung speaks pretty well. I heard him myself. He makes some sense. He presents a good case but I don't know how many minds he changed. That land is already sold and just because the enemy has burned some folks out don't mean they won't come back expecting to rebuild once the peace returns. Excepting for those that's been killed. Even them folks may have kin to claim the land when the shooting stops.

But, Governor Morris thinks they have reached agreement. He says there will be peace. If you recall Governor Denny said that same thing in July after the first Indian Conference at Easton. That looked good till the Munsee found out their old enemy the Cherokee were going to fight for the Virginians. That soured things pretty quick if you remember.

This time may be different. I don't know. Plenty of food got eaten. Lots of rum was drunk, lots of rum. Papers was signed, presents were given, hands shook, pipes smoked and speeches aplenty. Was a peace made? Maybe. I hope so. But I didn't see anyone that wasn't still armed when we left to come home."

Stands-often had seen Otter and Red corn when they broke out of the trees into the meadow. He, with others, had been guarding the trail. He had rushed to meet his uncle leaving two younger boys to continue the vigil.

"Will there be peace with the white man, uncle?"

"We will see nephew," said Otter as they walked on. "Teedyuscung spoke well. The Pennsylvanians have a new Governor. William Johnson is restored to his old position of honor. There are presents for the people, which will follow. But the white men have not agreed we may return to our former homes. They will keep the land."

"The war goes well," said Stands-often. "Even now there are war parties in the village preparing to go out against the white men on the Juniata, at the Minisnks and those building the new fort at Shamokin."

"Yes there is much to consider," said Otter, but he was worried.

168

The past winter Otter had gone to Fort Niagara with a war party to meet with the Frenchmen and sell scalps. He had been surprised at the limited supplies. Much was promised for the future but little had been available to make the winter better for the People. They had been forced to leave their homes and fields in Wyoming and flee. They had suffered devastating crop failures and were able to bring only a little food with them.

Brother Onas had tried to murder them instead of sending help. The French it seemed were long on promises but so far had little to share with their new allies. Now 'The People' faced another difficult winter even with all they had carried home from raiding white farms.

Otter knew that Teedyuscung had led the white man to understand that he was made King of all the Indian people. He had promised much in order to collect many gifts and payments. He had amassed so much in fact that he had cached the items in the woods and was waiting now at Fort Allen until help could be sent him to carry it home.

Otter thought about all this as he walked beside his nephew. *Teedyuscung is only a spokesman for the people. He is not a true Sachem as he has said. He leads only a few followers. The real chiefs will decide about the war. I think it will continue.*

Otter's old friend, Red-corn, had been with him in Niagara and at Easton. Together they had witnessed the string of forts spread out now along the Blue Mountains. Others had told them about the new forts along the Delaware.

It's becoming increasingly difficult to conduct raids without losing men. Still, the desire for revenge runs deep in the young men. Otter had lived close to the white man all his life. He had studied them carefully. He understood their differences, their weaknesses, their greed, and their strengths. He did not believe they could be driven into the sea as some men said. The time for that had past long ago.

The English have many more men behind those mountains, which they have not yet brought forward to fight. Without the French we will fail and be pushed west again. With French help we may still be forced away from our homes.

I'm but one voice. All the people will have a say. There will be much to discuss around our fires this winter and little to eat.

Chapter 37

"**D**id you hear about the mutiny," asked Lieutenant Hyndshaw.

"Where?" asked Elias, as he entered the open gates at Hyndshaw's Fort."

Elias was just returned from delivering a message to New Jersey's Fort Johns across the river. It was a cold December day. The banks of the river had ice at its edges. The late morning sky was populated with migrating fowl winging their way south—the last of the season—mostly ducks, geese and herons.

"At Fort Allen," answered James.

"When?"

"Week ago. Captain Reynolds was gone to Philadelphia. Lieutenant Miller was in charge."

"What happened."

"Miller was selling rum out of them big hogsheads they got. You know like they always do keeping the men broke and in debt."

"Yeah I know. But that ain't just Miller their captain's in on that too."

"I know. But that old Teedyuscung was there after the big conference in Easton. He hadn't got home yet. Miller got him drunk to cheat him out of some skins he had. That would have been bad enough but then some corporal named Christian something-er-nother got hot over some Indian women with the old man. I guess they were something special.

This corporal was a big feller and he and Miller got into it and a fight broke out and the corporal with some of his friends beat hell out of the Lieutenant and a couple privates throwing them out of the fort."

"What happened next?"

"The Corporal and his friends spent the night very indecently with them Indian women.

Sergeant Bossing finally sobered up. He'd past out drunk while Miller and he were plying the old Indian with rum to get the skins. When he woke up and saw what had happened he snuck out quiet like and came all the way to Fort Hamilton fer help.

Sergeant McPherson went back with some men and took control of the situation next morning. Most of the boys at Fort Allen were sober by the time he arrived. They knew they were in big trouble. The fort was totally tore up inside. It's a wonder the place didn't burn down. The corporal's in the guardhouse down in Easton. A couple of the men ran off. Van Etten has recommended to the Major that Captain Reynolds might do better assigned elsewhere."

"Hope it was worth it," said Elias.

"I bet it seemed like it in the beginning but I doubt they think so now."

"Where is Captain Van Etten?" Asked Elias.

"Took some men out on a scout down toward Hamilton. Says we're to cut some more wood before he gets back tonight. Want to help us?"

"He didn't leave no such orders fer me did he."

"Not exactly. Didn't mention you by name. But he didn't say you couldn't help."

"Think I'll just keep to the fort here with the guards and the women folk. I'll keep my eye on the fire in the cabin; maybe I'll take a little nap.

Elias did fall asleep sitting in a chair in front of the fire. They were sharing the cabin at this time with the Demack family, space lacking as it was in the fort. Some families had gone back to their homes following the council in Easton but most remained at the fort or very nearby. The log house was the only building with a real fireplace so folks moved in and out sharing the space and sleeping in shifts.

When he woke, Mrs. Demack was puttering about the fire and her husband Stosel was carrying in an armful of firewood through the open door. There was a cold wind.

"We need to get these coals right for cooking," she said.

Suddenly Captain Van Etten stomped in behind Stosel through the open doorway.

He had a look. Elias stood.

"The peace didn't hold," he said, "big raid down near Oblinger's block house."

"They okay?" asked Elias.

"Some are." Van Etten stepped past Elias and leaned his musket in the corner. He turned drawing a breath. He looked tired. "Two Indians fired on the block-house and ran off. Half a dozen men gave chase. It was an ambush. Luckily, four men stayed back. With the women and kids they were able to defend themselves fer another day till help came.

Since then several more barns have been burned in the neighborhood and a family of four were caught on the road. Three of them were butchered and a boy, eleven-year-old, carried off. We'll send messages out here to everyone and across the river. Better get people brought in close. This winter may not be as safe as we'd hoped."

Christmas came. It was a wet Christmas but not a white one. The rain continued for three days making life miserable. Old Mrs. Weirick caught a cough and died the next day. Everyone spoke about how sweet life was, though fleeting.

Her sons dug the grave outside the fort at the edge of the trees where a new cemetery had been begun last year. Grave digging was difficult in the rain but it would not get easier anytime soon. The rain finally stopped and it grew colder. In a day the ground froze on top and people were able to stand without sinking in muck, dressed warm, and huddled together for the graveside funeral.

Mrs. Weirick had lived a long life. She had buried two husbands and three children before her death. She had lost a grandson killed last spring by Indians. Her funeral was a somber occasion. Tears were shed but not like when a child dies before its' time.

In difficult circumstances, Mrs. Weirick's neighbors and friends did the best they could for her and her family. They held a wake at the cabin inside the fort. There was tea and rum, sausages, and sauerkraut. There was even some buckwheat cakes served with honey. Supplies were short this year after Christmas.

By New Year's day a dozen youngsters had a bad cough. Mother faces were taut and stern. The weather turned colder. The snow came and lay deep on the ground through most of January. One by one the children recovered—coughs faded and then went away altogether. The community within Hyndshaw's fort could relax again. Smiles returned to those faces accustomed to smiling.

Today was 15 February, 1757. It was overcast and cold. More snow had fallen yesterday. It was nearly a foot deep and a dry snow with little drifting. There had been no wind.

Elias was out hunting with Lieutenant Hyndshaw. They had walked about three miles north and then upslope till they came to the Bushkill bending back on itself. The water was frozen at the surface but they could hear it flowing over rocks below. It was a quiet day. Little moved in the whiteness. A jay called somewhere up in the trees. There was no answer and quiet returned. They could barely hear their footsteps in the snow.

Elias and Hyndshaw followed the Bushkill on its east bank through a little meadow where they cut across the fresh trail of deer. It was a big track, alone, which seemed odd this time of year. They followed the tracks through the meadow and up slope to a cluster of laurel bushes. The deer's tracks went to the right around the thicket. Elias nodded right to Hyndshaw and the lieutenant pointed at Elias and nodded left. Cautiously, each moved ahead circling different directions stopping every few paces to watch and listen. Elias saw his friend move ahead out of sight behind the laurel and he stopped and waited. A minute passed and another. Then he saw movement. A big buck was loping quietly through the
174

snow backtracking on the hunter he had seen. He glanced backward, big antlers flashing. He never saw Elias, his musket raised and ready.

After the kill Hyndshaw came around the laurel thicket and found Elias with his knife slitting open the buck's belly.

"We got trouble."

"What?"

Elias stopped and looked at his musket leaning against the tree. He sheathed his knife went to his weapon and started to reload."

"Yeah. Tracks say two," said James. "But there may be more somewhere."

"They can't be far. The snow came yesterday. Tracks today, It's hard to tell how old. They came from northeast on the river, headin up slope so they're above us somewhere. Let's get back and alert the captain. The meat will keep unless the wolves get it. I want to keep my hair and they sure as hell know we're here."

Chapter 38

Most of the land around Cole's Fort drained down toward the Machackemack River. It was a gradual slope. The river flowed south-southwest to meet the Delaware in a couple more miles flowing on toward the Water Gap. Just outside the walls on the southwest corner of the fort, Daniel Cole and his friends Anthony Westbrook and Daniel Davids, plowed for a garden in early March. It was a three-acre patch. Cabbage, peas, onions, turnips, parsnips, and potatoes were quickly planted. The vegetables were growing well, three weeks later when news came of the attack on Fort William Henry at the southern tip of Lake George in New York. Fifteen hundred strong, the Frenchmen had laid siege. But the fort held and the French retreated three days later back up the lake to Fort Carillon— the new French fort between Lake George and Lake Champlain.

The attack had been a shock to folks in Albany. Lord Loudon had dispatched reinforcements under Colonel Monro placing him in command at William Henry. Loudon also called for more provincial troops to be raised to fight on the northern frontier. The Hudson Valley was critical to all the northern colonies and had to be protected at all costs.

"Has Jacob said anything about joining the Jersey Blues," asked Sara?

"I don't think he will," said Beletje. "What about Anthony?"

Today, Beletje Davids and her cousin Sara Decker were pulling weeds and hoeing around cabbage in the garden. They knew a few of the local boys were going to join the fight up north and the New Jersey Blues was a new regiment being organized in Elizabethtown to answer that call.

"Peter Grubb is going and Elijah Kuckendal, I hear Daniel is thinking about it."

"He is not," said Beletje.

"Is too."

"I guess I would know."

"Not your brother Daniel. Daniel Cole."

"Oh. Well I hadn't heard that."

"No, I reckon not. You and he don't speak as often as you did last summer now that Jacob has come back."

"We still talk."

"Yeah but not as much. He sees the same thing we all see. Your eyes are always on Jacob when he is about and his eyes are always on you."

"Well... Jacob and I have been keeping company in church and on social occasions such as they are these days. But Daniel and I have always been friends I think he would have told me," said Beletje.

"Well you and Daniel may be friends. And you and Jacob may be friends. But I think them boys want to be more than just your friend and you are going to have to choose one or the other someday soon."

"Maybe I'll choose Anthony."

"No, you will not. He wouldn't have anything to do with you anyhow. I have him mooning over me and I aim to keep it that way," said Sara.

Anthony Westbrook like Peter, Elijah, and Daniel had been born and raised here at Machackemack. Jacob Fegley had arrived only last year with the New Jersey Frontier Guard.

"I saw Anthony looking at Jenneke Quik yesterday."

"Did you truly?" said Sara.

"No, not really."

"I didn't think so."

An eagle soared over the Fishkill which people now called the Delaware. Beletje paused to watch. It circled low for an eagle. *Maybe it will dive. No I guess not, it's too high for that,* she decided.

It was a pretty day. There was a smell of fresh turned earth in the air. Dogs barked from the fort. A hound bayed somewhere from over the Machackemack.

Most of the men were out working the surrounding farms. The frontier guard provided protection. There were thirty guardsmen assigned to Cole's Fort. During winter they had been down to only six. The threat had been lower then and men had little reason to leave the fort. Now it was different. People had to get their work done.

"I hope Jacob and Anthony stay here. I hope neither go to the Jersey Blues."

"What about Daniel?"

"I don't want him going either, nor Peter nor Elijah. I don't want any of them leaving. We need everyone we have right here to keep people safe. I see no reason fer boys to go north to fight when we keep getting murdered right here. It was just last week somebody got killed down south of Van Campen's. That's close enough. Since Simon Westfall's barn got burned last Spring we have lived in that damned old fort most of the time. Packed together like apples in a barrel. The savages were right at our walls last summer if you recall. Just cause we ain't seen too many this Spring don't mean they won't come back.

Suddenly Beletje noticed smoke rising across the Fishkill—a lot of smoke.

Newspapers in Philadelphia read: "May 11, 1757: We have advice from Northampton County, that on Monday, the second instant, fourteen people were killed there by the Indians, and the house and barn of one Abraham Miller burnt; also that two people have been lately murdered by them on the Jersey Side."

At Elizabethtown New Jersey they read "June 10, 1757 Last Sunday three Indians fired upon 8 men and 2 women in a scow, going over from our fort at Walpack, to Hyndshaw's Fort: They killed Stosel Demak, wounded his wife thro' both thighs near the kness, thou't to be mortal, and her sister through the side, grazed the ribs. On Wednesday some Indians called to our men at Cole's fort, to come out but being only a sergient and 7 men, they refused. The same evening the Indians were heard on the hill near Hyndshaw's Fort, which is opposite to Walpack."

Lieutenant Hyndshaw had come to Cole's Fort to see John Decker. It was unofficial business. He waited now at the church.

"Morning James."

"Morning to you sir."

"What can I do for you."

" I wanted to ask if you were willing to sell that forty acres near the Modderkill.

"Hadn't thought about that," said Decker. "I would think there are plenty of farms to be sold on your Pennsylvania side of the river."

"I think maybe I'd like to buy something this side," said Hyndshaw.

"This war won't last forever James."

"Just the same I like that little piece of land down by Shimers' place south of Joris Davids' plantation. You still own it don't you? Joris said you owned it."

"Yes I do, but I hadn't thought of selling it. I tell you what, I'll think on it, but I don't know? Someone in my family may need it when the war ends. I'll think on it. You're not in a hurry are you?"

"No sir. I guess not."

"How'd you and Van Etten feel about the big conference with the Indians this time."

There had been a third Indian Conference in Easton Pennsylvania July 21-August 7, 1757.

"Were you at Easton, James?"

"Not me, not this time," said Hyndshaw. "Van Etten was there. He said it was about like the two last summer—lots of talk about land fraud and such, lots of promises from both sides but little decided. He thinks old Teedyuscung is trying to straddle a fence and keep options open in case we start winning instead of the French."

"Well maybe it's us need to be looking fer options. We don't seem to be winning too many of these fights. I'm worried. Did you hear about the massacre on Lake George?" asked Decker.

"I heard some talk as I came in just now. Thought I'd get the details on the way out."

"New York newspaper posted at the blockhouse came over from Goshen yesterday. Read it before you go south. It ain't good. Tell that Van Etten boy that John Decker sends his regards."

"Yes sir."

Hyndshaw left the church and walked straight to the blockhouse. There was the posted newspaper and he stepped up to read it. A man and woman stood nearby who had been waiting. Hyndshaw didn't know them.

"Will you read it aloud Sir? It was read before we came in."

"I will."

He looked at the heading.

"It was printed three days ago August 1ˢᵗ," he said.

> *"Last night arrived here the post from Albany: by whom we have the following extract of a letter, from a Gentleman at Fort William-Henry, to his friend in New York."*

Fort William Henry, July 26, 1757

Sir.

I am sorry that I have nothing better to relate to you than the following melancholy affair, Viz. Colonel John Parker, with three of his Captains, and six or seven subalterns, with Captain Robert Maginis, Captain Jonathan Ogdon, Lieutenants Cambell and Coats, of the New York Regiment, with about 350 men went out on the 21st instant, in order to attack the advance guard at Ticonderoga by water, in whale boats and bay boats. They landed that night on an island, and sent before Break of Day to the Main Land three battoes, which the enemy way-laid, and took. They being taken, gave the enemy intelligence. Our men next morning at day break, made for said point, and the enemy contrived as a decoy, to have three battoes making for the same, which our people took as the three battoes sent out the evening before, eagerly put to land, where about three hundred men lay in ambush, and from behind the point came out 40 or 50 canoes, whale and bay boats, which surrounded them entirely. Colonel Parker and Captain Ogdon, are the only two officers that have escaped with life. The latter much wounded in the head. Captain Maginis, and everyone in the boat with him, are killed; and not one man left alive that were in the bay-boats. Captain Woodward being terrible wounded, jumped over board, and was drown'd, Capt. Shaw killed, Lieutenants Cambell and Coats of the New York Regiment they say are for certain killed; a captain of the New Jersey Regiment is also killed, but have not yet learned his name. Upon the whole, only

181

Parker and Ogden, with about 70 men escaped, all the remainder, being 280 men are killed or taken."

"We have a boy up north at Fort William-Henry. I hope he wasn't in them Bay-boats," said the man, whose wife sobbed beside him. "Much obliged sir."

"Your welcome," said Hyndshaw.

It was bad, he thought, *like Decker said.*

It had all happened while the peace negotiations were being conducted in Easton. *I hope their boy is still alive,* he thought. He hadn't asked their name and they were across the parade ground as Hyndshaw walked out the gate heading for the ford on the Machackemack River.

Their name was Sweetman and though they had no way to know their son Jacob was alive at Fort William-Henry. He had not been with the Bay-boats. He had remained behind in the fort. However, Jacob Sweetman, at this very moment, was struggling desperately to get the harness off a dead horse killed moments ago by a cannonball.

Fort William Henry was once again besieged by Frenchmen and savages. Unfortunately because curriers had been killed in the forests, no other Englishman outside the fort was yet aware of its peril.

Chapter 39

Abraham VanAken had recovered from his wounds of almost exactly a year ago. The middle finger on his right hand was shot away and the bullet hole in his left arm had healed leaving the limb stiff but usable. His daughter Lydia had not been hurt. Many other families in the Minisink Valley were less fortunate.

Today a dozen men along with Abraham were making steady progress cutting a six-acre field of flax near the horseshoe pond, on VanAken's farm. Cole's Fort was easily visible directly across the Machackemack River about a mile south. The men had brought weapons as well as scythes. The muskets were all stacked nearby, primed and ready. Three guards were posted with weapons set at the north and east edges of the field.

The mature flax was three foot tall with long stems. It still had much of the blue flower in bloom. Bees buzzed about the field harvesting pollen for their hives ahead of the reapers. It was a hot dry day.

Noon had passed. The laughter of morning was gone. The reapers had killed a rattlesnake but let the other snakes slither away unmolested. The men were hot, sweaty, and looking forward to washing up in the river on their way back to the fort.

Each man's scythe whispered a quiet, steady, yeoman-like rhythm. Locust sang from the surrounding forests. Suddenly, one of the guards to the north let out a cry.

Everyone grounded their blades peering northward. A horse and rider were coming up the road at a gallop. *Animal and rider are traveling fast for such a hot day. Must be carrying a message rather than trying to out run a bullet,* thought Abraham. Some of the men went back to work, others started moving to the center of the field where the weapons were stacked.

The rider turned in when he got to where they were working. All stopped then and gathered to hear what was said. The horseman was Jacob Fegley one of the New Jersey Frontier

Guards. He did most of the courier work when messages went north or south. As he rode up to the knot of gathered men he didn't bother to dismount.

Simon Westfall handed him a jug with a nod in greeting. Jacob gulped down a couple quick swigs to clear his throat handing it back.

"Just came from Marbletown," he said. "The French have taken Fort William Henry. Colonel Monro surrendered on the Ninth. Next day the French allowed the soldiers and settlers inside the fort to leave with their weapons. The Frenchmen guaranteed safe passage.

On the road south savages ambushed them. Most are dead. Some got back but no one seems to know how many. I best get the message to the fort."

He reined his mount back toward the road urging the well-lathered animal reluctantly back into a slow gallop.

"I bet everyone in Albany is in a panic." "Who knows where they will attack next." "Savages can travel as fast as this news." "They could be out in that woods already." "French cannon could be blowing up Albany right now."

They were all talking over one another like geese in a barnyard.

"Alright!" said Abraham in a firm voice. "Calm down. Leave the rest of the flax for later. Let's head in to see what needs to be done.

The French did not march on Albany. August passed in the Minisink Valley with little enemy activity except a few Indian sightings which, when investigated, showed scant evidence of having actually been Indians. In September, however, Peter Decker found two of his horses shot to death in his meadow.

Scouts went out again to scour the countryside for sign. They found little other than some tracks beside the Fishkill. It was thought the Indians had crossed back into Pennsylvania.

Harvest continued throughout the Minisink area. The weather cooled. Most leaves turned color. The sky once again came alive with migrating fowl. Huge flocks of passenger pigeons sometimes blotted out the sun as they flew south.

Early snow appeared a couple weeks later. It was wet snow. It hung heavy on the tree branches bringing down the last of the colored leaves.

" I hear Gideon Westbrook and John Pressor were killed near Brink's Fort," said James Hyndshaw.

He had just walked in the door of the small cabin inside Fort Johns—headquarters for New Jersey's frontier forts along the Delaware. An officer sat at a table by the fireplace with an ink bottle on the table, a pen in his hand and paper before him.

"That's right Lieutenant, last week. And day before yesterday John Doty and Sergeant Mahurin got killed in another ambush up that direction. A private with them is certain he shot one of the savages but he is pretty shook up. He barely got off with his scalp. He thought he counted five but wasn't sure. If he hadn't got mounted he'd be laying butchered with the other two. That was a mess. I helped bury them myself. I'm writing to a friend of Doty's right now."

The New Jersey Lieutenant returned to his writing. James stepped to the fireplace, and warmed his hands, staring into the flames.

A week later the Pennsylvania Gazette printed the following:

An extract of a letter from lieutenant Rickey dated at the headquarters, on the frontiers of New Jersey, Nov17. Sir, I have the melancholy news to tell you, that your friend John Doty was killed, scalped, and butchered in a barbarous manner yesterday, within two miles of the fort; as was likewise Sergeant Mahurin; there was a soldier with them, all on horseback, when five Indians in ambush fired, killed two, and then shot through the soldiers great coat, when he immediately got down, and one of the savages run toward him with his tomahawk, but the soldier fired his

185

piece and stopped him, then took Doty's piece and snapt it (for by Doty's fall he had hurt the lock) However he kept it presented until he mounted and rode off. This alarmed the people but as yet we have discovered nothing more than the usual marks, and a quantity of blood. The soldier is positive he killed one of them. The inhabitants on the whole frontier are so terrified, that they are moving, the rest gathering together, and stockading themselves in the best manner they can."

When the article appeared in the Philadelphia newspaper Jacob Fegley was at Cole's Fort. They were holding a hog-butchering frolic. It had started at first light and it was just after noon now. They had already made scrabble, sausages, hogs head-cheese, and they had salted ten barrels of pork. At the moment everyone had paused to eat a noon meal. Jacob was approaching the table where the food was spread. He wanted more apple pie. Beletje Davids was there to serve it to him.

"Thank you," he said with a smile. " I have an important question to ask you."

"What is it," she asked?

Lydia VanAken listened carefully from a few paces away.

"Well it's a bit of a business proposition."

"What might that be?"

"Would you mend this hole I have in my coat?"

Beletje hesitated. Then smiled.

"Sure, how did it get torn?"

"It's a long a story," he said, "I'll tell you about it sometime, but not now if you please."

"I'll mend your coat, Jacob."

It was a white Christmas though cold with a low hanging grey sky. There was no room for a Christmas tree inside any of the buildings at Cole's Fort, though there were simple decorations. A large fir tree was erected outside in the middle of the parade ground. It was dressed up with a few seasonal adornments. For light there were five candle lanterns, which at night were constantly blowing out and having to be relit.

Several folks with houses nearby went home and invited friends to join them for the Holy celebration. A few took the risk to stay overnight on Christmas Eve, and for a few days beyond. Others returned to the fort as the sun sank low each day.

Next week would be the New Year—1758.

It had been three and a half years since they had heard about the fight at Great Meadows in Virginia and nothing had gone well for the English in this War with the French.

Morale was low. It was hard for people to plan their next day let alone their future. But, life had to go on for those left living.

Chapter 40

*T*he smoke choked him. He woke disoriented.

"Mother of god what are you doing Pierre," said Jacque Ravelette in a hoarse whisper.

"Starting a fire mon ami."

Outside a dripping, drizzly late February rain fell.

"Don't open the door it will just make it worse."

They coughed and laughed quietly for a few moments until the chimney warmed and began to draw.

The other eight soldiers in the cabin continued to snore though more than one coughed and sputtered a little.

"A wet blanket over the chimney would be a good way for the English to kill us all in our sleep," said Jacque. Pierre chuckled.

The wind had died overnight and the air in the room began to clear. On windy days, down drafts sometimes filled the room with smoke even with a hot fire burning.

"The chimney needs to be taller. It would draw better," said Jacque.

"You tell the captain I'm sure he will be very concerned."

The soldiers lived in small cabins outside the walls of Fort Machault. The Officers lived inside the picketed palisades in their barracks, a two-story affair with a fireplace on both ends and tall chimneys that towered well above the roof. The soldier cabins naturally were short-changed on materials.

Life here is better than living in the woods, thought Jacque, *on the move most of the time, worried about ambush, sometimes sleeping without a fire.* But he missed Vincennes. He was tired of the War. He wanted to go home.

"This beats the long houses and wigwams at Venango," said Pierre.

"I 'm not so sure," said Jacque, "I was over there the other day and they're pretty tight. Those women know how to build houses, I think. The wigwams may be a little smoky on a day like this but when it's cold they're cozy."

"Your missing that Piankashaw girl again, ain't you."

"Shut up Pierre."

For a mile up French Creek on the right bank it was high ground, which sloped gently toward the stream. Two small runs flowed in from the northeast about a quarter mile apart. Between these streams, in a meadow on a rise slightly above the rest was situated the permanent Delaware Indian village of Venango. The surrounding forests included huge hickory, sycamore, beech, and sugar maples towering above an open understory.

This winter, in addition to its normal residents, the village was overburdened with Delaware and Shawnee refugees from the Wyoming Valley. Under the trees between the fort and the village were camped warriors from many French allied tribes: Miami, Huron, Ottawa, and Sauk. Some of these peoples were enemies of one another in earlier times. But today all were friends to the French. The war against the English had gone well. The fort, the village and the camps were packed with trophies. Scalps hung on belts, from lodge poles and on round stretchers drying near the fires. Copper pots, pans and teakettles surrounded the cook fires. Even a few clocks ticked and sometimes chimed though never on the right hour.

Scattered about were dozens of English prisoners— trophies also—men, women and children living day-to-day not knowing if they would survive the next. A few had already been sold to the French to be transported elsewhere in New France to be used as slaves or ransomed back to the English. Most waited to learn their fate. Some were bound securely. Others huddled together forlorn, dejected, trying to stay warm and keep their wits.

Zack Miller was here tied to a post in a Delaware Longhouse. He was only fed every other day. While on the trail from the

Juniata, he and Jesse had been separated. They had not seen one another since.

Jenny and Nathan Morrison from the Maryland backcountry were in the Munsee village—separated in different lodges. Neither of the Morrison siblings were bound but they were limited in travel to a small area around their assigned lodge. They were under consideration for adoption into the tribe. They had been separated from their other siblings and feared for their fate.

Prisoners were sometimes paraded through the village naked, painted black, their hands bound behind, led by a rope around their neck. Screams were often heard at night— agonizing screams out in the forest darkness to the south. The other prisoners knew what that meant, but they tried hard not to hear, or think, or feel.

"Will you fight the English when the geese fly north uncle," asked Stands-often.

"Yes nephew, said Otter, "If French gunpowder arrives as promised."

"Will it come?"

Otter thought about that as he drew in the smoke from his pipe. They sat alone at the fire, staring into the flames. It was late. Nothing could be heard but the flames of the fire licking at a dry hickory log.

"I believe it will. The French fathers want the war to continue."

"Why do our French fathers provide so poorly for their Indian brothers."

"The French Captain says it is because they too have had crop failures."

"Why are their trade goods so expensive and poor in quality."

"You ask troubling questions nephew. I do not have the answer.

Otter paused again drawing on his pipe.

190

"The women tapped sugar trees today. The geese will come soon. You are a man now. Are you ready to seek your own answers."

"Yes uncle, I will fight the English."

Stands often continued to look into the fire.

"But, I do not like the burning of prisoners. I have watched the Ottawa at their torture fire. I saw no honor in it. Yet many of our own people cheered and joined in."

Otter looked at his nephew before speaking.

"Each warrior must decide how he will fight, and when. There are those who burn with hate and seek revenge. Each has his reason. Some have been treated very badly by the white-man.

Others are fearful and they become angry at the English for making them confront their own weakness. They seek courage by torturing the helpless Englishmen. It makes them feel strong. Of those who burn the white-men some draw strength from it and afterward fight well, others do not. Courage is not known until it is challenged. Englishmen are the same. Some are weak. Others show great courage when tested at the fire.

You must decide why you fight and how. You will choose the warriors who you wish to fight beside. No one in the tribe will make that choice for you. No one will force you to go or to stay. That is not our way. That is the way of the white man. Among 'The People' each man decides for himself. You will choose well. Your Manitou, the bobcat, will help you decide. That is our way.

Chapter 41

"Get off the horse Jacob."

Jacob Fegley had just ridden in through the gate at Fort Johns.

"Yes sir. What's up?"

"Here, take these."

Captain Jonathan Hampton handed Jacob a musket, powder horn and bullet pouch. Jacob slung the leather straps, affixed the pouch and horn over his neck and checked the priming in the musket.

"It's dry," said the captain. You're with Lieutenant Hyndshaw and Ward. They'll fill you in."

"Let's go," said Hyndshaw, and out the gate they rushed, afoot, south on the road.

"What's happened?" asked Jacob as they settled in to a pace comfortable for Hyndshaw and a little fast for anyone else.

"You know Nicholas Cole?"

"I don't think so."

"He lives up toward the old beaver ponds on the Modderkill. He came home and found five of his children killed and scalped. His wife and eight-year-old boy are missing."

"When?"

"This afternoon. He came to the fort looking fer help. Captain sent some men with him to track them. The savages were headed up slope. Captain figures they may circle back. Lots of sign must be a dozen or more. I came in after the search party left. Just after I arrived in comes Anthony Westbrook to report a German fella killed and two others missing. He had the three planting a cornfield and he himself had left to look for a cow that hadn't come home. When he got back he found the one dead and scalped, the other two gone."

"Were we going?"

At this moment they were moving quickly away from both scenes Hyndshaw had just described.

"Captain wants us to circle out and scout back up the river from the south. See if we can find any signs where they may have crossed. Tonight we'll meet up with the other search party at Chambers place on the road back toward Nominack, above the crossroad leading to the Fishkill. If no one has found anything this side, we plan to cross the river before first light and waylay the road to Wyoming. It's a long shot but it's the best plan we got."

Jacob was beginning to lose his wind so he didn't ask any more questions. A couple miles along the road, Hyndshaw slowed and moved quietly into the forest on the right. Soon they were stalking their way along, fifteen or twenty yards apart. They moved in unison a few paces at a time then paused to study their surroundings and listen. It was familiar hunting. Jacob found the activity strangely comforting if he didn't think too much about why they were doing it.

The forest bustled with new life this time of year. The songbirds were back. Bear, deer, turkey signs were everywhere. May-apples, wild ginger and trilliums covered the ground. Leaf canopy above was fresh though not quite complete.

What was that smell? Jacob wondered. *Horse? No, deer. What was that scurrying in the leaves, coon? No, opossum. Why are those branches moving?* Then he saw the squirrel leap branch to branch. A hawk screamed.

The usual. Nothing amiss here. They have to be somewhere. They must have left behind some sign of their passing. He thought. *But we may not find 'em. It's a big forest and when they chose, Indians can move leaving damn little sign.*

The big water flowed smoothly along on the left as the sun sank behind the mountains in Pennsylvania. Quietly Hyndshaw snapped his fingers to get their attention without alerting anyone further away. He motioned Ward and Jacob to him. Quietly and slowly they eased in.

"Let's move up around the next bend where we have a good view of the Fishkill," he whispered. "We'll hunker down there, watch up river. We can move later to the rendezvous."

They spread apart and moved through the forest in the fading light. They rounded the bend in the river. Each found his separate place to wait and watch.

Songbirds stopped singing and the bullfrogs, peepers, and crickets took over. The forest was dark but Jacob could still see clearly upriver for a quarter mile. The reflective water seemed to provide it's own illuminated pathway through the dark trees lining the river's banks. A fish jumped and it's splash created a glimmer of rings emanating from the tiny waves. Swallows swept down to skim a drink, leaving a clearly visible streak across the wet surface.

No people appeared as they watched. Jacob wondered about the Cole family. What must they be feeling right now, those still alive.

Were the mother and son still among the living? Had the father rescued them? Jacob didn't think so. They had heard no sounds of a fight. *We would have heard the muskets. Maybe? Maybe not, the wind has been blowing to the east.*

What will happen tomorrow? Will we get lucky and catch the savages on the road? I doubt it.

A whip-poor-will began its repetitive call upriver. An owl sounded back from the darkness. A light breeze ruffled leaves.

It was dark now. He could see little on the river but the stars above it were bright. He heard Hyndshaw snap his fingers twice. He knew James wanted he and Ward to close in again, so Jacob stood and moved quietly a few paces. He felt his way along. He could see little but blackness before him. Then he recognized the outline of a man. *Hyndshaw? No, Ward.* There was Hyndshaw's dark form leaning against the tree. A few more steps and he stood beside them.

"Moon will be up soon," whispered the lieutenant. "We can watch this stretch of water till after midnight then we'll move up slope until we cut the road and follow it to the Chambers place. We'll take shifts on watch; you two try to get some rest. I'll wake one of you when I need to.

It was well past midnight. The moon was moving lower in the sky. Each had found some sleep. Now they were moving to the rendezvous so they could cross the river before first light. They had cut into the Kings Road a few moments ago and were proceeding north. Soon they would pass a crossroad leading down to the river. It was quieter moving on the road but they still stopped every few paces to listen.

Suddenly James reached across their path with his musket and they all froze in place. Something was moving through the woods on their right coming toward the road. Whatever it was, its present direction would bring it into the road twenty or thirty yards ahead of them. Then, in a shaft of moonlight coming down through an opening in the canopy above, they saw the confirmation they needed: savages, moving silently one after another unaware of their momentary illumination and then a smaller figure followed by more savages. By the time the last one had passed, the first in the line was about to step onto the road ahead of them. Another splash of moonlight beyond created an opportunity. Hyndshaw crouched and brought his musket up. Jacob and Ward eased silently into the bushes. All was still except the crickets.

The first and second silhouettes stepped into the road and continued ahead. They were heading toward the river crossroad. Then a third savage came out following the others. Hyndshaw's shot killed him instantly. The crash of the weapon shattered the stillness for only a second then there was almost complete silence while everyone and everything in that next instant formulated a plan for survival. There was a loud yelp and the forest was suddenly alive with crackling brush and shuffling leaves.

Jacob and Ward shouldered their weapons but were presented with no visible targets. Then Jacob realized the noise was moving not toward him, but away.

"Let's go!" said Hyndshaw, "before they circle back on us."

And then Hyndshaw, Jacob and Ward were running back up the road the way they had come.

They ran a mile. Then circling way around toward the higher ground they crossed the kings road above the spur leading to the river.

They headed for the Chambers' place. Soon they came to the cabin of James McCarty a little ways this side of the rendezvous point. They could hear a commotion ahead so they approached with a loud "hello the cabin" to keep from being shot themselves.

Captain Hampton met them.

"Trouble on the road?" asked the Captain.

"A little. I think we got one," said Hyndshaw, there were a few more. I think they had the boy."

"Not anymore." said Hampton, "Mrs. Cole and her boy are inside with Nicholas. She said they got away when somebody ambushed the savages. That must have been you fellas."

"They okay? I didn't see the woman," asked the Lieutenant.

"As much as they can be, considering. You boys go on to Chambers' place. Get some rest. We'll reconsider our plan. Start at first light. I already got six boys across the river.

Next morning Hyndshaw found and scalped the Indian he had killed. They drug him off the road but left him for the wolves. They found no sign of the other savages.

Mrs. Cole reported that thirteen Indians had attacked her house and killed her children. They had taken her and her son to a temporary camp higher up in the Kittatinnys where two more Indians waited with another two prisoners likely the two who had been captured at Westbrook's. The camp looked as if many other Savages had been here for at least a week. She supposed dozens more.

After arguing among themselves for some time the savages suddenly killed the two other prisoners and scalped them. Mrs. Cole had given up all hope as they came that night to
196

cross the river. She was much relieved now to be back among the living.

Two days later, within a mile of Samuel Dupui's plantation, a man splitting wood was shot in the arm. He saw two Indians running toward him but he was young and fit and able to outrun them.

Jacob reflected upon all this in his mind, now, as he rode the big roan back toward Machackemack. He had just left Brink's Fort. *I wonder what Beletje is doing. I hope she is staying in the fort.*

Chapter 42

"Hello Jake."

"Hey Jacob."

Jakey Davids was at the gate of Cole's Fort when Jacob Fegely rode in.

"How's your sister."

"Which one?" He asked smiling, and then he added, "They're all fine. Beletje's in the meeting house."

"Any trouble here the past couple days."

"Not here; not yet. Heard about the troubles down your way. Were you in on it?"

"Some. Not much."

"There was trouble over near Fort Gardner," said Jake.

"What kind?"

"The usual kind. John Walling's widow was at her home with her family a mile or so from the fort. Her oldest daughter was out picking up wood chips for the fire. They heard a scream and looked out the window just in time to see two Indians kill her with tomahawks. When they stooped to take the scalp her brother shot one with his rifle. Walling's got one of them long rifles—a good one. Both savages ran off, but one ran poorly. After that, the widow Walling, another daughter and the son all got back to the fort. Later a group of men found a blood trail for a ways but it disappeared, and they never found the Indians. There must be a lot of them out there this summer. They seem to be attacking all over the valley. Forts are all getting crowded again even with the extra houses that have been stockaded."

"Yeah. I guess we're lucky the French army hasn't showed up yet with their cannon," said Jacob. "But, I hear Lord Howe is putting together a big army near Albany to see that don't happen."

"Hope your right Jacob, but we've heard that before ain't we. They're taking more men out of Sussex County to fight up north. Uncle Joris and Daniel left before this recent trouble started. Where does that leave us? A lot of New York boys are going north to fight too. We got a mighty thin line of a few stockaded houses north of here. It's a long way to Marbletown. Lots of folks are thinking again about moving to Deckertown."

"Probably safer," said Jacob, "Got to take care of my horse."

He dismounted and led the animal off toward the lean-to stable across the parade ground. It was Monday 8 June, 1758.

Two days later a barrage of musket fire broke the early morning calm..

Jacob Fegley and Jake Davids were on scout with Simon Westfall. They had been out since before first light. They were heading back toward the fort.

"Sound came from over near the Westbrook place," said Jake.

"Them boys took the scout along the river," said Simon. "They'd be coming in about now. They'd likely come past to check on their place. Let's go see." He hesitated. "We don't know who fired that barrage but it sounded like several muskets. More than the Westbrooks had. Let's keep to the woods and move slow. The firing's stopped. It may all be over. Whoever's left standing we want to see before they see us."

It was slow going. They were close to the road but not on it. Easing along parallel they had not gone far when movement ahead caught their eye. They took cover and watched. Two men frantically stumbled up the road one helping the other who appeared to be wounded. As they closed the distance Westfall's eyes widened with recognition.

"That's Gilbert VanGorden. I don't see the enemy. Get em off the road. We'll cover you."

Jacob moved quickly up and emitted a soft whistle. The men stopped to examine who was hailing them. Recognizing Jacob they hustled off the road toward him and quickly joined Westfall who had taken cover behind a big rock.

"How many?" asked Simon.

Half dozen, maybe couple more. We came round a bend in the road at the same moment and stumbled into each other. Both groups threw up their weapons and let go at each other at the same time. I caught a ball. The Westbrook brothers are both down. The Indians took to the brush and so did we. The Grub boys were both moving back up the road but Helin and I went left and got separated from the others. Helin helped me get this far. The boy, Helin, was shaking but he had his weapon. Westfall nodded at it.

"Is it loaded?"

"Not now, there hasn't been time."

"Always take time, son, soon as possible."

Helin didn't need to be told twice. He started reloading.

"At least three of the Injins were down," VanGorden said, "I saw two dragging one off the road as we looked back through the brush. Others may have been hit.

"There may be other groups out there," said Westfall. "Like us they're curious. Helin, you take your Pa back to Cole's. We'll go check on the Westfalls and the Grub brothers. Stay off that road and go slow. Keep your senses." He looked at Gilbert. "Your arms bleeding some but I think not too much."

"It will be alright," said Gilbert.

Westfall, Jake and Jacob left the VanGordens by the rock and slipped back into the woods. The VanGordens soon slid away in the other direction and were quickly out of sight in the laurel thickets.

The Westbrook brothers were both dead. The Savages had stayed long enough to lift their scalps. Nearby were three of the Indians also dead. "Munsee," said Westfall, looking at the bodies. Jacob and Jakey quickly took their scalps.

Later that morning Westfalls' group and the Grub brothers
came in to Cole's fort with the news.

Chapter 43

Two days passed at Cole's Fort after the brothers were killed. Scouts went out. No signs of the enemy were found.

"Were the Westbrook's cut up like some people have been?" Beletje asked.

"No. The savages didn't have time for that nonsense."

Beletje and Jacob were sitting on short three-legged-stools shelling peas from a basket into a copper fish kettle. They were outside the fort. They had brought the peas, kettle and stools to the east side so they could sit in the shade of the stockade wall. It was a warm afternoon.

"But they were scalped?"

"Yes."

"And you scalped the dead savages."

"Yes we did."

"You didn't feel bad doing it?"

Jacob gazed beyond the meadow full of grazing sheep to the trees along the river. Leaves ruffled and boughs swayed in a gentle breeze. Red birds sang to one another accompanied by meadowlarks. It was a pleasant day.

"The French pay cash money for scalps so Pennsylvania and New Jersey do too. It's hard to blame anyone for collecting it. After a man is killed it don't really matter much to him." Jacob listened to the birds a moment. "As long as there is money offered people will take scalps."

He really wasn't as certain as he declared. But it was the law and cash money would help buy land if this war ever ended.

"I guess you're right," said Beletje. "I didn't know Lieutenant Westbrook well or the brother. They were older and lived south a ways. Though I'm glad they weren't cut up in pieces. Their cousin Anthony is my age. I've known him forever.

Jacob glanced at her.   She was looking toward the river and the hills beyond.

"Are you thinking about moving over them hills east to Deckertown," he asked.

"I am.   Mother and Lea are already living there with the children.   I hate to leave Jakey and grandpa Decker and..." she hesitated.

"It would be safer," he said.

"I know, but I hate to leave my friends."

"Daniel Cole has gone to join the New Jersey Blue," said Jacob.

"I know, but I have other friends."

"Are you sorry he went."

"Yes, I'm sorry," she said, "But I'm glad you didn't go."

"Me too."

"Do you think Lord Howe will be able to drive the French away," she asked, "That's why Daniel and Uncle Jorris and Daniel Cole went north."

Jacob thought a moment before answering.

"They say he's building a big army near Albany, bigger than anyone has ever seen here in the colonies. Folks say lots of ships are moving up the Hudson with more supplies and English Regulars. New Jersey and New York boys are joining up to fight. The King has another army being assembled from Pennsylvania, Maryland and Virginia to drive the French away from the Forks of the Ohio where all this trouble started."

He paused to take more pea-pods from the basket.   He held them in his lap on a small cloth.   He wasn't very good at shelling peas, but that wasn't why he was here.

"Our Frontier Guard is getting better organized," he went on. "We're beginning to make some of them Red Devils pay when they come across that river.   We ain't caught up with all of them yet but I think we will.   We just wasn't ready when this war started.   But now that we're working together there will be a price to pay for them Frenchmen and their Indians. I think someday soon they may wish they hadn't started this War.

A horse galloped in from the north on the road. They couldn't see him but they heard the thundering hooves on the hard packed clay. He was running hard no doubt urged on by a rider. Then they heard the call to the women still working in the garden.

"Trouble at Westfall's! Come on in!" The animal and rider didn't stop or even slow down but charged on into the gate. A bell inside started ringing.

"We better go," said Jacob.

He grabbed the basket and his stool and headed for the gate. The cloth fell out of his lap. He left it. Beletje scooped up the copper kettle, her stool and started to follow. She saw the cloth and took time to grab it. As they rounded the southeast corner, Jacob waited for her to catch up. They could see three young women running hard from the garden toward the gate. They all arrived at about the same moment, just as Mr. Cole dashed out with his spotted dog.

"Go Junior, get em." He shouted, and the dog took off like a streak running downhill toward the sheep spread out grazing beside the river.

More hooves were heard rushing down the road from the north. Around the southwest corner raced a dozen horses kicking and nipping at one another but herded together by one of the VanAken youngsters waving a coiled whip and yelling—a boy of about eleven riding a big black horse doing a fine job of getting his small herd down the road and through the gate. No sooner than the horses were in here followed nine brindled cows trotting at the quick step, bellowing their displeasure, ringing cow-bells, heads and udders swinging with every step. The eight-year-old Miller twins flanked them from behind flailing feverishly with hickory sticks and glancing over their shoulders as they came.

Soon the Miller boys had their cows in. Mr. Cole strode quickly then to stand blocking the road west of the gate.

"Bring 'em in Junior," he shouted.

The dog was bringing in his sheep. He nipped a heel here and a rump there but he kept the tight little knot of twenty sheep moving ahead quickly, bleating, and nervous, as they came on at a steady trot which Junior knew just how not to rush. Through the gate they went followed by the dog and Mr. Cole. Two of the Frontier Guard leaped out grabbed hold the gates and swung them closed with a thump. A second bump and a heavy wooden bar locked them in place.

Outside, it grew quiet. Inside the walls was a bedlam of people and animals, as in the landlocked ark of old, preparing for a great flood.

Chapter 44

 $\mathcal{T}$ he day passed slowly inside Cole's Fort and the night crawled by with a clear sky and three/quarter moon. Scouts were sent out. The light came and dawn broke bright.

"Can they attack the fort," asked Beletje.

"No."

"What about that Fort Granville in Pennsylvania, last summer, they took it and the hundred people in it?

"That was way out on the Juniata," said Jacob, "and they got in the gate somehow. Cole's fort is stronger. The savages yesterday didn't even overrun Westfall's. They just attacked it and killed some folks. The stockade held. The people who got inside are mostly okay."

Jurian Westfall's was a stockaded house four miles north of Cole's Fort in New York. Actually, according to many, Cole's Fort was in New York but the border was still under dispute. New Jersey supplied men and material to the fort and even people on the New York side of the border quarrel saw no reason at present to complain.

"How many people did they kill," she asked.

"Seven New York soldiers from Wassing and three locals are dead. We don't know, who, yet. A boy and a woman are missing. Three other soldiers are wounded.

But, we should be safe here. Another rider has been sent south to alert headquarters. Scouts are out. More will go out from Brink's and Nominack. We will know more soon."

"I'm worried."

"So am I," said Jacob, "but we have the swivel guns. Indians don't like them swivel guns. They won't rush this fort."

The days were long this time of year. But when the dusk turned to darkness it seemed forever to the people inside Cole's Fort until the first light of the next dawn. Their spies came back during the night.

"I have a hunch they're leaving and hoping to cross above us and take the trail to Coshecton. That's what I would do," said Sergeant Vantuyl who had been out on a scout. "I say we cross down here and move up the Pennsylvania side to see if we can catch 'em before they get too far."

"What if we catch 'em and there are too many fer us to handle," asked a voice in the crowd that had assembled to hear his report.

"What if it was your woman and boy? Wouldn't you want someone to try and get 'em back," responded another voice that sounded like Jakey.

Beletje was listening from the back.

"If we wait fer help they'll be gone again. We got to teach them Red Devils they can't cross that river," offered another voice.

"Who's coming with me," asked the Sergeant.

"Now hold on Sergeant." John Decker's word carried sway at Machackemack and everyone hushed for a moment. "You can't take more than a dozen men. We need the rest right here. We got to use our head. If too many go out we endanger this Fort and everyone in it. There may be a hundred or more savages out there. We don't know."

"You're right John. I'll take a dozen."

In the end only eight stepped forward to go with Vantuyl. Within the hour the nine men trotted out the gate toward the Machackemack River. Three canoes carried them quickly down to the confluence with the Delaware. Then not quite so fast they paddled back up the big river a mile, where they beached their craft on the Pennsylvania side hiding them in the brush and proceeding northwest on foot.

All morning and well into the afternoon they stalked the riverbank looking for sign.

Presently Jake Davids was on point with Jacob Fegely to his left flank about ten yards behind. Simon Westfall was on Jakey's right flank along the river bank. Sergeant Vantuyl was behind another twenty paces with Anthony Westbrook and Gerret Ditsoort. Twenty more paces to the rear were Mateus

Cool, Phillip DeWitt and William Ward.   Ward glancing occasionally backward.

Jakey stopped behind a big rock and glanced back himself. He saw the Sergeant motion for a halt and start up to join him. Vantuel crept up slow and cautious untill he stood beside Jake.

"How's it look up ahead, Jakey."

"More of the same Sergeant."

"Well Gerrit and Mateus are thinkin we should head back. They've been whining for a while. Maybe we've done all we can. If we head back we could get into the fort after the moon rises. If we go on we'll be sleeping out for the night in a cold camp.

"It's plenty warm Sergeant we sure don't need a fire."

Something snapped behind them and they looked back to see Westbrook pointing like a statue toward the New York side of the river and slowly lowering his profile.

"He's seen something.   Get in a hole. I'll go find out what." Slowly the Sergeant retraced his steps while everyone made himself as invisible as possible, when viewed from the river.

In a while the Sergeant appeared again slinking his way to Jakey.

"Anthony saw one, just one, he seemed to be watching down river. Not moving, more like waiting on something. We'll wait ourselves to see what develops. Fall back on Anthony, it's higher ground."

The vigil continued until evening when two Indians appeared on a wooded island near the New Jersey side of the river. Soon they noticed others. They thought they counted ten before nightfall. It was difficult to tell. They were never all visible at once.   They were building rafts.

"The water is deep here. Not an easy crossing. Not where we would expect them to be. But it looks like that's their plan. They'll likely put in and float across with the current. We'll sit tight and catch them on the water."

"You think they will come tonight."

"Probably wait till morning."

"I hope they do, we won't get em all in the dark."

"No, but either way we should be in a good position here."

"Wonder where the woman and boy are?"

"Haven't seen any sign of prisoners."

"No, me neither."

Nightfall turned to blackness. Later a quarter moon rose and the water twinkled here and there as it flowed downstream. The island stood dark and quiet. Owls called to each other from both sides of the river.

"Wake up."

It was Simon whispering. Jacob's eyes popped open. Instantly alert, he said nothing.

It was still dark in the forest but he could see a faint hazy illumination, more than moonlight on the river. Whip-poor-wills called. The breeze had shifted. He could smell the water.

Soon they were all lined up along the high ground watching the men on the Island loading gear onto rafts, preparing to cross.

"That current should bring them right to us. Spread out a bit more and get ready."

Minutes passed while each man prepared.

Jacob picked his spot and replaced the powder in the flash pan of his musket. They had lain all night on the ground. *I hope the powder charge is dry.* He wanted to do his duty. *They'll be sitting ducks on those rafts.*

What are they doing?

They got paddles. They're going upstream, thought Jacob.

That changes everything. They aren't drifting into the kill like we expected. Who would think they would paddle rafts upstream. But that's exactly what they're doing.

"Okay boys slow and quiet," said Sergeant Vantuel. "We have to ease along till they get close enough to our side. Don't let 'em spot us. Keep your hands off the bushes. Move slow. Keep low. Crawl if you have too.

Jacob was forward and they were moving again northwest along the river trying hard to keep back in the brush enough not to be seen while keeping the rafts in sight.

Jacob was worried. This wasn't the plan. *Where are they heading? Where are the prisoners they should have with 'em?*

They had moved about two hundred yards upriver. The rafts were still on the far side where the current was less and they could make better headway. Just now, they began to come west into the current, which would help push the rafts across.

Suddenly Jacob caught sight of a movement to his left on his side of the river. He froze. An Indian brave had stood from the forests floor and was walking toward him. He was unarmed. Casually the brave paused, turned suddenly and walked back the way he had come.

Has he seen us?

The brave reached down and came up with a musket. He gave a yell! Suddenly there was brush crackling and Indians popping up everywhere in front of them. Jacob heard the ball whiz by before he heard the discharge from the Indians' weapon. His own musket stock was against his cheek. He aimed and fired. The brave fell.

Other weapons were firing it seemed from all around him. He was on the ground trying frantically to reload. One of the savages ran toward him screaming with a raised tomahawk. The Indian's forehead suddenly exploded with blood flying backward as the brave fell forward onto Jacob.

Now, in a panic Jacob pushed the body off only to have another brave jump atop him slashing with a knife. He felt the blade cut his arm; miraculously he got hold of the Indians wrist above the hand, which held the knife. But the sinewy brave pulled free and drew back to plunge his blade into Jacobs chest. As the fatal stroke came forward the Indians arm became snagged on a laurel branch sending his knife swirling out into the air. He grabbed for the weapon and Jacob kicked free and was now atop the brave who found himself on his back in a depression of soil left by a decayed stump.

Jacob, with his hands on his attackers throat and his feet against a big fallen log behind him had the advantage. He could hear men shouting and muskets firing but he could not understand anything that was going on beyond his own death struggle with the desperate man in the hole. Jacob's legs braced themselves and pushed against the log forcing the struggling adversary deeper into the forest duff. The savage smelled of bear grease and old sweat. Gasping for air the Indian clawed frantically at Jacob's arms.

Beyond Jacob's battle the others were firing, reloading and trying to keep themselves from harm by hiding behind anything, which provided cover. Three of the Indians on the rafts had been shot and fell into the river. The others took to the water and were swimming back to New Jersey. The Indians on the Pennsylvania side were providing a heavy cover fire. Bullets flew every few seconds Mateus was wounded in the leg. No one else had been hit yet.

When the last Indian in the river stumbled out of the water, and disappeared into the brush, the shooting on this side of the river slowed and then gradually ceased completely. It was over in less than twenty minutes.

"Have they gone?" Mateus shouted.

"Maybe. Sit tight. Jacob you alright?"

Jacob did not answer.

"Jacob?" Vantuel called again.

"Yes."

"Simon?"

"I'm good"

"Everyone's still with us then," said the Sergeant. "Stay put fer a spell.

Simon, see about Mateus he's been hit.

Chapter 45

"La Belle Rivere is a southern branch of the Ouabache, Lieutenant" said the French Captain.

Lafollette listened excitedly. He had never been to the Ouabache country. He had never been inside the officer's quarters here at Fort Machault nor had he ever before been addressed as Lieutenant.

This was a day to remember. He had just been promoted, moments ago, by the Captain who sat now at a wooden table writing orders and reports for him to carry on an important mission. Two other Lieutenants he had never met witnessed the proceedings and waited now for their own orders.

"Your job is simple Lieutenant. Take these English prisoners to Fort De Chartres. The authorities there will decide their fate. Most are very lucky people I think. They have been chosen specifically for this journey. A few may yet end up in the Savages' fires but not so many as if they remain here."

"I have never been downriver Captain."

"I know, and I send with you only two of our countrymen. It is all I can spare. One is a young soldier who is from the Illinois country. He has been to Fort De Chartres and lived among the Miami. He speaks the local dialect. He has a Priest and a Commandant who wish his services back at Post Vincennes."

"And our native escort?" asked Lafollotte.

"You are to take along a few Munsee who wish to visit the country downriver."

"Munsee sir?"

The captain paused in his writing to look at the new Lieutenant. Lafollette stood before him looking every bit the coureur des bois (runner of the woods) he was, dressed in: canvas leggings, green linin shirt, woolen belt about his middle, a tied red scarf covering his head, possible bag hanging from a leather strap thrown over his shoulder,

moccasins, powder horn, bullet pouch, musket—
could live in the woods for months at a time.

"Some of them grow weary of the war," said the
"They may be savages but they do not all possess a
heart. You have, no doubt, told them but it is impor...
think, for them to see for themselves how Frenchmen
among their cousins without taking so much land as do ...
English. It may stiffen their resolve for the fight ahead."

The Captain sighed as he studied the three young men
standing before him.

"This war drags on gentlemen. The English are an arrogant
but also a proud people. We have bloodied them badly but
they are not destroyed. The war, which began near here almost
four years ago, has spread all over the world; anywhere there
are Frenchmen and Englishmen to fight it. Our supply lines
are drawn out and difficult. We may soon be forgotten as the
war rages elsewhere. We need our Indian brothers to keep up
the pressure." He paused. "Many of them I fear have had their
revenge. Their hatchets are red with English blood and their
honor is now restored. It is not their way to stay at war for
years at a time. Some have already returned to their homes to
bask in glory."

"What about the Ottawa who arrived in Venango yesterday?"

"Ah, yes young men do continue to flow in from the west to
burnish their reputations as great warriors but the numbers are
fewer every month. When they have scalps on their belts to
carry home and others to sell at Niagara for powder and lead
they too may leave us."

He dipped his quill in the ink, scratched more on the paper and
then looked up again.

"Our spy's tell us that the English still disembark immigrants
from their ships in Philadelphia. Lord Howe's army grows
ever larger near Albany. General Forbes builds an army like
Braddock's to come against our Fort Duquesne. They will not
make the same mistakes they made before. I fear we will need
our allies most just as they tire of the fight."

e lifted his paper and blew gently on its surface to dry his cript.

" Some of the prisoners have been kept by the Munsee in Venango. Some have been purchased from the other tribes camped near here. They have been brought in from all directions. Most do not know one other, except for about a dozen from Fort Granville. They have been told we have spies placed among them and that if they are caught trying to escape they will be given to the savages to burn in the fires. I do not expect you will have trouble with them. Use them to paddle and do the work but keep them healthy. They will be of no value dead."

Lafallotte could not believe his good fortune. He was to have a trip away from the fighting, an adventure into the interior where he had never traveled, to visit French settlements he had only recently heard about—prosperous trading communities, connected by way of a big river to the new French settlements in Louisiana. His future was looking brighter. Opportunity was knocking at his door.

He knew the two lieutenants awaiting their orders were jealous. But he could not help himself. A toothy smile spread across his face as he remained standing at attention as the captain resumed his writing.

Outside the walls Jacque Ravelette and his friend Pierre stood watch at the boats as some ragged looking men toted supplies to an experienced voyager who packed the items into canoe or bateau. French trade goods were rare these days. They had been replaced by all kinds of plunder taken from the farms of Virginia, Pennsylvania, Maryland and New Jersey. Moments ago they had witnessed the demonstration of a Swiss made wooden cuckoo clock to the great delight of themselves and a group of Munsee children who gathered to watch. The clock was then boxed and stored in one of the bateau. Jacque wondered to himself where the strange instrument had been acquired, how it had journeyed here from Switzerland, and where it would end its days: perhaps in a French cottage on the Ouabache or possibly in a savages lodge somewhere in the Illinois tall grass prairie country.

Zack Miller had heard the coo-coo, coo-coo, of the clock. He had stopped working for a moment. He had never seen such a timepiece. But he did not wonder about where it might end its days. Rather, he pondered what might happen to him someday soon.

Terrified, painful, screams from the darkness did not occur nightly at Venango, but they were heard frequently. Strive as one might, most prisoners could not push the sounds out of their memory for weeks after. Zack had tried.

He was happy today to be working. Hungry and weak as he was he enjoyed the movement and being near other white men even if they were Frenchmen. Occasionally he thought he saw pity in the eyes of the French. Not from all of them but from a few. He never saw that from the savages.

The Munsee had not been particularly cruel to Zack as he had witnessed them being to some other prisoners. They just seemed to always be watching and assessing without really showing any emotion. They didn't seem to think like Europeans.

He had noticed their behavior among themselves. They showed great respect for one another and especially for their old people and children. He didn't understand what any of them were thinking. But he was beginning to believe that he might have value to them and the Frenchmen as a beast of burden. He was fed better when there was work to be done. *If that's what it takes to survive*, he thought, *I'll work.*

"Will we see the great river Uncle," asked Stands-often?

"Yes," said Otter.

They were watching the English slaves load the bateau and canoes at the landing.

"How many will go."

"Ten Munsee, three Frenchmen and forty of the English. But more than half of the prisoners will be women and children."

"What will become of them, Uncle."

"Some will be gifts for the tribes along the big river. Some will become slaves in the French villages. Others may be sent down river and sold to different Frenchmen in Louisiana." Otter paused to watch an eagle soaring above. "A few very lucky ones may find themselves sold back to the English. White men are very strange. They are not like us, nephew. They seldom adopt people into their own tribe." The eagle soared lower, observing from above everything happening on the creek below. "We will watch and see if these Frenchmen are really any different from their cousins the English or are they just angry at each other today. They are alike in many ways but always it seems these particular white men, war with one another. They often times drag us into their fights. It has been so since the time of our grandfather's grandfathers when white men first arrived in our country."

Just after first light, next morning, four canoes and six bateaus shoved off and floated downstream from the landing at Fort Machault. Zack Miller was at the oars in one of the bateau. Two of the women prisoners faced him.

"What are yer names? Where you from?" he whispered, as he rowed.

"Delilah Lapp from the Northkill in Pennsylvania," said one softly.

"Jenny Morrison, Little Owens Creek near South Mountain," said the other.

The flotilla soon swept from French Creek into the faster currents of the Allegheny heading toward Fort Duquesne where they would meet La Bella Riviere. Jacque Ravalette had never been on this branch of the Ouabache below Fort Duquesne. He knew where it went; the Lieutenant had a map; Jacque was heading home. It was nearly 900 miles downriver. He would recognize the main branch when he saw it. He smiled at the thought. Of all the people in the four canoes and six bateaus he and the Lieutenant were the only ones smiling.

Chapter 46

William was in the woods. He did not intend to go far. He had been surprised to see a bear track this close to the fort. But it was fresh and he followed it now. The bear was headed upslope away from the river. The afternoon was getting on. Black- berries were ripe. *He's in the meadow.*

William stalked along the edge of the trees. He saw him. But it was too late. The bullet caught Ward in the chest.

"Did you hear about William Ward," asked Lieutenant Hyndshaw.

"What about him?" asked Elias Knepp.

"Killed, by Indians yesterday half mile from Fort Johns, while he was hunting," replied Hyndshaw.

They were standing outside the cabin at Hyndshaw's Fort in northeast Pennsylvania. The palisade gates were closed. Several women were doing their laundry at half a dozen different fires.

"Day before that some man and a boy were out near Brink's. The man was killed. The boy saw the savages and ran. One of the devils in hot pursuit got a surprise when the boy turned and shot him. Four others continued the chase. The boy saw he wasn't going to outrun them with his rifle so he broke the stock against a big rock and then outdistanced them. Damn smart boy, I'm thinkin. Most men wouldn't have had the wisdom to disable the weapon, they would have just tossed it in a panic."

"What was his name?"

"No one knew but I aim to find out. I want to shake that boys hand," said Hyndshaw.

"Ward was a good man, " said Elias.

"Yeah he was, answered James. It can happen to anyone who goes out alone. They're crawling all over these woods; burning houses and barns, stealing horses, shootin milk cows. They ain't so much looking for a real fight as they are keeping us off balance and out of our fields.

I heard your Moravian friends are moving their Christian Indians all the way to Philadelphia to keep them safe."

"Really, where did you hear that?"

"Over at the New Jersey headquarters, where we hear most things. News gets here quicker through them than through our own channels," said Hyndshaw.

"Well I guess south of Ellison's their roads may be a little safer than ours and they get messages over the Mountains from Newton as well. We're kinda isolated way up here from our other Pennsylvania forts. Sometimes they forget about us. Have any more of the Moravian Indians been killed."

"Not that I know. Couple missing I heard."

"Yeah, well their scalps can be sold for the same price as a hostile's can. Who would know the difference? And most people wouldn't care. You know that."

"Some people maybe, I wouldn't say most."

"I would," said Elias. "Most folks just lump Indians together and hate 'em all. They don't know any personally and they don't want to."

"Well all the more reason to get the Christian Indians south to Philadelphia where they can be protected. We can't be worryin' about them. We got our own problems with their cousins who are sure as hell trying to kill us."

In early July, Lord Howe moved his 15,000 man British and colonial army against The Marquis de Montcalm's French forces totaling 3,600 men at Fort Carillon situated on the bluffs between Lake George and Lake Champlain. On July 8th the main attack was an all-day affair, which cost the English 1,950 killed or wounded, including Lord Howe himself, killed. It was another horrible demoralizing loss.

On July 28th the English finally had a glimmer of good news. In far north Nova Scotia, the British General Jeffery Amhurst captured the French fortress at Louisburg. This success would severely restrict French shipping into the St. Lawrence Seaway—the main supply route for New France.

After four years of war the English had finally won a major battle in their American colonies. Maybe there was yet hope.

He rolled off her. Tiny rivulets of sweat flowed gently from her breasts across the skin of her flat tummy. She lay naked in the darkness enjoying the feel of the air moving over her—cooling her.

Recent days and nights had been exceptionally hot. August lovemaking was best left until the very early morning hours when temperature in the stone house moderated.

The room was engulfed, now, in darkness but she could see starlight out the small attic room window. Her linen shift was visible between the bed and the window laying across the back of the tall chair. Occasionally the light garment fluttered gently as the early morning breeze blew into their room. Beletje thought she might smell rain. That would be good. They needed a soaker to break the heat and renew the crops.

Whip-poor-wills sang from the river and crickets chirped from the meadow. John Decker's extended family had come home to the farm for a few nights. The house was not stockaded but the downstairs wooden shutters were closed and doors were locked. Everyone was armed and armed men were on watch outside.

Jacob was already snoring beside her. Beletje took a deep breath and turned to embrace him lightly. She was still too warm to cuddle close.

In the darkness she smiled. They had been married in the church a few weeks ago. Not everything could wait for the war to end. Some of her family and friends had been there for the simple celebration. This was their time, they would face it—together.

Chapter 47

Dark clouds were forming over the Poconos. A brisk wind blew from that way too. Everyone was hoping for rain.

Lizabeth Dewitt and Sara Shammers worked in the garden ahead of the wished for rain. Some of the men were searching for animals to bring in closer to the fort. Everyone watched the sky. Far to the west, thunder muttered.

Beletje and her cousin Sara Decker were pealing apples. Jakey and Jacob had brought them in from granddads orchard. There were three bushel. The girls planned to use some for baking pies tonight when it was cooler. August was almost past. Everyone was back inside the fort again. The girls had not anticipated rain this morning. It was an outside community oven, built inside the stockade walls. If it rained they would wait. The apples would keep.

"It's good to have Daniel Cole back home," said Sara.

"Yes it is. I just wish brother Daniel and Uncle Joris had come home with him."

"Well just be happy they weren't wounded or killed at Carillon."

"I'm thankful for that. But I wish they were home."

"Me to. Do you think this war will ever end, Beletje."

"I don't know. It has to end sometime doesn't it?"

"It's over for some folks that's for sure," said Sara.

"Yes, I guess it is."

"Do you ever wonder about those folks that are carried off as captives like the Westfall boy or the Swartwout family."

"All the time, but I try not to," said Beletje.

"I think I'd rather be killed than captured."

"I'd rather kill them."

"Could you do that," asked Sara, "kill another person?"

"Like wringing the head off a chicken. I hate them all. I don't care how many Uncle Joris and Pa used to have as friends. They aren't my friends. They're killing my friends. When this war ends I hope there isn't a savage within a thousand miles of the Minsink Valley."

"What was that?"

"What?"

"I thought I heard a gunshot," said Sara.

"Probably more thunder."

The women in the garden were standing, looking southward. The clouds rolled and the wind picked up. She heard something else—a shout.

Someone was running in. He was waving his rifle in the air and yelling but it was hard to hear through the rushing wind gusts of the approaching storm. The women in the garden suddenly dropped their baskets and in two steps lengthened their stride to full extension running hard for the gate.

The bell rang inside the fort. Men on the wall pointed south. The approaching man was closer now. Beletje could see who it was. It was Jacobus Middag.

"What you reading?" asked Ezekiel.

"News from up near the Minisink's."

Heinrich was back at the mill. It was dusty and hot for early September He had just noted one particular article from the New York Mercury with two stories:

> *"August 28th, 1758.   The 11th instant, Jacobus Middag and his son, were fired upon by the Indians in a field near Coles Fort, on the frontiers of New Jersey, the boy was killed on the spot, and Middag died a few minutes after he got into the fort."*

> *"and last Friday week, a woman was killed and two others carried off, by the Indians also, within a few rods of Gardners Fort, on the Frontiers of New Jersey likewise."*

Ezekiel Graber scanned the article quickly.

"Well Maybe all that is going to change now that Colonel Bradstreet and his militia destroyed Frontenac," said Ezekiel.

"Where is dat Frontenac, exactly," asked Heinrich.

"Up on the north shores of Lake Ontario. It was a major French supply center where they stockpiled war materials and stuff. Bradstreet's men burned what they couldn't carry home. They were almost all militia you know. With that success powder and shot may get scarce for French war parties."

He listened a moment. The big waterwheel and grinding-stones had stopped moving. Rushing water could suddenly be heard. There was a wooden thump and then another and the big wheel turned again spinning the shafts and grinding-stones drowning out the sounds of nature.

"The other good news is the Iroquois up North," Ezekiel said in a loud voice. "They have agreed to fight for King George. Old Johnson finally convinced them to break their neutrality and get on the right side. That will help. Our General Stanwix and his men are building a new fort up between Oswego and the Mohawk river."

"I tink we need new forts near here."

"We do Heinrich but you got to see the big picture. We're in this war together remember. We can't forget about New York. They got to control the Mohawk Valley to protect Albany. The key to the Mohawk is the Oneida Carry where they portage goods over to Wood Creek and float 'em north to Lake Ontario. When the French held it last summer they destroyed German Flatts and threatened Albany, remember? It's an important place and this new fort will help keep the French off us up North.

Forbes is building his army south of here. He'll move on Fort Duquesne soon. He's just getting ready."

"Well I still say we need more forts on the Susquehanna and along the Blue Mountains," said Heinrich, furrowing his brow.

"It's about strategy Heinrich, not just protection. Folks say the momentum may swing our way soon. We need to control the key points on the rivers and through the mountain passes. That's how we will win. That's probably why the Ohio Indians are coming back in for another parley up in Easton. Maybe they've got wind of the trouble comin their way."

"Vhen?" asked Heinrich.

"What?"

"Another Indian conference at Easton, when?"

"This month. It may be happening right now."

"I hope you're right, Ezekiel, but we haf heard all dis before avn't we. I hope dis General Forbes don't step into anudder ambush like Braddock and get hisself kilt. If he does we may haf to move to Germantown or Philadelphia.

The wheel had stopped again. The sounds of flowing water and songbirds returned inside the mill on Swamp Creek.

Chapter 48

The moss covered waterwheel turned powering the large millstones at the Davids' Mill, grinding corn today. A fresh breeze separated red leaves from the sugar maple tree. They spiraled down and settled over the wet surface of the tailrace after that water had finished its work and flowed on toward the Machackemack River.

Sheep tore at the grass in the upper pasture where they had not grazed for three summers. Wood smoke rose from the chimney of the stone house across the road where Beletje and cousin Sara puttered about pots and pans cooking over coals of a large fire.

It's good to be home thought Beletje, *even with armed guards posted on the hillside.*

No sign of the enemy had been seen in almost a month. Another treaty had been agreed upon in Easton, this one signed by the Munsee and several other tribes.

People in the Minisink area were hopeful. In the past two days many had returned to their homes. At least until news came that the treaty had been broken, or smoke *god forbid* rose ominously to raise alarm.

"It's good having you back, brother," said Jakey.

"It's good to be back. And it's good to be here at home."

"Yes it is."

Daniel Davids and his uncle Joris Davids had returned home last week.

"I hope Ma and the youngsters can come home soon," said Daniel.

"Some who've been living in Deckertown are starting to think about coming back," said Jake. "Ma is waiting for us to tell her when it's safe. I reckon we should be ready to send that message soon. Maybe everything can get back to normal by

Christmas. But, the war aint over yet. The French could still send Huron or Ottawa against us."

"Maybe," said Daniel, "but they would have to come through Iroquois or Munsee territory. The Iroquois are fighting for us now. And the Munsee agreed not to fight *for* the French. I don't think they want other tribes coming through, stirring people up. I think they have had enough and see what is coming. General Forbes is on the move. He's cutting a new road through Pennsylvania, north of Braddock's old trace."

"Well what about that little problem we heard about the other day. Some of his advance forces were ambushed—350 killed. The Virginians lost six of their eight officers. Sounds a lot like Braddock's debacle," said Jake.

"Well that was an advance party who overloaded their ass before they should have. Forbes is no fool. His army is building forts to fall back on as they go forward.

When he gets to the Forks of the Ohio with his main army I think the French at Fort Duquesne may get what they got comin to 'em," said Daniel.

"I hope you're right but we heard that four years ago."

In late November General Forbes' 6,000 man army finally reached the Forks of the Ohio. Fort Duquesne's 600 French defenders burned the fort and retreated north two days before the English arrived. King Georges red-coated Army once again controlled the Forks and promptly started construction of another fortress to be named Fort Pitt.

In early December it snowed in Philadelphia. It was a cold, dry snow blowing and drifting in a westerly breeze. Tuesday evening at eight of the clock, according to the chiming of the bells, two men bundled up in gray woolen coats and felt hats stepped out of the brick meeting hall onto the stoop.

"I'm happy you came with me tonight, Elias," said John Branch, "and I'm happy you are back from the frontiers."

"Thanks John. I'm glad to be back and I'm pleased you invited me."

"It's too bad Henry couldn't be here. He wanted to come tonight. He loves these meetings. It may not be Mr. Franklin's Leather Apron Club but there are all kinds of people interested in learning here in Philadelphia. What did you think of our speaker?"

"He was interesting. Not as good a speaker as Reverend Antes though. I don't know much about astrology or the stars. I didn't understand a lot of what was said. I know nothing about comets and had never heard of that Halley guy. But it was interesting and I'm going to be watching. A bright light in the sky at Christmas time will be something to see. Like the star of Bethlehem. Some folks may take it as a sign that peace is really at hand. Maybe this godforsaken war is coming to an end. That's sure how I would like to think. I hope that comet appears just like he predicted."

"Let's get us a warm brew down at Town Tavern. Have you been there since you've been back."

"I've never been inside Town Tavern John."

"Well all the more reason to go now, it will be my treat."

Off the steps they went striding down the cobblestone street, collars and shoulders up, heads tucked, trudging through the snow. As they walked along Elias marveled at the light shining out the windows of the brick homes, lining the street. I'm a long way from Hyndshaw's fort, he thought, I wonder if things are quiet along the Delaware.

It was quiet at Hyndshaw's Fort and Dupuis'. People still lived at the forts but not quite as many. A few who still had houses or barns to live in went home and took extended family and neighbors with them. Maybe this spring, if peace held, rebuilding could start.

On the New Jersey side of the river up through the Minsink Valley it was the same although there were more homes or buildings left standing.

At Machackemack many folks went home before Christmas. Jacob and Beletje Fegley were at the Davids Mill. Ma and the children had not come home from Deckertown yet and her Sister Lea had married Jeremiah Kittle and remained there with a new baby.

Beletje and Jacob had the attic bedroom to themselves. It was late but they were awake—talking.

"People say it won't hold, Jacob."

"I know but it was agreed. It was in the documents that were signed in Easton. The Governor signed. Everyone knows, this time, they will have to enforce it. The Government will have to keep people from going over the Alleghenys. The Indians have agreed to move out to the Ohio country. There is plenty of land this side of those mountains for everyone who wants it. No need to cross over and start another war. I'm not saying I want any of it. But some people will."

"Well this is my home. All my family and friends are here. I'll be happy to get plenty more folks between us and the savages," said Beletje.

Jacob knew that some of Beletje's friends were already talking about that land in western Pennsylvania. But he saw no reason to discuss that any more at the moment. He wanted to cuddle under the covers.

"Get up and look out; see if it's still there?" said Beletje.

"What?'

"The Christmas star."

He got up and glanced out the window.

"Yep."

She pulled the blanket from the bed and came to the window to look out with him. She covered them both and gazed out the attic window. The fields were beautiful looking down toward the river. Snow cover on the land reflected the light from a nearly half full waxing moon.

There it was a strange star brighter than the others low in the western sky. They had noticed it last night.

227

"Was it there Christmas night."

"I don't know. It was snowing then."

"Well it's beautiful tonight. With that moon, and the snow, and the season, I think it's good luck.

"Me too. Let's go back to bed. I'm cold."

Afterword

The French and Indian war was not over. There would be more fighting far to the north. The Treaty of Easton with the Munsee and the Ohio tribes would be honored for a few years. The Iroquois would fight for the English against the French.

White farmers seeking more land quickly questioned the agreement, within the Treaty of Easton, for white settlements to remain east of the Allegheny Mountains. However, following the peace treaty between France and England came a proclamation from the English King known thereafter as The Proclamation of 1763, which forbad any further settlement beyond those mountains.

The English government by right of conquest had a vast new territory now to administer in the Province of Quebec. Good relations with Indians would profit the fur trade. The English government decided they would keep a permanent army of ten thousand men in the colonies to protect their interests and enforce the proclamation. England had incurred a great amount of debt fighting this war in America and they expected the colonies to repay some of that debt through an increase in taxation.

The author intends to continue telling this story with a third book due out in 2019.

You may contact him at stormsatkendiamong@gmail.com

About the Author

The author holds an Associate of Science Degree from Vincennes University, a Bachelor of Science Degree in Education from Indiana State University and a Master's Degree from Southern Illinois University. He is an amateur historian and genealogist. He is, or has been during his life, an avid hunter, fly fisherman, mountain backpacker, canoer of rivers, farmer, antique collector, poet, husband, father, and grandfather.

Michael Phegley's love of the individual stories, which en masse make up our collective history, was sparked first in John Hodge's 1958 sixth-grade history class, Busseron Township School, Oaktown, Indiana.

The author lived for many years in the oldest continually inhabited European community in Indiana—Vincennes.

The author traced his family roots in America, back to the eighteenth century Delaware River Valley described in this book. Phegleys (then spelled most often Fegely, Fegley, or Feagley) were always farmers. The author as genealogist was never satisfied with finding documents or cemetery markers. He had to locate parcels of land, stand upon those homesteads, and personally experience the natural surroundings his ancestors had so intimately known centuries before. That research, those deeply personal pilgrimages, and the subsequent questions awakened in the author's imagination, inspired and powered this story.

The author now lives with his wife and two dogs in Evansville, Indiana.

Acknowledgments

The closest we get to truth in our history is when we read source material written or told of by actual participants or contemporary witnesses. Even then facts are skewed by prejudices and opinions.

I am grateful for letters, journals, diaries, baptismal records, land registrations, newspapers and all other original documents. I also appreciate the people throughout the centuries who have secured, protected, and preserved these treasures.

I would be remiss without mentioning and thanking particularly the following groups:

Sussex County Historical Society; 82 Main St., Newton NJ.

Minisink Valley Historical Society; 125-133 W. Main St. Port Jervis NY.

Montague Association of the Restoration of Community History, Foster Armstrong House, Montague NJ.

Sandyston Township Historical Society, Sandyston Township NJ.

Knox County Public Library, McGrady Brochman House, 614 n 7th St. Vincennes IN.

Bibliography

King of the Delawares, Teedyuscung 1700-1763, by Anthony F.C. Wallace;

Syracuse University press, 1949

Peaceable Kingdom Lost (The Paxton Boys and the Destruction of William Penn's holy Experiment); by Kevin Kenny, Oxford University Press, 2009

The Indian Chiefs of Pennsylvania; by C. Hale Sipe; Wennawoods Publishing, Louisburg Pennsylvania,1999

Minisink Valley Reformed Dutch Church Records, 1716-1830; the New York Genealogical and Biographical Society; Edited by Royden Woodward Vosburgh; a reprint published by Heritage Books Inc.; Westminster Maryland, 2004

History of Sussex and Warren Counties, NJ; by: James Snell; published by Everts and Peck; Philadelphia, 1881

History of Wayne, Pike and Monroe Counties Pennsylvania; by Alfred Mathews; R.T. Peck, Publisher; Philadelphia, 1886

History of Orange County, New York ; by Russel Headley; Van Dusen & Elms, Publisher; Middletown New York, 1908

Orange County History; by Edward Manning Ruttenber and Lois H. Clark; Everts & Peck publisher; Philadelphia, 1881

The First Peoples of Ohio and Indiana; by Jessica Diemer Eaton; Diemer Eaton Publishing, Bloomington, 2001

Swamp, New Hanover Vol. II; by Robert Wood; New Hanover Township Historical Society, publisher; Gilbertsville PA, 2007

The Indians of New Jersey (Dicken Among The Lenape); by M. R. Harrington Rutgers University Press; New Brunswick NJ, 1966

Documents relating to the Colonial History of the State of New Jersey, Volume XX, Extracts From American Newpapers , relating to New Jersey Vol. IV. 1756-1761; The Call Printing and Publishing Company; Patterson New Jersey, 1898

For King and country (the maturing of George Washington 1748-1760); by Thomas A. Lewis; Harper Collins, publishing; New York ,1993

General William Maxwell and the New Jersey Continentals; by Harry M. Ward; Greenwood Press; Westport, Connecticut, 1997

Ouabache; by David A. Lottes; 2011

Printed in Great Britain
by Amazon